"Dana, I don't want to play this game. I want you to be honest with yourself and admit that you still want and need me. Because I damn sure want and need you more than ever."

There was no way that she'd give him the satisfaction of knowing that she still craved his touch, yearned for his taste, and needed his heat. Hell no! She would not . . .

Adrian lifted her chin and pressed his nose against hers. Dana's lips quivered as she felt the warmness of his breath teasing her mouth. *Step away!* her good sense called out. But Dana ignored it, pressing her mouth against his and kissing him with zeal. Her words didn't have to admit what she felt for Adrian because her kiss said it all.

Though he was briefly taken aback by the sheer force of her kiss, Adrian received what she was saying and cupped her bottom, drawing her closer to him. She gasped when she felt the bulge in his pants. Pulling back from him, she felt drunk, felt as if she was about to make a bad decision that she would regret in the morning. "I want you, Adrian," she moaned.

"Say it again," he commanded.

"I. Want. You. Now."

Also by Cheris Hodges

Just Can't Get Enough

Let's Get It On

More than He Can Handle

Betting on Love

No Other Lover Will Do

His Sexy Bad Habit

Too Hot for TV

Recipe for Desire

Forces of Nature

Published by Dafina Books

Love
After War

CHERIS
HODGES

Kensington Publishing Corp.
www.kensingtonbooks.com

DAFINA BOOKS are published by

Kensington Publishing Corp.
119 West 40th Street
New York, NY 10018

All Kensington Titles, Imprints, and Distributed Lines are available at special quantity discounts for bulk purchases for sales promotions, premiums, fund-raising, and educational or institutional use. Special book excerpts or customized printings can also be created to fit specific needs. For details, write or phone the office of the Kensington special sales manager: Kensington Publishing Corp119 West 40th Street, New York, NY 10018, attn: Special Sales Department, Phone: 1-800-221-2647.

Dafina and the Dafina logo Reg. U.S. Pat. & TM Off.

ISBN-13: 978-0-7582-7662-9
ISBN-10: 0-7582-7662-1
First Kensington Mass Market Edition: November 2013

eISBN-13: 978-0-7582-7663-6
eISBN-10: 0-7582-7663-X
First Kensington Electronic Edition: November 2013

10 9 8 7 6 5 4 3 2 1

Printed in the United States of America

Acknowledgments

This book was a labor of love. Dysfunction and happiness don't usually go hand in hand, but that describes Dana and Adrian's love story. Sometimes it takes love to combat anger and hurt. I hope you enjoy the roller-coaster ride.

Thank you to some of the most supportive people I could ever have on my side: my agent, Sha-Shana Crichton; my sister, Adrienne Hodges Dease; Greg and Sonya Purvis; my wonderful editor, Selena James; Sonia Corley; Ronda Renee Tankson; Viola DeWitt; Louise Brown; Michele Grant, Farrah Rochon; Phyllis Bourne; Yolanda Gore; Beverly McDuffie; Erica Singleton; Wendy Covington; Tiffany Strange-Wilson; Tashmir Parks; Connie Banks Smith; Victoria Christopher Murray; Lasheera Lee; Wendy Harris; Nila Brown; Harley Davidson of Charlotte and, as always, my mom and dad, Doris and Freddie Hodges.

I have to give a big thank you to my Hot Mama Land sister writers, Kianna Alexander, Angie Daniels, AlTonya Washington, Monique Lamont, Denise

Jefferies, Iris Bolling, Bridget Midway and Loretta R. Walls. Have you followed our blog yet? It's http://hotsouthernwriters.blogspot.com.

I'd like to thank the book clubs who have hosted me and supported my work including The Sistah-friends Bookclub (Columbia, Charleston, and Atlanta), the Building Relationships Around Books group, Real Readers Real Words group, the Black Romance and Women's Fiction Book Club.

This is always the hardest part of writing a book, because I feel like I'm always forgetting someone, but charge it to my head and not my heart.

Follow me on Twitter, @cherishodges, log on to my blog, www.cherishodges.blogspot.com, and be sure to friend me on Facebook/cherishodges.

Chapter 1

The last thing Dana Singleton ever wanted was to find herself alone with the man who'd broken her heart two years ago. She'd put three thousand miles between them twenty-four months ago only to find that the moment she returned to Los Angeles, she was trapped with him in the middle of a brownout.

Adrian Bryant.

God, she thought, *why do you hate me?*

"This is insane," Adrian said, then looked over at Dana. And a slow smile spread across his face when he recognized her. "Long time no see." When he reached out to embrace her, Dana pushed back.

"Don't you dare touch me," she said. "How dare you even look at me or expect me to be thrilled to see you?"

"Don't act like that," he said, offering her a sizzling smile. In the near darkness of the coffee shop, his smile damn near lit up the place.

"Act like what? Like I can't stand to be in the

same room with you? Trust and believe, it is not an act," she snapped. Oh, she hated him and the way he still made her heart flutter with a powerful yearning to fall into those strong arms and press her mouth against his while he slowly kissed her until her body melted against his. Looking away from him, she forced herself to remember being dumped by text message. *It's for the best. I'm moving on and you should do the same,* the message had read. She closed her eyes and rubbed her temples. That night replayed in her mind like a bad movie in a broken DVD player. She'd felt stupid, confused, and disappointed. But she had taken the hint and left. If only she'd told Imani and Universal Studios no. Then she'd still be in New York and not running into Adrian on his home turf, Los Angeles.

She expelled a frustrated sigh because when she opened her eyes, he was still there. Still staring at her with that spectacular smile on his face.

"Dana, I know I owe you a huge apology and an explanation as to why—"

"You don't owe me a damned thing, and I definitely don't want to hear any apology you took two years to come up with."

Adrian stared at her, soaking up Dana's unique beauty. The long dreadlocks were new and very sexy. She had caramel-colored skin that made him salivate as he thought about all the places he used to lick and how sweet she tasted between her thighs. Letting her go had been the worst thing he'd ever had to do. But it was necessary. He only wished he could come clean with her now. But his mission wasn't complete and the last thing he wanted was to get her caught up in his plan.

Dana snapped her fingers in Adrian's face. "Thinking of a pretty lie to tell me?"

"Can we talk about it over a cup of coffee?" he asked, smiling at her and making Dana snarl in response.

"You know what, Adrian? I've grown up since the last time I saw you. Decided that I deserve someone who knows how to treat me and that isn't you. So, hell no. I don't want to talk to you over coffee. I don't want to talk to you period."

"I was trying to protect you, Dana," he said, his voice low, a sexy growl that made her body twitch. The same voice that he used to whisper sweet promises in her ear. Turning her back to him, Dana tried to pretend she wasn't affected. *As long as he doesn't touch me, I'll be fine,* she thought. Then she felt his hand on her shoulder. "I'm sorry," he said. "Sorry for what I did and the way things looked. But it was for the best."

"It was. And when the power comes back on, we can pretend you're still gone."

Adrian spun her around, drinking in her delicate features. Though her eyes flashed anger and resentment, she was still the most beautiful woman he'd ever seen. The love of his life. The only thing not touched by his need for revenge. What could he say to her to explain what his life had become?

"What?" she snapped, locking eyes with him.

He knew the right thing to do when it came to Dana was to leave her alone, to walk away and continue his quest. But at that moment, in the silence of the darkened coffee shop, all he wanted was a sweet taste of his past. A kiss from Dana. He leaned in, pressing his lips against hers. He felt her heat, passion, and want. When her lips parted and his tongue slipped inside, her sweetness nearly brought him to his knees. Closer. He had to be closer to her, and he wrapped her in his arms as if he were a blanket. She didn't resist him, didn't push him away. Instead, she kissed him back as if no time had passed since their lips last touched. She made him feel as if her mouth had been waiting for his. That couldn't be the case . . . could it?

Dana's brain clicked and she realized she wasn't dreaming about kissing Adrian; she *was* kissing him. Relishing in the touch of his tongue against her lips and savoring the hint of mint that his mouth always held. She wasn't imagining that his fingers were gliding up and down her spine; it was actually happening. The man she loved. The man who'd broken her heart with a text message. Kiss over. She pulled back, snatched away from him, and angrily eyed him. "What in the hell is wrong with you?" Dana demanded.

"Me? I didn't kiss myself and from what I felt, you're happy to see me."

"You cocky son of a—"

"I know I am. Glad you agree," he quipped.

"This may be a game to you—one kiss and I'm

supposed to bend to your will and let you back between my thighs because you think you belong there? Go to hell, Adrian."

Between her thighs . . . was that supposed to push him away? That was his place and he would reclaim it, just as soon as he put his father where he belonged. "Dana, Dana, Dana, you wanted that kiss, needed it just as much as I did, if for nothing more than closure."

"How about you close your mouth?" Dana snapped. Before she could say another word, the power popped on and Dana bolted out of Starbucks and away from Adrian. But the memory of that kiss haunted her and reminded her of hot LA nights on the beach when they were in love. When things between them had been easy and sunny, bright and filled with the promise of a future filled with love. A future that Dana thought would mean her as a fashion photographer and the wife of Adrian Bryant. The latter dream ended with a text message. Still, she wanted to know why and what changed his mind. She knew his mother's death changed him, but the coldness she'd seen on his face the day of the funeral and later at his penthouse kept her awake at night. Was someone to blame for Mrs. Bryant's death?

Did Adrian believe he'd done something to cause his mother's death? She'd wrestled with these questions for two years, and the moment she'd resolved to forget about him, there he was. Sexier and more mysterious than ever. But not this time. She was not, in no way, shape, or form, going to allow him to suck her into his atmosphere again. Not when she was about to embark on her biggest and most exciting assignment of her career—shooting publicity shots for one of the biggest film studios in America. Sure part of the reason why she'd gotten the gig had been because of her best friend and current Hollywood it girl, Imani Thomas, but the fact of the matter was, Dana's career was on the uptick and Adrian Bryant could go to hell, twice. She had her closure, even if the taste of his kiss burned in her mouth.

Chapter 2

Two days had passed since the blackout at Starbucks, and Adrian couldn't get Dana off his mind. He'd been so distracted that he'd almost missed the reason why he'd come back to LA—the opening of Crawford Towers and his chance to confront his absentee father, Elliot Crawford.

Elliot and his son Solomon Crawford were opening the chain's first hotel on the West Coast. Adrian had followed the construction of the project, smiling at the stumbling blocks that cropped up, like the zoning dispute between the city and the contractor. Then there was the Sierra Club's opposition to the project, which made Crawford Hotels spend an additional forty million dollars on LEED certification for the project. But the most interesting part of the project had been the public sparring between Richmond—Elliot's oldest son—Solomon, and Elliot, which made the building of the towers more dramatic than *General Hospital*. And this was his "family." Whatever. Why had this man, with two overgrown spoiled sons, turned his back on him and his mother?

Adrian hated that the last conversation he had with his mother was about that man. That piece of shit who donated sperm, because he was not a father in Adrian's eyes.

Pamela clinched her son's hand in hers and smiled at him. They'd always been so close and watching cancer suck the life from her made him want to cry and Adrian wasn't an emotional man. "I love you, son," she said, her voice frail and quiet. The whirling of the oxygen machine filled the air as Adrian kissed his mother's bony hand.

"I love you, too."

Pamela broke into a fit of coughing and Adrian reached for the nurse's call button. She grabbed his hand and shook her head. "No, no. I have to tell you."

"Mama, you need to rest."

Pamela coughed again as Adrian stared into her ashen face. He hated feeling powerless and helpless. He stroked her hand and closed his eyes. "Mama, I wish you would rest."

She shook her head. "Not until I tell you."

He wanted to tell her that it could wait, that they had time. But he knew nothing could be further from the truth, Pamela was slipping away with every breath she took. "Mama," he said.

"Your father."

"What about my father?" he asked, thinking about Paul Wallace, the man his mother said was his father. "He died when I was seven."

She squeezed his hand again. "Your father is a power-
ful man and I loved him very much."

Adrian wrinkled his nose and cocked his head to the
side. "Powerful?"

"But . . ." She began coughing again, this time her body
shook like a leaf and Adrian worried if she would be able
to take another breath.

"Just rest, Mommy," he said sounding like the helpless
12-year-old that he felt he was as her hand slipped from his
grip. Again, he reached for the call button, but Pamela
grabbed his hand again.

"If things had been different, we would've been together
and given you a real family," she said. "I know he loved
me. He took care of you from a far and I wish I had never
agreed to her deal."

"Mama, it doesn't matter." Adrian kissed her hand.
"Rest."

"I want you to know . . . know the truth. Elliot loved
you. When you were a baby and he held you in his arms,
I knew he would've been there for us, but she wouldn't let
him go, not without taking everything he'd built. I tried to
stay in New York, but she let me know that you would
never be accepted as Elliot's son, not like her sons."

"Mama, what are you talking about? Who is Elliot?
What does all of this mean?"

"Elliot Crawford is your real father. I told him I'd never
tell you, but I can't go to my grave holding this secret any
longer."

"Who is Elliot Crawford and it doesn't matter that he's
my father. You've been there for me all my life, I don't give

a damn about him," Adrian raged as his mother took a ragged breath.

"Don't say that. Get to know him."

"Know him? Why would I want to get to know the loser who didn't stick around to be a part of my life and if he loved you so much, where the hell is he now?"

Pamela's glassy eyes searched her son's face and her mouth fell open. Her hand slipped from his and Adrian knew one thing, he was going to find Elliot Crawford and make him pay.

The more he'd looked into the Crawford family, the more he wondered if his mother had dodged a bullet by not being involved with that family. Still, as he remembered reading the journal that his mother kept about the love she felt for Elliot, he knew that he had to bring that man down for stringing his mother along for all of those years. The words that poured from Pamela's heart had only worked to anger Adrian more and more. Why hadn't Elliot Crawford seen that his denial of their relationship and being away from him had taken a toll on his mother? While he hid Pamela away on the West Coast, she'd watched and kept heartbreaking notes about what he was up to and how his family grew. She'd even talked about how his visits to LA stopped after Adrian was born.

Every time he thought about his father's cowardly actions, he wanted to light a fire to the Crawford Towers construction site. He'd even had an alleged arsonist on his speed dial. The plan would be perfect: the hotel would burn and no one would suspect

Elliot's bastard son—because no one knew about him in the first place.

He knew the element of surprise would work in his favor, and he planned to use it to his advantage. Adrian had already gotten to Richmond, since he figured he was the weakest link. The men were scheduled to meet about a club in the hotel. His goal was to get his foot in the door so that he could have direct access to the hotel and create a lot of scandals. He had already decided to drop a nugget to any madame looking for a new hotel for client meetings. Then he'd call in the police, FBI, hell, even the CIA to make this story explode. Adrian knew there was a book in the works about the family, and he wanted to turn the tender family book into a tell-all exposé.

But since seeing Dana, he'd rethought the arson part of his plan. He knew she wouldn't approve of his scheme, especially the idea of setting anything on fire. After being apart for over two years, he was surprised that her opinion would still mean so much to him. Yes, he wanted her back and had plans to win her love again. But he'd pushed her away with the mission of bringing the Crawford family down. He didn't want her touched by his pain and anger and need for revenge. But he did want her.

Glancing down at his watch, Adrian realized that he had to leave now if he was going to make it to the press conference in enough time to make his presence known.

* * *

The weather was perfect for snapping pictures, and though Dana had completed her work with the studio, she decided to drive around the city to take some shots for her personal collection. People knew of Dana's work in glossy magazines and fashion pictorials, but her real love was to capture real people. Sort of like the work of Gordon Parks and his images of migrant workers. She'd hoped to find a buyer for her photography book. Imani was on her bandwagon and working her contacts to help Dana get a deal. Unfortunately, everyone wanted the glamour and celebrity shots.

The deals had been lucrative, but money wasn't everything to Dana. She wanted to publish pictures of real people living real lives. Sadly, publishers weren't feeling that idea. But as her mother, Whitney Singleton, always told her, there will be hundreds of nos before you get that one yes. Thinking of her mother, she smiled. Whitney had been her biggest cheerleader when Dana decided she wanted to be a photographer. She'd taken Dana to the Art Institute of New York City and told her that if this was her dream, she'd have to stick to it. When Dana had told her mother that this was what she was born to do, Whitney purchased her an old camera and twelve rolls of film and told her to trust her eye.

Dana hated that her mother never got to see her

dream come true, and she hated that she'd wasted her time with Adrian.

Where did that come from? She pulled into the parking lot of a Starbucks, grabbed her camera from the passenger seat, and walked toward the entrance. Immediately her mind returned to the last time she'd stopped for coffee and ended up with a mouthful of Adrian.

"Stop it," she whispered. "He threw you away when you'd been there for him and that's how he repaid you."

"Damn it," a voice behind her muttered.

Dana turned and saw a comely woman dressed in an ivory pantsuit kicking off a shoe with a broken heel.

"Are you okay?" Dana asked, wanting to snap a picture but refraining.

The woman smiled at Dana and she shook her head. "Unless you have a pair of shoes on you, I'm pretty much out of luck."

Dana held up her camera and asked, "Do you mind?"

The woman eyed her as if she'd asked her for a million dollars. "Why?"

"Because the typical Hollywood woman would be whining and you have a broken expensive shoe in your hand and a slight smile on your face," Dana said.

"That's because I'm a New York Southerner," she said, then held up her shoe while Dana took a couple of shots.

"A New York Southerner in California?" she asked when she put her camera down. "Interesting."

The woman frowned. "No, it really isn't."

Dana held the door open as she and her subject entered the coffee shop. "So, are you from LA?" she asked Dana.

"No, I'm a New Yorker working for Universal."

"I'm Kandace," the woman said as she extended her hand to Dana.

"Dana Singleton," she replied. The women took a seat near the front window after they ordered a couple of lattes and slices of banana bread.

"People in LA love Starbucks more than New Yorkers, for sure," Kandace said. "I think I know you or at least your work. Didn't you shoot a spread in *Elle*?"

"I did." Dana smiled, excited that someone noticed her work.

"Black girl in Paris. I'm keeping that magazine for my daughter. The layout was so tastefully done and I'm now a fan of Imani Thomas."

"She's good people," Dana said as she sipped her drink.

"Not one of those Hollywood types? Since my husband and I have been here, I've met more phony people than the law should allow." Kandace broke off a piece of her bread and popped it into her mouth.

"And no one around here eats," Dana laughed. Then she glanced down at her latte. She remembered the first time she and Adrian had met for Starbucks and how he'd told her that he knew she wasn't from LA when she had ordered a pastry with her coffee. Why did that man keep creeping into her thoughts? That kiss. She knew better than to think she could've been unaffected by having his lips pressed against hers and tasting the tongue that had brought her so much pleasure.

"Dana?" Kandace asked. "Are you all right?"

"I'm sorry, just a little preoccupied. That's why I decided to get out and shoot some photos."

Kandace nodded. "I had to get away from my husband and his family. I've never met three men who are so pigheaded and have to be right all the time."

Dana snorted. "I can relate to that." Shaking her head, she wondered why pigheaded men always captured seemingly smart women by the heart and never let go.

"Honey," Kandace said, exposing her Southern roots, "these people have more issues than *Ebony, Jet,* and *Essence.* But I love them anyway. I hope there isn't another family out there like these guys."

Dana shrugged, thinking that Adrian could probably give them a run for their money. "Thanks for letting me shoot you," Dana said, then reached into her bag and handed Kandace one of her business cards. "Send me an e-mail and I'll send you a copy of the picture. One day a publisher will understand that women want to see something other than high fashion and glamour shots."

"If my broken shoe makes it into your book, I'd be so honored," Kandace said. "And I'll throw you a hell of a party in Charlotte and New York."

"Charlotte? Oh, right, New York Southerner."

"My friends and I own a restaurant down there, Hometown Delights."

"Wait, not the restaurant where Emerson Bradford tried to kill his ex?" Dana bit down on her bottom lip.

"One in the same. Sometimes I wonder if it's better to be famous or infamous. When people think of Hometown Delights, no one ever thinks of the world-class chef who created our menu."

Though Dana heard annoyance in Kandace's voice, she could tell this was a conversation she'd had before. "But," Kandace said, "we have had a run of bad luck."

Dana nodded and decided not to say anything about the murder Kandace had been a party to at that same restaurant. It had been big news in New York because of Solomon Crawford's involvement and subsequent marriage to Kandace. She and Kandace locked eyes.

"I know what you're thinking," Kandace said.

"But I don't know you well enough to ask, so let's get more coffee."

Kandace laughed and drained the rest of her drink. "As much as I'd love to sit in here and pretend that whatever is going on at the Crawford Towers construction site has nothing to do with me, I'd better go and play the role of referee." She held up her broken shoe. "And find another pair of shoes."

"There is a shoe store two blocks over. So at least one problem is solved."

Kandace nodded at her. "Well, let's hope the rest of my problems today are solved this easily." As Kandace headed for the door, Dana drained the rest of her cold latte.

Morbid curiosity tugged at her otherwise logical mind. She'd moved on with her life, sort of . . . It wasn't as if she were pining away for Adrian Bryant. Granted, her career kept her too busy to have a serious relationship, but she dated. Secretly, she hoped to find someone like Imani's husband, Raymond. Kind, sweet, considerate, and understanding.

If Dana was honest with herself, she'd admit that Adrian really was nothing like Dr. Raymond Thomas. Her best friend's husband ran a free clinic in Harlem. Adrian was a club owner and promoter. He'd been the co-owner of several nightclubs, including Crimson. Dana hated that place, with all of the half-naked girls vying for A-list attention. Adrian had been on the receiving end of that attention, though he'd sworn to Dana that he'd never cheated. But she believed that their text message breakup had something to do with activities going on in the club. Dana wanted to believe that she was wrong about that, but she thought she was proven right the night she'd shown up at his penthouse following his mother's funeral.

"Dana?" Imani asked. "Are you all right? I've been calling your name since I walked in here."

"Oh, yes. I'm sorry, I'm a little distracted."

Imani raised her right eyebrow. "Are you getting stressed out by the studio? I know Willard Maines, the director of public relations, is getting on my last nerve!"

Dana waved her hand and *psst* at Imani. "Willard and I have already had our come-to-Jesus meeting about these shots. He, of course, blames you actors and your unrelenting schedules for the reason why things have fallen behind. I was just thinking about something that happened in another Starbucks a few days ago."

"You've been holding out on me," Imani said as she waved for the barista and ordered a skinny vanilla latte with soy milk and no whipped cream. Dana shook her head, ready to tell her friend that she'd taken the fun and taste out of the drink.

"You've been busy and I don't want to talk about it."

"It's that guy, isn't it?"

"What guy?"

"The fool who dumped you by text message."

Dana waited for the barista to finish making their drinks before she answered Imani. "It's not that serious, all right?"

Imani rolled her eyes and placed her hand on

Dana's shoulder. "Girl, if he's on your mind, then it is that serious. I know you, D. You have the tendency to obsess and hop inside your camera to forget that there's a big world out there you should be a part of."

"Been doing yoga and talking karma with some of your Hollywood friends? I need to talk to Imani from Brooklyn."

"No, you need to talk to Imani from Harlem. Because if you are considering talking to that ass again, I need to slap you."

"Did I say that? But how weird is it that we run into each other at Starbucks during a blackout?"

"Maybe the blackout was a sign?" Imani shrugged. "Listen, if this guy was dumb enough to let you go, then let it be."

"Maybe I need closure, a period at the end of all this so that I—"

"Closure? You know that's just an excuse to hit the sack one more time."

"Whatever."

"I'm just saying, you are better than this and you shouldn't—"

"I get it," Dana said, stopping what was surely going to be an infamous Imani rant. As much as she didn't want to admit it, her friend was right. Adrian had gone dark on her, evident by his cruel breakup. But his kiss made her wonder if he'd finished fighting his demons and could be the man she loved again.

"Dana?"

"Yeah?"

"I said I'm going back to New York for a few days. Why don't you come back with me and get your mind off that dude?"

"I'm not running away from Adrian, and I have a schedule that I have to keep."

"Speaking of schedules," Imani said. "Edward said if I can get the studio to sign off on it, the producers of *Cat on a Hot Tin Roof* want me to do a week's run as Maggie."

"That's big! Congratulations."

"I know and I get to spend a week with my husband. God, I miss that man so much."

"I bet you do. He's coming out here for the premiere of the movie, right?"

"You know it," Imani said with a gleam in her eye.

Dana couldn't help but smile at her friend's happiness. Dana glanced at her watch. "Playtime is over. I have to head back to Culver City. Lawrence Miller is supposed to actually show up today."

Imani rolled her eyes. "He puts the *D* in *diva*."

Dana nodded. "Tell me about it. Maybe I should start taking notes and write a tell-all book."

"No way! Then I'd have to disassociate myself from you."

"The first ten chapters would be all about you," Dana quipped.

Imani narrowed her eyes at her and pretended

to be appalled. "At least the pictures would look good."

The two women finished their coffees and headed outside. Dana tried to focus on her upcoming photo shoot with megastar Lawrence Miller, but as she headed for her car, Adrian was front and center in her mind.

Adrian shook hands with Richmond Crawford. "Nice to meet you, Mr. Bryant," Richmond said. "I went over the proposal about the nightclub for Crawford Tower. Impressive."

"I know what makes LA tick, and I can make your hotel the hottest spot in the city," Adrian said as he searched Richmond's face for any similarities. After all, this stiff, buttoned-up New Yorker was his brother. They had comparable hazel eyes. Richmond caught Adrian's intense gaze. He shot him a look that asked, *what's that all about?*

"You know, our other hotels don't have anything like a nightclub. Why should this one be any different?"

"Because it's LA. People don't just come to hotels because they're visiting the area. They come for dinner, for parties, and for hooking up."

Richmond cleared his throat and uncomfortably tugged at his tie. "I'm not really sure if that's the—"

"What's going on back here?" a deep voice boomed.

Richmond and Adrian turned around and watched Solomon cross the construction site and approach them. His eyes held untold accusations and questions. Without a doubt, Adrian recognized himself in his younger brother. Younger by four months. Solomon sized him up as Richmond made the introductions.

"Why is this the first time that I'm hearing about a nightclub in the towers?" Solomon demanded, ignoring Adrian's outstretched hand.

Pompous jackass, Adrian thought. He must take after his mother. Hell, he could be just like our sperm donor.

"Because the decision hasn't been finalized. Get over yourself, Solomon," Richmond snapped.

"Gentlemen," Adrian said, reminding the bickering brothers of his presence. "I don't think this is the time or the place. We can meet after the presser and have a drink. Relax, we're in California, not Manhattan."

Solomon raised his eyebrow at Adrian. "What the hell is that supposed to mean?"

"That you East Coast types need to mellow out."

"And that's supposed to make me want to do business with you?" Solomon sniped.

"It's not your decision to make alone. This isn't the Solomon Show," Richmond retorted. "And I'm getting pretty sick of you—"

"Why is it always an argument with you two?" Elliot Crawford said as he walked over to his sons.

He didn't give Adrian a second look as he stepped between Solomon and Richmond. The man with an ebony cane; caramel-brown skin, which was slightly wrinkled; and a bald head was the man who had ruined his mother's life. This man, with a slight curve in his spine and bass voice, was his father. The man who had just walked away from him and his mother, the man he was going to make pay for breaking his mom's heart. While the Crawford men argued, Adrian slipped away, not ready to come face-to-face with Elliot. Part of him wondered if the man would've recognized him anyway. Had he ever visited him or requested pictures of him? Adrian knew from reading his mother's words that New York had been a dream for her. But she left because of this bastard. Maybe Elliot figured throwing enough money at him and his mother would make them disappear. Deep inside, though, the little boy who wanted a father still yearned to know Elliot Crawford.

Walking out of the construction area, Adrian bumped into the woman he knew from his research was Solomon Crawford's wife, Kandace. He smiled at the comely woman and who he assumed was her assistant as he nearly collided into them. Placing his hand on Kandace's shoulder, he smiled at her. "Excuse me," he said. She looked up at him and blanched a bit.

"I didn't see you there," she said.

"No problem," he said, then extended his hand to her. "I'm Adrian Bryant."

"Bryant? I swear you wouldn't have surprised me at all if you'd said your last name was Crawford," she replied as she shook his hand and smiled. "I'm Kandace Crawford, by the way." The irony of Kandace's recognition of the family resemblance and the fact that his father and brothers didn't seem to get it at all wasn't lost on him.

"I've just had a conversation with the Crawfords . . . I'm pretty sure they don't want to claim me as a family member," Adrian said, chuckling.

The other woman pointed toward Solomon, who was scowling at the trio. "I think Mr. Crawford is ready to get this press conference over with."

"You're right, Nadia. I know that look." Kandace turned to Adrian. "It was nice to meet you, Mr. Bryant."

Adrian nodded in her direction and then gave Solomon an arrogant wink. He could nearly see the steam puffing from his brother's ears. Watching the interaction between Solomon and Kandace did something unexpected to Adrian. It made him yearn for Dana. He didn't know how long he stood there watching the subtle touches and sly smiles between them as if they knew a secret that they weren't going to share with the rest of the world.

He and Dana had had a connection like that once. He remembered the night she'd come to his club opening to take pictures for the *LA Weekly*. An hour earlier, they'd made love and joked about the groupies Atlanta rapper TI would attract. When she'd arrived and found Adrian and TI surrounded by half-naked women vying for a chance to get in VIP, they'd shared a smile that had meaning to them, and the rest of the world just wondered why they were so happy. He missed that more than he ever thought he would.

When Solomon caught Adrian's stare, he turned away and headed for his car. He didn't have time to be nostalgic. He had to plan for his meeting with his brothers.

Reaching into his pocket, Adrian retrieved his cell phone and dialed Louise Kilpatrick, an underground madam one of his employees had told him about. The plan was to get pictures of Richmond in a compromising position with a call girl. That would definitely puncture the good family image the Crawfords were trying to convey.

"Yes?" the woman said when she answered the phone.

"This is Easterling," Adrian said. "Are we still on for tonight?"

"I just checked the wire transfer and the money's there. In other words, the answer is yes."

"Like I said when we talked before, this is a surprise gift for my boy, so she needs to pretend she's happy to meet him."

"Look, Mr. Easterling, my girls are professionals,

and they know how to provide a surprise. But if there is any kinky extras, then expect a bill."

"I'll be happy to pay any additional costs," he said as he crossed the lot to his car. Looking up, he saw a car speeding his way. Just as he was about to curse at the driver, he saw it was Dana. Hanging up the phone, he flagged her down. Adrian half expected Dana to keep going or drive over him, so when she stopped, he was shocked.

"Are you stalking me?" she asked after rolling her window down.

"Glad to see you in a car," he said. "I think we should talk."

"I have to go to Culver City, and I'm not sure that we have anything to talk about."

Adrian wanted to reach inside the car and kiss her again. Wanted to tell her that they had a lot to talk about, and he had a lot to atone for.

"Dana, this is the second time we've run into each other by chance. Maybe somebody upstairs wants us to work this thing out."

"You're really bringing God into this?" She shook her head and rolled her eyes. "I don't think Jesus would've dumped me by text message. There would've been a bolt of lightning or an explanation."

Adrian winked at Dana, then pulled a business card from his pocket. "Dana, why don't we talk about that later?" He held the card out to her, and she looked at it as if it were the forbidden fruit that the serpent in the Garden of Eden offered to Eve. And just like Eve, she wanted to take it. However, she knew she wouldn't be able to handle the consequences. *Ignore him and this stupid heart of yours,* Dana thought. Still, she took the card.

Chapter 3

On the drive to Culver City, Dana glanced at the business card in the passenger seat. Why had she stopped? Why had she fooled herself into believing she needed closure with Adrian?

"Pandora's box," she muttered as she turned her attention back to the road. Dana knew she had to clear her mind before she dealt with Lawrence and his photo shoot. He may have been a great actor, but he was a horrible man. If she heard the words *Get my good side* again, she would bash him with her camera lens. Besides, the man had had so many Botox injections that his fifty-five-year-old face looked like plastic. Shaking her head, Dana decided that she was going to put her foot down and get this shoot done at a decent hour. There would be no diva attitude today, and if Lawrence and the studio didn't adhere to her schedule, she was going to walk. After all, Imani and hottie Ian Kelly were the stars of the film, not Lawrence.

As she pulled onto the lot of the Sony studio, she looked at Adrian's card once again. Lifting it from the seat, she tucked it in her pocket. She needed to try this foolish notion of closure and get an explanation for why Adrian walked when he'd supposedly loved her. Granted, she had moved on, dated again, but a piece of her never allowed herself to open up and give her everything to a man.

Her reasoning was self-preservation. Yes, it was the easy way out—the punk way. But Dana never again wanted to feel the pain that she felt after Adrian walked out of her life. Some people called it serial dating, but she didn't care. Even if Imani had taken to calling her a New York player.

When she walked into the studio, Dana wasn't surprised to see that Lawrence wasn't there but his "staff" was. Sighing, she walked over to the set and pulled out her camera.

"Dana, glad you're here," Sasha Mitchell, Lawrence's overworked and underpaid assistant, said. "L is on his way. He's having a bad day."

"When is he not having a bad day?" Dana snipped as she set up her equipment.

"That's funny," she replied with a nervous laugh. "Please don't mention his hair, though."

"Are you kidding me?" Dana snapped. "He's holding up this photo shoot because he's having a bad hair day?"

Sasha held her index finger up to her lips. "You know L is very sensitive about—"

"Are we ready to get this over with?" a thunderous

voice boomed from the doorway. Dana held back a laugh as Lawrence walked into the studio wearing an ill-fitting toupee. It was shaped like a box and reminded her of Steve Harvey's old do, which Dana always believed was a bad toupee.

"Good afternoon, Lawrence," Dana said, still trying not to laugh as she got a closer look at the hair. "I'm ready when you are."

"I'm here, aren't I? Where's the little reality TV star? Aren't you two joined at the hip or something?"

Dana shook her head and lifted her camera to her shoulder. "Today is all about you. If you would kindly head over here to the backdrop, we can start and finish."

He rolled his eyes, mumbling about how every day should be about him and that without his name, this movie would head straight to DVD. As much as Dana wanted to tell him that his five scenes didn't make him the star of the movie and that his hair was ridiculous, she didn't. She simply held up her camera to evoke a big smile from his plastic face.

"Wait, wait, wait," he said after Dana had fired off a few test shots. "Make sure you get me from my best side."

Dana gritted her teeth and made a mental note to shoot him from his right side just on general principle. After three wardrobe changes, one straightening of the toupee, and a shouting match, the photo shoot was finally over. Dana was tired, hungry, and happy to see Lawrence go. Packing her camera equipment, she grabbed her memory card and started to stick it into her jacket pocket. That's when she felt Adrian's card. Pulling it out, she was tempted to toss it. But she knew she had to call him, because if she didn't, it was going to eat away at her.

Dana plucked her cell phone from her camera bag and dialed his number.

"Bryant."

"Adrian," Dana said, then sighed. "It's Dana."

"I'm glad you called. Really didn't think you were going to."

"Don't make me regret it. What do you want?" *No need to beat around the bush,* she thought as she waited for his reply.

"We need to talk. I need to talk and I hope you'll listen," he said.

Dana rolled her eyes and blew into the phone. "Talk about what, Adrian? Those two women you flaunted in my face after texting me that I should move on? Or are we going to talk about how you went from loving me to being a block of ice?"

"I know you don't believe this, but I was trying to protect you. There was a lot going on in my life."

"And I was trying to support you and be there for you," she snapped. "Don't you think I know how much it hurt you to lose your mother? I was trying to be there for you and you shut me out as if I'd done something wrong to you."

"Can we talk about this at Starbucks? Better yet,

the least I can do is buy you a nice dinner and show you a good time."

"Whatever," she said. "Starbucks is fine."

"Dana. Dinner and a movie premiere is all I'm talking about," he replied, then laughed. "Unless you—"

"That. Is. Not. Going. To. Happen!"

"And just what is *that*?"

"If I decide to go to dinner with you, I'll call you back. You should be thankful that I'm willing to meet you at Starbucks," she said, then ended the call. What had she gotten herself into? Why did she fall for that closure bull? All she'd really done was open an old wound.

Adrian glanced at his phone and smiled. Hearing Dana's voice almost took his mind off his plans for Richmond Crawford and the call girl. Hearing her voice almost made him forget that his sole purpose in Los Angeles right now was to bring down his father and those sons of his. For that reason, he should've walked away and left Dana alone. He didn't want her involved in this, and he didn't want her to be touched by any of this family war that he was about wage. That's why he'd ended their relationship and watched her walk out of his life and go back to New York. Having her back in Los Angeles couldn't change his plans; he wanted revenge, and he would get it no matter what. But he wanted

Dana back in his life in the worst way. He wanted and needed her softness around him more than ever. He'd never loved anyone the way he loved her. He craved her touch, her kisses, and her taste. He hadn't thought about her much while developing his plan to bring the Crawfords down, but just one kiss from her put Dana back in the forefront of his mind. How could he not yearn for this woman, though? She was sensual, independent, and sexy as hell. When he held Dana in his arms, her sweet kisses and tender touches made him feel alive and needed. How in the hell did he allow her to walk out of his life? Would he be able to convince her to fall in love with him again while he was trying to bring his family down? Would she ever forgive him for that night? Adrian hadn't thought about the hurt he saw etched across Dana's face that night, because thinking about it reminded him of what an asshole he'd been. Sighing, he sat on the edge of his desk and squeezed the bridge of his nose. He couldn't get off track. Richmond, he believed, was his key to getting the inside track to the man who ruined his mother's life, and once he had the information he needed, he'd rip Elliot's mask right off.

For a split second, he heard his mother telling him what he was doing was wrong. He could feel her spirit frowning down on him. If his mother made peace with Elliot abandoning them, why couldn't he? Easy—he didn't take kindly to people hurting his mother, and after discovering her diary,

Adrian knew that Elliot had hurt his mother deeply. It was only fair that the old bastard felt some pain of his own. Even though Adrian knew one of his mother's final wishes had been for him to get to know his father, the bitter and disappointed child in him was not going to make the effort. Why in the hell should he? Elliot never tried to know him. He strengthened his resolve and decided that his plan would go ahead.

Leaping off the edge of the desk, he grabbed his phone and called Richmond.

"Hello?"

"Richmond, this is Adrian Bryant. I was just calling to confirm our meeting tonight," he replied in an überprofessional tone.

"Ah, Mr. Bryant, I'm not sure if I want to sit in some loud, smoky club tonight."

"Then you're in luck. It's illegal to smoke indoors here and I run lounges—not just clubs. You and your brother should come check it out."

"My brother and I won't be checking out— You know what, I will meet you and check out your operation. It's time that I put my mark on this madness," Richmond said.

"I'll send a car for you," Adrian said, pumping his fist happily.

"Wow, very classy of you."

Adrian gripped his phone and swallowed a caustic reply. "I run a very classy organization," he replied, deciding that having Richmond set up with the call girl was for the best because he was a pompous jackass.

After hanging up with his brother, Adrian called the car company and gave them instructions to pick up Richmond and the call girl he'd hired. He wanted the woman in the car before Richmond. Once he'd given the instructions to the driver, Adrian grinned, thinking that tonight would be an evening Richmond would never forget.

"Hello," Imani said, snapping her fingers in front of Dana's face. "Are you listening?"

"What?" Dana asked as she looked up at her friend.

"All right, Dana, what's going on with you? You've been acting strange since Raymond and I got here."

Dana sighed and lifted her half-empty coffee cup to her lips. "I'm just a little preoccupied with work."

"Not buying it. What's really going on?" Raymond asked as he shared a piece of pecan pie with his wife. Dana grinned at the couple. Raymond had become like a brother to her, and maybe he could offer some advice from a male's point of view. Setting her coffee cup on the table, she looked up at Raymond and said, "Tell me what you think about this."

"Okay," Raymond said, then took a sip of his coffee. Imani rolled her eyes.

"Remember when Imani filmed that movie with

Bradley Cooper and I came out here with her? I met someone."

"I figured as much," Raymond said. "My wife was really sad when you didn't come back to New York."

"She should've come back," Imani mumbled.

"Hush," Dana said. "I'm talking to Raymond. Anyway, things didn't work out. It was like one day we were in love and the next day I got a text message saying it was over."

"That's cold as hell," Raymond said as he shook his head.

"Tell me about it. I knew he was hurting after his mother's death, but I didn't think he'd lash out at me, because all I'd done was be there for him."

"Not to defend him, but some people deal with grief by hurting the people closest to them," Raymond said. "I've been guilty of that."

"At least you had the good sense to apologize immediately," Imani said.

Dana flashed her a look informing her to be quiet as Raymond stroked the back of Imani's hand.

"Well, it's been two years but who did I run into twice in the last few days? Adrian."

"What did he have to say for himself?" Raymond asked.

"That we should talk. I mean, why now?" Dana sighed and toyed with her coffee cup.

"It takes some men a long time to realize that they made a big mistake. Maybe you should hear him out and see where his head is," Raymond said.

"Absolutely not!" Imani exclaimed. "That's the worst advice you could give her."

"Drama queen," Dana said, causing Raymond to snicker.

"Imani," Raymond said. "If they keep running into each other, then maybe—"

"He's stalking her?"

"Imani," Dana said. "You really should switch to decaf."

"If I'd been the asshole to dump you through a text message but had a chance to right the wrong and possibly get forgiveness, I'd try it as well. What could talking to him hurt?"

My heart, my soul? she thought as she picked up her cup again.

"Dana," Imani said. "I wouldn't do it. If anything, you should text him and tell him where he can go and how to get there."

Raymond kissed Imani's cheek. "I wonder about you sometimes," he said.

Dana was wondering as well, wondering if she should call him back and agree to dinner. Yes, she owed it to herself to find out why he'd been so cold and ended their relationship. But did she want to rip the old scab off an old wound? Her mind wandered back to that night.

Dana waited outside Adrian's penthouse, wanting—no, needing—an explanation of his text message. Just as she pulled out the phone to read the three-line message again, she heard the ding of the elevator and the laughter. Those were female voices and Adrian's.

"And you have a rooftop pool?" one of the voices cooed.

"Can we skinny-dip?" another asked.

Dana gritted her teeth as she saw them turn the corner. Adrian was flanked by two half-naked broads, one of whom was actually unzipping his slacks.

"What is this?" Dana demanded, wishing there was something in reach to hurl at him. This son of a . . ."

"Dana?" he asked, pushing Thing One's hand away. "What are you doing here?"

She shook her head, refusing to let the tears burning in her eyes drop. "Getting the answers I need."

"Didn't you get my text?" he asked.

Crossing over to him, she slapped his smooth cheek with all the fury inside her. "Damn you."

Adrian rubbed his face and snorted. "Look, I told you to move on. As you can clearly see, I have."

"And to think I was concerned about you because your mother passed away. I thought . . . Never mind. Enjoy your whores."

"Just who are you talking to?" one of the women shouted.

"Stalker," the other called out.

"Stop it," Adrian said, and nodded toward the door. "I'll handle this." He gripped Dana's elbow and whispered in her ear, "I was trying to protect you."

She smiled sardonically, thinking that all she'd done was love him, support him, and hurt for him as he watched his mother die. Dana swiftly kneed him in the family jewels. "Maybe one of those bitches will kiss it and make it better," she snapped, then dashed to the elevator.

She couldn't wait to get away from Adrian, Los Angeles, and everything else that reminded her of his trifling ass. She was going back to New York City.

Imani watched her friend in breathless disbelief. "I don't get it. If he dropkicked your heart like that, then why do you want to talk to him at all? This is the one time when I'm going to tell you, don't listen to him." She threw her thumb in Raymond's direction.

"So, this is the thanks I get for taking time off from work and flying halfway across the country to be with you and you're telling folks not to listen to me. Maybe I should—"

"Lean over here and give me a kiss, Dr. Thomas."

"Hello!" Dana exclaimed as the couple shared a kiss. "I'm still here, sitting at this table with you two. No one wants to witness your PDA anymore."

Imani rolled her eyes at Dana and Raymond while they laughed. "I don't think either of you are funny. But I will say this—if you do have dinner with him, make sure you go someplace expensive and order caviar."

"Why would I do that? I don't even like caviar."

"I know. Just order it and throw it in his face."

"That's cold, babe," Raymond said.

Dana shook her head as she rose from the table. "And on that note, I'm out. I have pictures to edit. Thanks for listening, Raymond."

He smiled and stood to give her a brotherly hug. "Anytime, and don't follow your friend's advice. Tossing caviar at people is never a good idea."

"I heard that," Imani shot back.

Dana laughed, then headed for the door. Imani quickly caught up with her friend. "You know, if you simply want a dinner date, I could make that happen for you."

"What are you talking about?" Dana asked with her hand on the door handle.

"I could hook you up with Ian Kelly."

Dana rolled her eyes. "Your costar?" Ian Kelly was touted in the media as the next Matthew McConaughey, just without the naked bongos and marijuana. The actor had been voted one of *People* magazine's sexiest men alive, and he stuck to his Southern roots despite his success as an actor. Was he attractive? Yes. But Dana couldn't say she was interested. She hadn't even met him yet; they were scheduled to do a photo shoot in a few days, and by all accounts, he was much less of a diva than Lawrence was and things would probably go well.

"My single, sexy, and sweet costar. You two already have something in common—he rides a motorcycle too. He's grounded because he splits his time between New York and New Orleans. Just think about it." Before Dana could object, agree, or tell Imani to mind her own business, her friend was on the phone with Ian Kelly. Dana started to bolt and leave Imani to her own devices when her cell phone chimed.

Glancing at the text message, her heart lurched. **Dinner tomorrow. Breakfast at Roscoe's in a few hours? Please. A.B**

I have plans, she quickly replied. **And I haven't agreed to dinner.**

But you will. Miss you. Want to see you, badly.

"Okay, Ian," Imani said. "Raymond, Dana, and I will see you there."

Dana looked up from her text message. "Did I just hear you commit me to something?"

"Get dressed and get ready for a night on the town," Imani said with a twinkle in her eye. "Ian told me about this hot club that's having an opening tonight."

She glanced at her phone. Well, she did tell Adrian she had plans and maybe having dinner with Adrian was a bad idea, despite what Raymond said. "All right," Dana said. "What time should I be ready?"

Imani looked down at her watch. "Shoot, I forgot to change my watch back to Pacific time since I thought I'd be going back to New York today."

"It's seven-thirty."

"All right, be ready at nine," Imani said as she tossed her cup in the recycling bin.

Dana nodded and then left. If she made it through traffic and got back to the hotel at decent hour, she could get the photos ready for the studio and make herself presentable for a night out with Imani and Ian. *And maybe I won't even think about Adrian.*

Chapter 4

Adrian sat in his office with his feet kicked up on his desk. He waited to hear if there was a sighting of Richmond and the call girl. When he looked out at the crowd coming into his club, he smiled. Opening night was looking like a success. Just as he was about to head downstairs to check out the scene, his cell phone rang.

"Yeah?"

"It's done," a voice said. "We have the pictures of Richmond Crawford and the call girl. They're en route to the club now."

"Cool. Call the police and send the pictures to my Gmail account and to Emily Burke at the *Los Angeles Times*."

"Got it."

"And dump the phone after you're done sending the pictures." Adrian ended the call with a big smile on his face. Now he was ready to bask in the success of his club opening and wake up to headlines of

Richmond's arrest. He was sure the news would make it back to New York. When he made it downstairs to the main floor of the club, Adrian was annoyed and surprised to see Richmond, looking a little disheveled, sitting at the far end of the bar.

What the hell? he thought as he crossed over to him. *Why hadn't the police gotten there yet? Typical LAPD.*

"Richmond, glad to see you made it," Adrian said with forced cheerfulness in his voice.

Richmond whirled around on the bar stool and glared at Adrian. "It's a good thing that I did make it here. What was the big idea?"

"What are you talking about?"

"You put a hooker in the car with me." Richmond downed the gin and tonic he'd been nursing.

"Wait a minute, I did no such thing. I don't own the car service that picked you up. How do you know the woman was a hooker?"

"The moment she saw the blue lights behind us, she started screaming at the driver about not being able to get caught because she had a pending prostitution case." Richmond tapped the bar, then rubbed his face. "If this gets out . . . It's bad enough that Solomon was involved with a lunatic and spent years screwing any woman with ovaries. I knew coming to Los Angeles was a mistake."

Adrian fought back a smirk. "So, how did you all elude the police?"

"She directed the driver here by some back streets. I'm not even sure the cops were after us," he said as the bartender placed another drink in front of him.

Obviously. I'm firing that fucking driver, Adrian thought. "So, I guess talking business is off tonight, huh?"

"What the hell do you think?" Richmond's mind flashed back to the scene in the back of the town car. He'd nearly had sex with a hooker. What if that got out? How would that affect the Crawford brand? He was supposed to be the responsible one. And Vivvy. This would be the ammunition she needed to get a huge divorce settlement.

He looked out on the crowd. Though his mind was clicking with thoughts of the huge mistake he'd just made, Richmond told Adrian he'd listen to his plan.

"This is a nice lounge. I see you draw a great crowd."

"People know I create excellent places to hang out. Stars can come in and not get hassled. The working man can come in and get treated like a star." Adrian snapped for his bartender, a shapely blonde dressed in a seventies-style white halter jumpsuit.

"Hey, A. B., what can I get for you?" she asked with a toothy smile.

Richmond focused on the bartender's breasts, then quickly chided himself. Breasts started his problems tonight.

"The usual and refill my friend's drink."

She glanced at Richmond and smiled. "And what can I get for you, handsome?"

"Umm, gin and tonic," he said.

"Top shelf," Adrian said, his special code for *make it extra strong*. With all of the photographers outside the club, someone would surely get a shot of drunken Richmond, which would add to the story. There was a silver lining.

"You got it," she said, then started making the drinks. For Adrian, a glass of orange juice and more gin than tonic for Richmond.

"How are things going with the hotel?" Adrian asked.

"What?" he asked, still distracted. "Will be an amazing feat if we get it done on time. I don't know who's worse to work with, Dad or Solomon."

Adrian cringed inwardly when Richmond said *Dad*. What made Solomon and Richmond Crawford worthy of their father's love while he and his mother were cast off from the family? "Why did you all decide to build in Los Angeles after all of these years? There's already plenty of luxury properties here."

"I asked that same question, but this is my father's pet project," Richmond said. "Which is odd, when my mother was alive, she hated Los Angeles and refused to entertain expanding to the West Coast—even after she retired."

Adrian folded his arms across his chest and leaned back on the bar, watching the door. "Interesting," he said absentmindedly.

"Why do you care, though?" Richmond asked as he followed Adrian's pose. "If we partner with you, all you have to worry about is keeping the club at the hotel packed like this."

"That's . . ." Adrian's voice trailed off when he saw Dana walk through the door with actress Imani Thomas, some tall dude, and freaking Ian Kelly. And Kelly had the nerve to have his arm about his woman's shoulders. And Dana was smiling as he whispered something in her ear. What in the blue hell was going on? These were her plans. Oh, hell no! Adrian was not about to watch Dana have a date in his damned club. Of course, the thought of her being with another man anywhere made him angry, sad, and disappointed. He couldn't have expected her to carry a torch for him for two years, though.

"What's wrong?" Richmond asked, taking note of Adrian's silence and following his gaze to the people who'd just entered the club. "Wow, that's the photographer Solomon tried to hire to work on our family book. No wonder she turned us down. A hotel company must be boring subject matter when you're hanging out with Hollywood stars."

"Family book?"

Richmond nodded as he accepted his drink from the comely bartender. "Another big idea by Dad. Said he wants to show that we're a family business, and no matter how big the Crawford empire is, family is the most important thing."

Between listening to Richmond and watching Dana flirt with Ian Kelly, Adrian felt ill. He gulped his orange juice and wished there was vodka in it. He turned to Richmond. "Excuse me for one minute." Rising from the bar stool, he crossed over to Dana and her crew. On the way over, he stopped one of the waiters and took a bottle of champagne from his tray. Adrian stood in front of Dana and set the bottle on the table. "Welcome to Allure," he said, attempting to sound jovial. "I'm the owner and I'd like to offer you a complimentary bottle of bubbly."

"Thank you," Imani replied.

"Adrian," Dana said.

"Adrian?" Imani furrowed her brows in confusion.

"This is your place?"

"Yes, Dana," he said, locking eyes with her. "Had you told me your plans included coming here, I would've rolled out the red carpet for you." Adrian glanced at Ian, who had his arm around Dana's shoulders, and sneered.

"You need to do more than that, jackass," Imani muttered, causing her husband to give her a cautioning look as he squeezed her hand.

"Had I known this was your spot, I would've suggested we go someplace else," Dana said coolly.

"I'm glad you and your friends are here," he said, forcing a smile.

"Thanks," Ian said as he took the bottle of champagne and passed it to Imani and Raymond. "Let's dance."

She hesitated for a moment and then nodded.

She and Ian rose from the table and brushed past Adrian to get to the dance floor. While he watched Dana bumping and grinding on the dance floor, Adrian saw red. Well, green actually. He was jealous beyond words as he saw his woman holding Ian tightly, just like when they used to go dancing. "That's just—"

"Karma," Imani shouted out as she and Raymond started for the dance floor.

Adrian narrowed his eyes at the actress and then returned to the bar where Richmond was in a conversation with the bartender's breasts.

"So, Richmond, tell me more about this book."

Across the room, Dana tried to pretend she wasn't looking at Adrian as she danced with Ian. But Imani caught her stare. "I'm hungry," Imani declared. "Babe, let's go to Roscoe's and bring those two along."

"Don't they have food here?" Raymond asked through a yawn.

"Do you want to leave?" Ian asked Dana. "Because your ex is shooting daggers with his eyes."

She laughed nervously. "How did you know that was my ex?"

"The look of 'damn, I messed up' gave it away."

Dana stroked Ian's shoulder as she held back more laughter. Why did he have to be so damned cute and nice? "Well, if you guys want to leave," she said, "we can."

"Great," Imani said.

"Um," Raymond groaned. "Jet lag is kicking in. Why don't you all go without me?"

"If you want to go back to the hotel, I'll go with you," Imani said. "I couldn't enjoy myself without you."

Raymond kissed her forehead. "Yeah, and you don't want to be a part of rumors about our marriage being over, either. There are a lot of reporters out there."

She thrust her hip into his. "I never had such a thought." Imani turned to Ian and Dana. "You guys can go eat without us, right?"

"That depends on Dana."

"Me?"

Ian nodded. "Do you mind riding on my Harley?"

"Not at all," she replied, excitement peppering her tone and causing her eyes to glitter. Her plan had been to rent a bike of her own next week and hit the PCH for old times' sake. Despite herself, she glanced in Adrian's direction and locked eyes with his angry glare. He had always hated the fact that she rode her motorcycle up and down the highway. His solution? He bought her a Corvette. Dana smiled, turned back to Ian, and followed him, Imani, and Raymond out of the club.

"That was strange," Raymond said once they were outside. "Was that about the conversation we had earlier? Otherwise, I'd like to know why my wife is picking fights with total strangers."

"Because you married a drama queen," Dana replied. "What did you do, Imani?"

Looking down at her nails, Imani pretended not to be paying attention to the conversation about her. "I'm sorry, I thought you two were talking about someone else. Raymond, let's talk about this later. Much, much later."

Ian laughed. "Imani, you're something. I'm going to get my bike. Be right back, Dana."

When Ian was out of earshot, Imani turned to Dana. "Don't fall for Mr. Slick's tricks."

"What are you talking about?"

"I'm not blind. I saw the looks you two were giving each other and—"

"Imani," Raymond interjected. "Leave Dana alone. When a man decides to alienate folks who can make or break his club, he has some deepseated affection for a woman. You should consider that dinner, Dana."

"No, you shouldn't," Imani shot back.

Dana reached out and hugged her friends. "I got this."

"Good," Raymond replied. "I need some sleep and I don't need my wife obsessing over someone else's business all night."

"I don't do that, Doctor," she snapped, then smiled. "Especially when there are so many other things we can do tonight."

"I think I feel my second wind kicking in."

"Eww," Dana said. "I'm standing here and this is

just uncomfortable. Like watching a reality show all over again."

Imani poked her friend on the shoulder. "Maybe you ought to . . ." She stopped talking when she heard the roar of Ian's Harley.

"Oh, that's sexy," Dana intoned as she watched Ian maneuver the Switchback up to the curb. Dana immediately recognized the rumbling of the twin cam 103 engine.

"Dangerous," Imani whispered.

"I don't know, honey, we'd look good on one of those."

Imani shot her husband a *get real* look. "Not on your life, Doctor. I can't believe you."

"When I hit my midlife crisis, expect to see me riding across 110th Street on one of those."

"Come on, Bobby Womack, our car is here." Imani linked arms with her husband as they headed for the limo. Dana walked over to Ian and ran her hand across the seat of the Harley.

"Nice."

"You ride?" he asked.

She nodded. "I had a Triumph once and against my better judgment, I sold it."

"I like those bikes, but this gives me all I need. Especially when I travel in New Orleans."

"New Orleans. I've always wanted to do a shoot down there."

"Oh no, *chere*, you've never been to New Orleans? Now, there's some beautiful scenery down by the bayou. You have to see it one day."

"It's definitely on my bucket list." Dana took the helmet Ian extended to her and snapped it on her head.

"Maybe I can be your tour guide—that is, if he doesn't have a problem with it." Ian nodded toward the entrance of Allure where Adrian was standing watching their every move.

Dana closed her eyes, willing him away. Willing her heart to stop pounding like a bass drum. "He's not a factor," she said as she climbed onto the back of Ian's bike and wrapped her arms around his waist. "Maybe we can use this bike in the shoot tomorrow." Glancing over her shoulder, she saw the anger clouding Adrian's face. What she didn't understand was why she cared. He'd done much worse to her, and now he had the nerve to be mad? Leaning closer to Ian, she closed her eyes and allowed the wind to blow Adrian out of her mind—for a little while at least.

"She really just hopped on a motorcycle with that fake-ass Tom Cruise," Adrian mumbled as he stomped back to the bar. Glancing at his brother, he saw Richmond was good and drunk. Unfortunately, the more Richmond drank, the more he complained about his wife, the more he talked about how he hoped being with that call girl wouldn't come back to bite him. Then he talked about Solomon and how his life seemed to be so perfect and all he wanted was a chance to be happy like his brother.

The only piece of information he gleaned from him was about the book. Elliot Crawford had a damned nerve trying to present a picture of being the perfect family when he ignored him and his mother. Adrian was going to make sure that the world knew it as well. Turning to his sad brother, he shook his head.

"Richmond, I'm going to have to cut you off and send you back to your hotel," Adrian said as Richmond prepared to launch into more complaints about Solomon.

"Yeah, yeah, back to my lonely hotel room. Nobody wants anything to do with me." He tilted his head toward the bartender. "She would've been all over Solomon. The only reason a woman let me touch her tonight was because she obviously wanted money." Richmond slurred his words so badly that Adrian wondered if he'd given him too much alcohol.

"You're married, right? Shouldn't you be trying to work things out with your wife?"

Richmond shrugged. "What difference does that make? She doesn't want anything but my name and my money. Sort of like what my dad wanted from my mother." He reached for his glass and Adrian moved it out of his way.

So, his mother knew about the affair and Elliot was too weak to accept his responsibilities. Richmond seemed to be just like his sorry excuse of a father, looking for someplace else to stick his pole. Rich married men seemed to love having something on the side. Adrian wondered if his mother had been mistaken about the love she thought Elliot had had for her. Maybe, like Richmond, he had a horrible marriage and used Pamela as an escape. He hated thinking about his mother as anyone's option; she was much more than that.

Looking at Richmond, he decided that it was time to get him back to the hotel before the photographers left and wouldn't be able to catch him stumbling to the car, making a further ass of himself. Adrian pulled out his cell phone and called a different car service to take Richmond back to his hotel; then he waved for the bartender to pour Richmond a cup of black coffee.

When the driver called from outside and Richmond had sipped half of his coffee, Adrian motioned for a security guard to escort his brother outside and he headed for his office. In the stillness of the dim office, his mind switched back to Dana and Ian Kelly. Had she gotten caught up in his celebrity image and that freaking motorcycle? Were they serious? Was she another one of Kelly's groupies? Wait a minute—Dana wasn't a groupie. If anything, that guy was head over heels in love with his woman. Adrian dropped down in the chair behind the desk and pulled his cell phone out again. He started to text Dana. But what would he say? He couldn't tell her the truth, couldn't type what he really wanted to say: *I still love you.* Adrian tossed the phone across the room.

"This is insane." Then an idea popped into his head. Dana was probably staying at a hotel near the movie studio, and if the studio was picking up the tab for it, then it was probably the same place where Dana was staying. It was off to Culver City. And he silently prayed she would be returning to her hotel room alone and not spending the night with Ian. Crossing the room and grabbing his smartphone, which now had a cracked screen, Adrian tried not to think about Ian's lips pressed against Dana's and he definitely wasn't trying to think about Ian making love to his woman.

He rushed down the back stairs and headed to the Culver Hotel, hoping that he was heading in the right direction.

Chapter 5

Ian's handling of the motorcycle was smooth, cautious, and not at all how Dana would've zipped down the highway. Then again, he was probably being courteous because she was riding with him.

They decided to skip Roscoe's and go to a nondescript diner instead. Ian wanted to avoid the paparazzi and Dana agreed. As they pulled into the diner's lot, Dana realized she was going to purchase another motorcycle and she would ride in New York.

"That was an amazing ride," Dana said as she pulled her helmet off.

"I could tell you enjoyed the ride. You were really comfortable back there," he said.

"Yeah," she said, then stretched her arms above her head. "I can't wait to get me another motorcycle. I might dump the Triumph for a Harley."

"Sounds like a plan. Glad I could assist in that decision." Ian placed his hand on the small of her back as he opened the door of the diner. It was nearly empty and Dana felt a twinge of nervousness, which was funny. She had no problem hopping on the back of his motorcycle, but now she was nervous about talking to him? *Get it together*, she thought as they headed for a booth.

"Imani's trying to play matchmaker with us, isn't she?"

Dana nodded. "That's my girl. Since her fairytale wedding, she's been on a mission to make sure no single people exist. Especially if the single people are a part of her inner circle."

Ian laughed and placed his hand on top of hers. "You're funny and very pretty. I don't know how you've spent your life behind the camera when I'm sure you'd look good in front of it."

Dana's cheeks burned under his compliment. "Thank you. But I wouldn't trade my camera for the stress you and Imani face on a daily basis. My idea of being camera ready is having an extra memory card and a fully charged battery."

Ian chuckled and leaned in close to her. "So, what's your story?"

"My story?"

"Yes, why are you single when you're obviously such a cool lady?"

Adrian's face flashed in her mind. Yes, he broke her heart into a million pieces, but that hadn't stopped her from comparing the men she dated to him. Dana remembered how they'd clicked on so many levels. Well, except for his inability to be faithful, truthful, and compassionate. Sadly, no one measured up to him. Would Ian be different? Should she even let her mind go there? *He's a movie star with all kinds of women at his disposal,* she thought as he focused his sky-blue eyes on her. "I guess my career comes first."

"I've seen your work, very artistic. Watching you on the set, I have to say, you have the patience of Job. If you ever do get to New Orleans, I will definitely be your tour guide. I'd love to show you a good time beyond Bourbon Street."

Dana laughed nervously and smiled. "Thank you."

"Are you shooting the premiere tomorrow night?"

"Nope. After I wrap up these publicity shots, my work with the studio will be done and I can work on my personal project."

Ian flashed the electrifying smile that shot him to the top of *People*'s Sexiest Man Alive list and said, "Great, you can be my date."

"Wow, that's . . . Sure."

"Don't worry, *chere,* we're just going as friends. Though, I'm not going to lie—I'd love to get to know you better. Especially since you have a taste for Harleys. Tell me about your project."

"I want to do a photography book. Something like Gordon Parks's work. Not just the glamorous shots of Hollywood stars," she said, then held up her finger. "No offense."

"None taken. It just sounds like more incentive to head down to New Orleans. There's still so much work to be done to recover from Katrina, even all these years later."

Dana nodded, thinking of the oil spill in the Gulf and all of the displaced residents who hadn't even made it back to the city following the 2005 storm. "I'd love to find Brownie and ask him some questions," she said. "The response to that storm made me so angry."

"Yeah, it was hard to watch my city drown. Even harder to see how many people wanted to come back but couldn't. That's one of the reasons why I established my foundation, to provide housing for many of the displaced residents of the lower ninth ward."

"This is the first I've heard of this," Dana said, thinking about all of the coverage Brad Pitt's efforts had gotten.

"I didn't do it for publicity. I just did it to help people who needed it."

"Wow." Dana smiled and decided that Ian had moved up ten spots on her list of Awesomeness.

He shrugged. "When you love New Orleans, you do what you have to do to make her whole again."

"A humble superstar?"

"I'm just trying to right some wrongs. I fell for the trappings of Hollywood after my first hit movie. Did some things I shouldn't have, was an asshole for a while. Then life showed me a few horrible things and I had to clean it up."

"That's admirable," Dana said. "It usually takes arrests and rehab for those epiphanies to happen."

"No arrests. No rehab. Just some common sense. We all have our vices, though."

Adrian crossed her mind and Dana had to admit that if she had a vice, it would be him. "You're right. Maybe we can work on being better people together. I just have one question."

"What's that?"

"Are we rolling up to the premiere on the hog?"

"A woman after my own heart. Of course, any excuse to have those arms around me again."

Dana blushed as the waitress walked over to their booth. After ordering, she and Ian fell into a comfortable conversation. Still, in the back of her mind, she was comparing Ian, one of *People*'s Sexiest Men Alive, to Adrian.

What in the hell is wrong with me? she thought as the waitress returned with their coffees.

Adrian sat in the hotel lobby staring at his watch. *Okay, where in the hell is Dana?* When he rose to his feet and began pacing—again—the front desk clerk cleared her throat. "Sir, I can try that guest's room again if you'd like."

"No," he said, and started for the door. Adrian was ready to assume that Dana and the fake-ass action hero were spending the night together. When he walked outside, he saw Kelly's motorcycle pulling up. Dana was all wrapped up with him. Well, he knew she had to hold on, but did she have to do it that tightly? He quickly moved back into the lobby. A million thoughts ran through his mind: Would she invite him up? How long had they been seeing each other? Was it serious? Adrian returned to the seat he'd been occupying for the last few hours and waited.

Five minutes passed.

Ten.

Fifteen. As he stood up again, Adrian saw Dana walking into the lobby—alone. Releasing a sigh of relief, he crossed over to her. "Dana."

She glared at him. "What are you doing here? How did you know I was staying here?"

"I wanted—need—to talk to you."

Slapping her hand on her hip, Dana shook her head. "Unbelievable. You're here because of Ian."

"I'm here because I . . . You're serious with him?"

"Why does it even matter? Remember you told me it was over and I needed to move on?"

Adrian closed the space between them, bringing his lips dangerously close to hers. "Because you're mine, Dana."

"Oh, am I? Was I yours when you showed up at your penthouse with your whores? Was I yours when you sent that text message telling me to move on with my life? Now you're pretending that you give a damn. Go to hell, Adrian."

He wrapped his arms around Dana's waist and pulled her against his chest. "I want to explain what that night was all about," he said as he ran his hand down her side.

She slapped his hand away, though his touch

made her body tingle all over. "I already told you I'm not interested in a lie it took—"

Adrian captured her mouth savagely, cajoling her tongue to join his. Dana's mind said, *Stop, back away, and run.* But her body responded, as it always had, from the wetness between her thighs to the way she melted against his broad chest. So she was surprised when Adrian abruptly broke the kiss and stepped back from her. Dana's body yearned for more. She needed to get herself together. But his probing stare made her feel as if she were on fire, consumed by lusty flames that no one but Adrian could extinguish.

"Dana, I don't want to play this game. I want you to be honest with yourself and admit that you still want and need me. Because I damn sure want and need you more than ever."

She sucked her teeth, telling herself that she'd admit no such thing. There was no way that she'd give him the satisfaction of knowing that she still craved his touch, yearned for his taste, and needed his heat. Hell no! She would not . . . Adrian lifted her chin and pressed his nose against hers. Dana's lips quivered as she felt the warmness of his breath teasing her mouth. *Step away!* her good sense called out. But Dana ignored it, pressing her mouth against his and kissing him with zeal. Her words didn't have to admit what she felt for Adrian because her kiss said it all.

Though he was briefly taken aback by the sheer force of her kiss, Adrian received what she was saying and cupped her bottom, drawing her closer to him. She gasped when she felt the bulge in his pants. Pulling back from him, she felt drunk, felt as if she was about to make a bad decision that she would regret in the morning. "I want you, Adrian," she moaned.

"Say it again," he commanded.

"I. Want. You. Now."

Adrian smiled and pointed toward the elevator. "Lead the way."

Dana gripped his hand and practically ran to the elevator. And despite hearing Imani's voice and the voice of reason telling her to stop, her heart screamed out for her to let Adrian make love to her. She was going to listen to her heart, give in to the lustful feelings flowing through her body. Maybe, just maybe, this was the closure she needed— right?

When the doors of the elevator opened, Adrian and Dana were happy to see they'd be alone in that car for a few floors at least. As soon as the doors closed, Adrian backed Dana against the mirrored wall and kissed her slowly while his hands roamed her body, touching her intimately. He lifted her leg around his waist, happy and disappointed that she had panties on underneath her skirt. At least he knew she wasn't about to sleep with Ian. Slipping his finger inside the crotch of her panties, her heat and wetness turned him on and made him harder than a cement block. Dana moaned as his finger found her throbbing bud. She shivered as he made small circles inside her.

Just as he was about to drop to his knees and lap the sweetness he felt pooling between her thighs, the elevator stopped on the third floor and the door opened. Adrian pulled Dana against his chest as a man stepped into the elevator. Dana pressed her lips against Adrian's neck.

"Oh, you're so bad," he whispered as he kept an eye on the older man, who was trying not to watch the couple and failing miserably. "You're going to give me and that man a heart attack."

"Is that so?" She flicked her tongue across his earlobe. Their passenger coughed and dropped his head.

"I'm going to get you for this," Adrian groaned as she sucked his earlobe.

"Thought this was what you wanted?"

The elevator stopped again, fourth floor. "Where's your room?" he asked as a less amorous couple stepped into the car.

"Two more," she replied, then slipped her hand in his pocket. Adrian's erection twitched as anticipation surged through his veins. Finally, the sixth floor. Adrian scooped Dana up in his arms and nearly bowled the other guests over as they made a hasty exit. Dana placed her hand on his chest. "Slow down. You almost knocked those people over."

"They will be all right," he replied, but did slow his gait a bit. Dana pointed to room 612. Adrian waited for her to dig the key out of her clutch; then he took it from her hands and opened it. Once they were inside, Dana expected Adrian to rip her clothes off and take her immediately. He didn't. Instead he sat her on the edge of the bed, stared at her for a beat, then said, "Dana, I love you."

"Adrian, don't do this. I don't need to hear sweet words—"

"But you need to know the truth. That night, the night you left, nothing happened with those women. I knew you'd be there. And I wanted you to be anywhere but here. I was—am—dealing with a lot of hurt and I wanted to keep the beautiful memories we had safe from the madness around me."

Dana shook her head. "I don't understand. If you love me, why couldn't you allow me to help you through this?"

"Because," he began, then sighed. "It's complicated and I don't want to get you involved."

"Involved in what?"

"My mess. When I saw you, I knew I couldn't let this thing consume me as it had over the last two years."

"I know losing your mother was hard, Adrian. I wanted to be there for you and—"

He brought his lips on top of hers, kissing her softly, tenderly—fighting telling her the truth. Was he still going to destroy the man who abandoned him and his mother? Yes. But right now, in this moment, it didn't matter. He needed Dana to remind him of love. Over the past two years, he hadn't allowed anyone to get close to him. No one, in his opinion, had the warmness he felt in Dana's kiss or the passion he felt in her touch. Slowly, he unbuttoned her blouse, reveling in the silkiness of her skin. Leaning in, he flicked his tongue across her neck, making her moan. Slipping her blouse off, Adrian cupped her breasts, using his thumbs to release them from the cups of her demi-bra. Her nipples reminded him of dark chocolate drops, and they were just as sweet. His mouth watered as he lowered his head and sucked her nipples until Dana cried out in delight. She held the nape of his neck as he licked and sucked her nipples. His tongue sent waves of pleasure vibrating through her body. Moaning, Dana lost herself in the moment, pushing all of the questions about his "mess" down deep in her subconscious. One nagging question still bit at her pleasure—why didn't he trust her enough to let her in? Did she mean as much to him as she thought? How much did he love her if he didn't trust her?

Adrian felt her tense up in his arms. He pulled back and focused his stare on her comely face. "What's wrong?"

"Nothing. Don't stop," she moaned. "Please."

"Are you sure you want to do this?"

"I need you."

Adrian slid her skirt down her hips; then she spread her thighs apart. He stroked her through her panties, making her legs shiver and shake as he pulled the crotch of the silky panties to the side.

Bringing her hips to his lips, Adrian licked and kissed her wet folds, seeking her throbbing bud. How he'd missed the sweetness of her. Dana wasn't like any other woman he'd ever known. And if someone had told him a week ago that he'd be able to taste her again, he wouldn't have believed it at all.

"Adrian!" she screamed as his lips closed around her clitoris. Adrian lapped her sweetness as she exploded in his mouth. Dana reached out and clawed at his shirt until she nearly ripped it off. He pulled back and stripped out of his clothes. Dana's eyes were drawn to his erection. Her mouth watered as he joined her on the bed. His body was still amazing, like caramel dripping over a delicious treat. He was much more than the fantasies she'd created in her mind over the last twenty-four months. When Adrian pulled her into his arms, Dana shivered from anticipation. The anticipation of feeling him deep inside her, the anticipation of tasting his lips again, and the anticipation of the pleasure she'd receive from the only man she'd ever been so free and open with. Gripping his shoulders, she pulled Adrian on top of her and kissed him with a burning passion, sucking his bottom lip as she wrapped her legs around his waist.

Adrian wanted to drive into her wetness, revel in the feel of their skin-to-skin contact as he was nearly burned by her heat, but with every ounce of strength in his body he pulled back.

"We need a condom," he said.

"Umm," she groaned. "I didn't pack any."

Adrian threw his head back and released a sigh; then he remembered his emergency package in the car. "Give me five minutes," he said as he hopped off the bed, pulled on his pants, and dashed out of the room.

Alone in the hotel suite, Dana's mind twisted and turned over what Adrian said about his mess. What was this mess? She sat up in the middle of the bed and ran her fingers through her locks as she waited for Adrian to return.

But if she asked him about it again, the mood would be killed, and she needed to be with Adrian in the worst way. She stroked her left thigh, eyes closed, imagining Adrian's hand there. Moving closer to her wet center, she moaned, shivering and whispering his name.

"Starting without me?" Adrian asked from the doorway. Dana opened her eyes and saw him, naked, sheathed, and ready.

"How long have you been there?" Her face was red with desire and a twinge of embarrassment.

"Long enough to get a view of what I've missed for so long." He stalked over to the bed. "The way you called my name made me harder than a diamond." He took her hand in his and kissed her fingertips, tasting the sweetness of her nectar. "I've never been so jealous of a hand before."

She spread her legs. "Need you."

Adrian entered her wet and awaiting valley with a thrust that made Dana groan. She was so hot, wet, and tighter than he expected. Part of him was happy to feel her tightness. Happy that she still fit him like a glove.

Another thrust.

Her moans punctuated the air like the perfect note from John Coltrane's immortal sax.

Another thrust.

Her desire poured down on him like rain. Adrian joined her chorus, crying out her name as Dana clenched her thighs around him and ground against him with the beat of a Latin groove. He fell deeper inside her, she felt so good. She thrashed against him, giving him everything and Adrian returned the favor, giving as good as he got. But when she flipped him over, mounted him, and gyrated her hips against his, he felt as if she were milking everything out of him—his heat, his desire, his love. Adrian tried to hold back his explosion, tried to save his climax. Dana wasn't going to allow that to happen as she tightened her grip around his penis and then she leaned forward and sucked his bottom lip as if he were the sweetest chocolate known to man.

Adrian was done.

Dana fell against his sweat-covered chest, nibbling on his earlobe.

"Oh, woman, don't touch me," Adrian groaned as she darted her tongue in and out of his ear.

"Umm, make me," she said as she tightened her thighs around him. Adrian palmed her round bottom and brushed his lips against her neck, then gave her a wonton lick across her collarbone. "Now you're cheating."

"And what do you call that sucking of my ear-lobe?"

"Tasty."

He circled her nipple with his index finger, making her shiver from the inside out.

"Stop," she moaned, feeling herself melt against him.

"You sure about that?" he asked, then replaced his finger with his tongue. He remembered how she would purr when he licked and sucked her nipples. Ah, there it was—soft and low like a happy kitten. Just as he felt his erection grow inside her, his cell phone rang.

"You'd better get that," Dana said.

"I can ignore it."

He thrust forward, and Dana answered with a thrust of her own. "What if it's important? About your club?"

She thrust again and Adrian gripped her hips. "I'm holding everything that matters." Grinding like gears, they ignored the ringing of Adrian's cell phone.

After making love again, Dana and Adrian fell asleep in each other's arms. When she snuggled against him and he wrapped his arms around her, Dana felt a warm feeling of peace envelop her. As much as she tried to deny it, as much as she tried to fight it, being in Adrian's arms was where she wanted to be. Tonight she'd enjoy the moment and live inside the maleness of Adrian, then deal with reality tomorrow. Was this the closure that she needed with him or had she opened the door to more heartache?

Adrian woke up thinking he was dreaming again. Nope. Dana was in his arms. Her warm breath was heating his chest.

And that damned phone was ringing again. Glancing at the clock above the thirty-two-inch flat-screen TV, he saw it was 5:45 a.m. Who was stupid enough to call him at this hour? The last thing he wanted was to move. Not when he knew, come first light, that Dana would call last night anything but a reunion. He peered at her sleeping frame. Beautiful. Angelic. Peaceful. Her lips were swollen from the attention he'd given them hours ago. Tempting. As he leaned in to wake his beauty with a kiss, his phone rang again.

Somebody was asking for trouble. Tearing himself away from Dana, Adrian crept from the bed and angrily grabbed his phone.

"What?" he grumbled.

"Is this Adrian Bryant?" a male voice asked.

"You've got about two seconds to state your name and your business."

The man chuckled. Adrian didn't get the joke. "My apologies, I'm still on East Coast time. This is Elliot Crawford."

Adrian's heart stopped for a split second; his mouth felt as if it had been stuffed with sand and cotton. Something made his words gather in his gut and fail to reach his lips.

"Again," Elliot said, sounding wide awake and in control. "Sorry about the hour. You've been in contact with my sons about putting a nightclub in Crawford Towers."

"We've talked about it, but nothing's written in stone."

"I have to say that I'm impressed with what I've heard about your business acumen and the establishments that you run in the greater Los Angeles area."

You son of a bitch. If you've checked me out, then you know exactly who I am. Adrian seethed as he listened to his father drone on about how he wanted to meet with him and get the details about the club in the hotel.

"I don't have my calendar on me. Why don't you adjust your time and get back to me so that we can make an appointment."

"I'll do that," Elliot said. Before he could say good-bye or when he would call him back, Adrian hung up the phone. He returned to the bed as Dana sat up and yawned. The white sheet fell from her body, exposing her supple breasts, and before his conversation with his father, he would've inched closer to her and taken her breasts into his hands, palming them and tweaking her nipples with his thumbs.

Then he would've licked and sucked her breasts until her body caught fire. But the only thing on fire right now was his anger. Well, if this would be the way he met his father, then so be it.

"She finally got you, huh?"

Adrian's eyebrow shot up and he scowled for a moment before his face softened. "That was some unpleasant business. You know how New Yorkers are—you all think when the sun rises on the east, the whole world is supposed to be awake."

Dana frowned. She used to love this game, their version of the East Coast–West Coast rivalry, but there was something in his eyes that told her he was really upset. "What's wrong?"

"Nothing, just an unexpected meeting, and you know how I feel about getting my sleep interrupted."

Dana wrapped her arms around Adrian's waist and rested her chin on his shoulder. "You know, I've slept through the night. I wasn't born last night. What's going on, Adrian?"

He turned to her and kissed her cheek. "You're the only person I know who's ever been able to read me like a book. Remember that mess I was telling you about?"

She nodded. "Adrian, why don't you tell me what this is all about?"

"It doesn't concern you and this is what I wanted to avoid." He sighed and rubbed his forehead. "Hey, let's get some breakfast."

"Breakfast?" she asked as she glanced at the clock. "It's barely six a.m."

Adrian smiled, then ripped the sheet from her

body. "Well, then, let's start with me having you for my breakfast."

He spread her thighs, kissing her hot wetness with a fervor that rendered her speechless. What about that phone call? Well, her mind clicked as his hot tongue lashed her throbbing bud, that could wait. Lusty feelings invaded her body, sapped her rational thoughts out of her head and her body, and made her give in to the desire. The passion and the skill of Adrian's tongue. Her legs shivered and her thighs quivered as Adrian deepened his kiss, pressed his tongue against her clitoris, and released a hot breath that made her love come down like rain.

Dana screamed his name as her thighs turned to jelly and she reached an explosive climax. Adrian pulled back and smiled at the sated expression on Dana's face. If he could cocoon himself in the room with her forever, he'd be happy. He wouldn't need to seek revenge on the father who never wanted him. Wouldn't need to avenge his mother, who died with that man on her mind. Her last breath whispered Elliot Crawford's name.

The soft stroke of Dana's hand against his cheek brought him back to this moment.

"Where did you go?" she asked.

"I'm right here."

She held his face with both hands, staring deep into his eyes. Adrian's body shifted. "I know you and I know that look. You're either going to tell me what's going on or tell me good-bye—again."

"Can we just have today? Let it be about me and you?"

"And if I want tomorrow?" Dana shook her head. "Your mess returns then, right?"

"Dana, if I could give you all of my tomorrows, I would. This—"

"Are you married?" she bellowed, then leaped from the bed. "Get the hell out of my room."

Adrian chuckled at her. Naked. Angry. So damned sexy. He didn't move a muscle, simply watched her heave.

"Think what you want about me, but I'm not a cheater and I ain't married."

Dana paused as if she realized she looked absolutely ridiculous. She wiped a few beads of sweat from her forehead and reached for the short white robe on the back of the desk chair. Slipping it on, she asked, "What is it, Adrian? What was that call about—and don't try to change the subject again."

He crossed over to her, leaving a sliver of space between them. While he wanted to wrap his arms around her and inhale her fragrance, he decided to be honest . . . sort of.

"All right, there are some issues with my clubs. I've been pretty hands-off and the wrong element has gotten involved. I'm trying to keep it quiet working with the LAPD to get things cleaned up without publicity."

"How long has this been going on?"

Hearing the concern and the tortured look in her eyes made his lies burn on his tongue like acid.

But telling the truth would compromise his second chance. "I don't want you worrying about this. I have to take care of my problems on my own."

"Adrian, I . . ." Dana's voice trailed off as she looked into his eyes. Did she see through the lie? "Where do we go from here? I thought I needed one last night with you to get you out of my system, to get closure. But now I feel . . ."

"Dana," he whispered. "I need you back in my life, but this isn't how I want it. I love you and I don't want any of this nastiness to touch you. But I can't push you away again. I will not make the same mistake twice."

A cell phone rang again. This time it was Dana's.

"Do you need to get that?" he asked.

She shook her head. "Should I wait for you? Am I supposed to sit back, constantly worrying about you and these shadows you're fighting until the time is right for you to bring me back into your world?"

"Dana." He inched closer to her. "Just tell me I'm not going to lose you to Hollywood Ken."

Pushing him forcefully, Dana glared at Adrian, feeling foolish and angry all at once. "You asshole! Is that what last night was all about? You see me with someone else and I become a temporary priority? Get out and this time I mean it."

"Dana—"

"Don't. Just don't. Go clean up your mess and I'll see if Hollywood Ken wants to have breakfast." She stalked over to the door as Adrian slipped his pants on. Maybe this was the blowup he needed to move Dana aside while he worked on his plan. But what if he lost her forever this time? Was revenge worth the anger he saw written all over her beautiful face?

"Can you move a little faster?" she snapped when she caught his glance.

"Dana . . ."

"Please, save it."

Adrian slipped his shirt over his head and crossed to the door. He stopped and stroked her cheek. "It will all make sense one day," he said.

Dana snatched away from him and slammed the door in his face so he wouldn't see the hot tears streaming down her cheeks.

Chapter 6

Adrian drove aimlessly around downtown LA, trying to get the image of Dana's hurt face off his mind. He'd meant what he said about losing her, not just to Ian, but to any man. Dana was his. *Then why do you keep hurting her? You're more like him than you want to admit. Is revenge really worth this?* Adrian slammed on his brakes to avoid hitting the car in front of him and to shake his thoughts clear. His mother was slick, naming him Adrian Elliot Bryant. Did she think giving him that bastard's name would mean something to him? Give him a piece of the father who wanted nothing to do with him?

The sound of a blaring horn alerted Adrian that he was holding up traffic. He sped through the intersection and headed back to his club. In his office he could think, plot, and plan for the meeting with his father. And, he hoped, forget that he'd hurt Dana again.

When he arrived at Allure, he smiled at what had

become LA's newest hot spot overnight because Imani and Ian showed up at his place the day before their red carpet premiere. Sure he'd helped it happen since he had photographers staking out the place because he'd planned to embarrass Richmond. He'd been so consumed with Dana that he hadn't checked to see what kind of waves the pictures of Richmond and the hooker made. Maybe that was why Elliot called him this morning.

Unlocking the door and picking up the *LA Times* and a discarded copy of the *LA Weekly,* Adrian entered the empty building ready to see if his plan worked at all. Instead of heading to the office, he took a seat at one of the tables and opened up the papers, searching for Richmond's picture. When he found it, Adrian smirked, glad to see that the *Times* gossip columnist used the photo where Richmond looked as if he were about to eat the call girl's breasts as if they were orbs of chocolate cake. Adrian began reading the column.

Crawford Hotel executive Richmond Crawford was caught with a well-known Los Angeles call girl last night, and it looks as if he paid for the whole package. As he and the call girl got close, they headed to the city's newest hot spot, Allure. However, when Crawford arrived at the club, he must have handled his business already because he arrived alone. On the flip side, Crawford's car mate, identified as LaTrell McClain, was arrested and charged with solicitation. There's no word if LAPD will charge the married Crawford. This is unusual behavior for the older brother of former tabloid star Solomon Crawford, the ex of Heather Williams. Solomon Crawford has been quiet since his marriage and the murder of his former partner. Then again, if my wife had taken her out, I'd be faithful too.

The other Mrs. Crawford, Vivian, couldn't be reached in New York for comment. Another interesting fact about the Crawford family—there's a rumored family business book in the works. I wonder if these pictures will make it into the book about one of New York's richest families.

This was a good start, Adrian decided as he folded the newspaper, but he wanted more. He considered getting Heather involved, but that wouldn't be enough. Two cheating sons could be brushed off by a forgiving public; however, if the call girl was arrested and Richmond was still free, then he was sure there had to be some angry feminists who'd mobilize and protest the at the construction site. Dashing up the stairs to his office, Adrian was about to add more fuel to the fire.

Dana pulled herself together after a long hot shower and a fifteen-minute sob. She couldn't understand why she'd allowed herself to think things would be different with Adrian just because he gave her an orgasm—well, multiple orgasms. Dana wasn't going to wallow in self-pity over Adrian again. She had work to do, and worrying about Adrian

Bryant wasn't going to get in the way. Dressing in a pair of leggings, a tank top, and black sneakers, Dana decided to walk over to the studio and take some shots of the people who made Hollywood tick—the stage hands, the set designers, and the like. Then she had her final set of publicity photos to shoot for the film. With Ian.

Dana had to admit that she had fun with him before getting sucked back into Adrian's orbit. Was she wrong not to give him a chance? As she headed out the door, her cell phone rang. She half hoped that it was Adrian but was surprised to see that it was Ian.

"Hi," she said.

"Good morning, sounds like you're up and out."

"I'm about to go shoot some pictures before we have our session and get some breakfast."

"That's what I was calling you about, breakfast. If you'd like some company, I can come and get you on my Harley."

"Now that is an offer I can't refuse." Dana smiled despite herself and the tumult of emotions tearing at her heart. "I'm ready when you are."

"I can be there in twenty minutes. You're in Culver City, right?"

"Yes. I'm staying at the Culver Hotel, but you can pick me up outside of the studio," she said.

"Will do. See you soon."

"Bye," she said, then ended the call.

Dana wondered if Ian would be game to take their photo shoot on location. She wanted to make a trip to Orange County for two reasons: to take pictures of Ian on his Harley and to get one of her own. Forget leasing—it was time for her to own a cycle. Was part of her getting the motorcycle because she knew it would piss Adrian off? Yes. But she told herself that she was simply getting her swagger back. And nothing said swag like a motorcycle, new helmet, and a hot pair of motorcycle boots. Dana couldn't wait. She was going to get her own Harley.

As she crossed the street, her cell phone rang again. Looking down at the phone, she saw that it was Imani. "I really hate LA," Imani groaned. "Raymond is still on East Coast time and he's already up as if we're supposed to be out and about."

"Good morning to you too," Dana quipped.

"Anyway, how did everything go last night? Isn't Ian just the sweetest? I bet he pushed all thoughts of Mr. Slick right out the window."

Dana shivered as she thought about last night. Adrian's arms around her. His lips. His touch. His bull. Sighing, she agreed with her friend. "As a matter of fact, Ian and I are having breakfast. I'm going to meet him now. And we're taking a little road trip to do his photo shoot."

"Ooh, this is promising. Wait, you aren't hopping on the back of that motorcycle of his again, are you? Thanks, babe."

"I'm guessing that 'thanks, babe' was directed at your husband?"

Imani laughed. "It was. He brought me a copy of the paper because we're in it."

"At Adrian's club?" Dana asked. She wondered if the activity at the club would come back and bite Imani, Ian, and other stars who made Adrian's clubs hot spots. Would they get questioned by the police?

"Yes. I hate that my presence there gave your heartbreak kid free publicity."

"Well, I wouldn't go back there if I were you."

"Trust me, I won't. Look, don't forget about our spa appointment at three. I have to go now," Imani said, the purr in her voice revealing that she and Raymond would be spending breakfast in bed.

Just like she and Adrian. Stop it. Adrian made his decision two years ago, and you can't allow him to come back into your life and turn things upside down again. You got your closure; now move on. Dana stepped on the elevator and pasted a smile on her lips. At least by the end of the day, she'd have her own Harley and tomorrow she'd be so busy shooting for her book and editing pictures that she wouldn't have time to think about Adrian, his mess, or his hot and tantalizing kisses.

"You look ready to ride," Ian said when he spotted Dana.

She smiled at him and drank in the image of him on that motorcycle. *Sexy* was an understatement. Dana lifted her camera and snapped a few shots of Ian. He smiled like the star he was. "You're the one who looks ready to ride," she said when she lowered her camera. "I don't have the proper gear, but I think it will keep me safe. How do you feel about going to Orange County this morning?"

"What's in Orange County?" he asked as he got off the bike and gave Dana a quick hug.

"My Fat Boy."

"You're getting a Fat Bob today?" Ian's eyes stretched to the size of silver dollars. "Color me impressed."

Dana shrugged and offered him a sweet smile. "And, since you look so great on this bike, I figured we could get some shots of you actually riding, instead of in the studio."

Ian wrapped his arm around her waist. "I like the sound of that. It's a good thing that I didn't drive the Corvette today."

Dana inhaled sharply at the mention of the sports car. Ian thought she was expressing her admiration of the car and smiled. "I know, I have all the trappings of a man going through a midlife crisis."

She returned his smile, not telling him the story of what a Corvette really meant to her. Adrian had wanted her off her motorcycle so badly that he'd gotten her a black one. She gave up the motorcycle and had only called him controlling once. When she'd walked in on him and those two women following his mother's death, she parked the car—with the keys in it and the engine running—on a random street near LAX, then walked to the airport to catch her flight to New York. She'd hoped someone had taken the car and had a better time with it than she had. Dana had decided that when she accepted that car, she lost a part of herself. And what was the purpose? Adrian still tossed her aside as if she'd never meant a damned thing to him.

"Let's go," she finally said.

"Do you want to eat first or are you as excited as I am to go to the Harley dealership?"

"The sooner we get to the dealership the better. I can't wait to roll back into LA on my new wheels."

"That is a sight I'm looking forward to seeing."

Ian handed Dana a helmet, which she snapped on her head, then climbed on the back of the bike. She leaned against Ian and told herself she could learn to like this—a man who appreciated her love of the open road.

But your heart isn't all in, she thought. Last night was not closure. You simply opened a wound that was healing just fine.

Suddenly, the warmth of Ian's body wasn't that comforting.

"This is unacceptable!" Elliot boomed as he thrust a copy of the *Times* in Richmond's face. Richmond took the paper and read the column with trepidation.

"I didn't know—"

Elliot held his hand up, cutting Richmond off. "You're the one who always called and complained about Solomon's exploits. Yet, you purchase sex while we're building this hotel and getting ready to do the family history book. How in the hell do you think this is going to play out?"

Solomon walked into the suite with Kandace and their daughter Kiana in tow. "What's all the yelling about?" he asked as Kandace and the baby crossed over to the breakfast buffet in the corner of the suite.

"This," Elliot said as he snatched the paper away from Richmond.

"I didn't know," Richmond said as Solomon scanned the paper. "It was a mistake and—"

"A mistake!" Elliot thundered as he rose from his chair. "It's a PR nightmare."

Richmond glared at his father. "So, what do you call what you did? Family building?"

Elliot looked down at his watch, then up at Solomon. "You two better fix this."

"Where are you going?" Solomon asked his father as he headed for the door.

"Out." Elliot slammed out of the suite.

Adrian checked the time on his iPhone. Elliot Crawford was late. Jackass. First he woke him up, and now this? He was wasting his time. Adrian didn't mind losing money—he could always get that back—but his time was priceless. Part of him wondered if his delay had anything to do with today's headlines. It was still no excuse for tardiness.

His time could've been used to find a way to win Dana back. Pacing in front of his desk, Adrian was losing his patience. Elliot could kiss his . . . There was the bell, alerting him that someone had come in. He didn't want to look overly anxious and rush into the lobby to greet his father . . . well, more accurately, his sperm donor. He let a few seconds pass; then he headed into the lobby. To his surprise, it was Solomon waiting for him and not his father.

"What kind of place are you running here? I know you sent the car for my brother. Did you pay for the hooker too?" Solomon bellowed when he saw Adrian.

"Don't come into my place of business hurling accusations. If your brother enjoys the company of hookers, what the hell does that have to do with me? Maybe you need to have this conversation with him," Adrian snarled.

"You son of a . . . I know my brother and he's not stupid. You're behind this. The question is why."

"Get out," Adrian growled.

"Not until I get answers." Solomon stood toe to toe with Adrian. Sizing him up, Adrian squared off with Solomon as if ready to fight.

"You're barking at the wrong person. I didn't get in a car with a hooker while the press took pictures. So, for the last time, get the hell out of here."

Solomon grabbed Adrian's collar. "I don't trust you and I don't know what your game is, but you'd better stay away from my family."

Adrian snatched away and glared at him. "You don't want to pick a fight with me," he snapped.

"And you think I'm some sort of lightweight?

If you want to go to war, get ready to lose," Solomon gritted.

"Be careful who you challenge," Adrian retorted.

"I don't know what your game is, Bryant, but this LA double-talk is not going to work. I don't trust you."

"This isn't about you, Solomon," Elliot said as he walked into the club.

Adrian looked from Solomon to Elliot, seeing more of himself in the two men than he wanted to admit. He and Solomon were four months apart in age. They had the same color and eye shape. When Solomon glared at his father and gritted his teeth, Adrian recognized that expression. He found himself doing that when he was angry as well.

"You don't think that it's pretty damned suspicious that Richmond was on his way over to this club and he gets caught with a hooker? You don't think this son of a bitch had something to do with it? And what are you doing here anyway? If you think you and Richmond can handle this idiotic project and deal with shysters like this assclown, then have at it. He is not to be trusted."

"Who in the hell do you think you're talking to, son?" Elliot asked.

Adrian shuddered inwardly at the word *son*. Did he even know that he was standing in a room with two of his sons? Did he even care?

"This is an important project to our company, and if you walk away, you can submit your resignation as

CEO. Richmond has been chomping at the bit to do this job."

"You're kidding, right?" Solomon laughed sardonically. "First you come up with this idea to build in an already saturated market, one that Mom was always against, and now you want to give Richmond a job we know he can't do? Yeah, go ahead and do that. And I'd love to see how you two are going to handle this scandal." He laughed and for a split second, Adrian was excited. There was already discord in the family, and he wouldn't have much work to do to create more.

"Do you think I need you to fix any problem that comes up with my company?" Elliot snapped, pointing his bony finger in Solomon's face. "You don't have your champion anymore. I'm going to finally do what I want to do with Crawford Hotels."

"Don't do that," Solomon growled. "Don't pretend that my mother wasn't the brains of Crawford Hotels. All you did was lend a name."

"You arrogant—"

"Hey!" Adrian exclaimed. "Why don't you take your family argument somewhere else. You're wasting my time." Inside, Adrian smiled because this little argument was captured on his security cameras. He was going to leak the video to the same gossip columnist who wrote about Richmond's arrest. He'd even send it to Page Six.

"I came here to talk about partnering with Mr. Bryant. You can join us or you can leave. What I won't have is you questioning him about your brother's bad choices."

Solomon glared at Adrian and his father. "Somebody has to look out for this company."

Adrian rolled his eyes and pointed the men toward his office. This wasn't the meeting he'd planned, but he'd make it work in his favor.

"What's your vision for the lounge in Crawford Towers?" Elliot asked once they were seated in the office.

"I know LA nightlife and I know people are always looking for the next big thing. You have to think ahead. A few years ago, it was beds in clubs; then it was signature drinks. Now people want to go back to basics, a place where they can drink, see beautiful people, and unwind."

"What's the difference between that and a regular hotel bar? Hell, we can hire a band on certain nights," Solomon interjected.

"This isn't Atlanta or New York. We're talking about the entertainment capital of the world. A hotel bar isn't going to cut it." Adrian sized Solomon up. He knew of his brother's reputation as a reformed ladies' man, but now that he'd married businesswoman Kandace Crawford, he'd changed his ways.

However, he'd left a string of broken hearts across the country and one powerful one here. If he had to, he'd play that card. Adrian and Heather Williams, the actress Solomon dumped three years ago, were LA friends—meaning they didn't hang out and share secrets, but they had each other's cell phone numbers.

"What do you get out of this deal? You just opened a club, where my responsible older brother made a spectacle of himself and got caught with a damned hooker!" Solomon looked pointedly at his father.

"I'll admit having a presence in downtown will enhance my portfolio," Adrian said. "More than anything, this gives your hotel more publicity."

Solomon snorted.

Elliot nodded thoughtfully as he examined Adrian's face. Did he see himself? Did he see Pamela? Adrian turned away from Elliot and pretended he was pulling up a file on the computer.

"Having entertainment in the hotel is a good idea and it will set this location apart from our others. Draw up some specs and we'll get down to business."

"Just like that?" Adrian looked into the older man's eyes, wondering if his pure hatred for him shone through. "We don't even know what role he played in Richmond's dalliance with the call girl."

"Whatever Richmond did doesn't have a bearing on what kind of business I decided to do with Mr. Bryant."

Solomon sat stone-faced. "I don't like this," he blurted out.

"Why don't you check my credentials?" Adrian said. "I'm the best at what I do."

"Don't think I won't." Solomon rose from his

seat and tore out of the office. Alone with Elliot, Adrian found himself at a loss for words. How was he supposed to handle this? Blurt out that he was Pamela's son, the bastard he'd ignored? Or just say nothing?

"Well, you have to excuse Solomon. Headstrong and loud like his mother."

Adrian grunted, picked up a pen, and twirled it. "Studies say that most men have more of their mother's qualities anyway," he said. "My mother had little choice but be my everything." His words were meant to be daggers—that is, if Elliot even gave a damn.

The older man inhaled sharply before saying, "Your mother was an amazing woman and I loved her."

Adrian dropped the pen. Did he really say he loved his mother? A woman he ignored and left broken? A woman he'd forced to give up her dreams because he wasn't man enough to leave his wife? How could he even say love when it came to his mother? "You're going to sit there and spew that bullshit when you exiled my mother to Los Angeles because—"

"I was a married man and I—"

"Couldn't be a man and accept your fucking re-sponsibilities."

"I provided for you and your mother. She under-stood that I couldn't—"

"My mother loved you. Even with her dying breath, you were on her mind. So don't tell me that you took care of me and my mother. Now you want to be a family man?"

"What do you want, Adrian?" Elliot asked quietly. "You've known who I was from the moment you decided to go into business with us. The day I saw you at the press conference, I saw your mother in you."

Adrian leaped from his seat. "Don't talk about her as if you gave a hot damn about her. I guess Solomon got his player ways from you. He was just smart enough to not get anyone pregnant."

Elliot rose to his feet, his face contorted in sadness and confusion. "Adrian, I wanted a life with you and your mother. But I couldn't lose everything. I wouldn't have been able to give you and Pamela what you deserved. I wasn't going to let a son of mine grow up the way I did. Poor, wondering where your next meal is coming from, and suffering."

"A life built on a lie? Yeah, I deserved that. Thanks, Dad. Or should I call you *Sperm Donor*?"

Elliot sighed and started for the door. "When you calm down, we can talk like men. But as long as you act like an angry child, then we'll just have this business arrangement."

Adrian wanted to reach out and wrap his hands around the older man's throat. Did he just talk to him as if he were some kind of idiot? Taking a calming breath, Adrian watched his father walk out of his office. What excuse could he possibly have for being a damned deadbeat father?

Chapter 7

Dana climbed on the back of the Fat Bob she'd just purchased. Her face lit up as she started the cycle. The roar of the engine made her giddy with excitement.

"You look good on that bike!" Ian exclaimed.

"And it feels good," she replied as she revved the engine again.

"I'm glad we took this field trip to do this photo shoot." Ian ran his hand across the silver handlebars. "This Fat Bob is hot and you look even hotter on it."

Dana smiled as she reached for her helmet on the back of the bike. "I would say let's race back to LA, but I'm going to take a slow ride back."

"Maybe after the premiere we can take a late-night ride together?" Ian suggested.

She nodded and pulled the helmet on her head. Flipping the shield up, she said, "I'd like that."

Ian waved good-bye to her as she tore out of the

dealership parking lot. Dana forced herself to slow down and enjoy the tingle of the wind. The vibration of the motorcycle made her feel alive, back to her old self. The woman who didn't give a damn what Adrian or anyone else thought about her riding a hog. Weaving in and out of traffic, Dana felt like a superhero. Too bad she was a mere mortal and her heart and mind were still weighed down with thoughts of Adrian.

About an hour later, and fifteen minutes late for her spa appointment, Dana was back at her hotel. When she reached in her pocket and looked at her cell phone, she had three missed calls. Two from Imani and one from Adrian. She immediately cleared his number from the list, then deleted his contact information. They had nothing left to say to each other.

Still, she needed to warn Imani and Ian to stay away from Adrian's clubs, especially if there was something illegal going on there. Pulling her bike into a motorcycle only spot, Dana headed inside and called Imani back.

"Just look up," her friend ordered when she answered. "And why are you carrying a motorcycle helmet?"

"Well, it's what you wear when you ride a motorcycle and it's the law."

"You and Ian are getting on my nerves. Motorcycles are dangerous, but at least he's there to protect you. So, how did the photo shoot go?"

"It was great and I have my own bike now. Ian

and I went to Orange County for the shoot. I got some amazing pictures of him on his bike and then I got my first Harley." Dana smiled broadly. "The ride back was such a rush! I don't even know if I need a spa treatment now."

Imani smacked her friend on the shoulder. "Really, Dana? That may be cool in LA or New Orleans, but you live in New York. Hello! Just imagine all of the accidents and—"

"You know, I allowed someone else's fears to cause me to give up my motorcycle before. I'm not going to let it happen again."

"That jab was not mine." Imani raised her eyebrow. "This is about Mr. Slick, huh? If he caused you to give up such a dangerous hobby, then he might be all right. Maybe."

Part of Dana actually wanted to defend him. Wanted to tell Imani that Adrian was . . . what? Amazing? The love of her life? Instead, she shrugged. "It's my life, Mani. I'm going to live it my way. You don't have to like it, because it's my choice."

"He really did a number on you, huh?"

Dana sighed and stroked the helmet in the crook of her arm. "He did and sadly, he still is. And you need to avoid his clubs and tell your friends to do the same for a while."

Imani snorted and furrowed her brow. "How about forever?"

"You can't say that. Adrian has been known to cater to A-listers, and he's having some issues that no one wants to be involved with right now. We know what the media does when it comes to scandals."

"Scandals? What aren't you telling me . . . Wait, are you seeing him? Because I haven't read anything about his club other than that guy getting caught with the hooker."

"We spent last night together," Dana admitted.

"You did what? But you went out with Ian. When? How? Are you insane?"

"I was, but I'm good now."

Imani shook her head. "That's what you say. I know he's cute, but he broke your heart and you hopped into bed with him after spending the night hugged up on a bike with Ian."

"Well, Mrs. Matchmaker, you should be happy to know that I'm going to the premiere tonight with Ian."

"Hope y'all are leaving the bikes behind and rolling in a limo like normal stars do," Imani said as she and Dana headed for the hotel's spa.

"You forget I'm not a star," Dana replied with a laugh.

Adrian picked up his cell phone and dialed Dana's number. He needed to apologize and he needed to see her, to be reminded of softness, love, and light. All he wanted was to have her in his arms and inhale the sweet smell of her hair.

Voice mail.

Adrian slammed out of his office and locked up

the club. He couldn't expect Dana to be his savior. He couldn't expect her to make him forget that his father was an asshole who thought DNA meant nothing and throwing money at a problem was supposed to make it disappear.

Well, he had news for his father and those selfish-ass brothers of his. They wanted to portray this nice little family image, but Adrian was going to bring it down piece by piece. He'd smack the smugness off Solomon's face. It was time for round two.

Adrian dialed Heather Williams. He wondered if he might be taking things too far. Heather's highly publicized breakup with Solomon was big news a few years ago. Did he want to hurt a total stranger just to humiliate his father? Before he could change his mind, he heard, "Heather Williams's phone."

"Is this Ms. Williams?"

"No, this is her assistant, Nichelle Marsh. Who's calling?"

"Adrian Bryant. I'm calling to invite Ms. Williams to an event at Allure tonight following the screening of *Black and Blue*."

"Let me check her calendar. I don't think she's attending tonight's premiere."

Adrian smirked. Heather Williams let everyone with a microphone or a video camera know about her simmering feud with Imani Thomas and the fact that she didn't get the lead in the movie and was forced to play a smaller role.

"I assume she wasn't happy with her supporting role," he said, buttering up the assistant. "I saw the preview and she stole every scene she was in. That's why I want her to be the guest of honor tonight."

"So, Imani Thomas won't be there?"

"Nope. She isn't on the guest list."

"I see an opening on Ms. Williams's calendar. She'll be there at eleven."

"Great. I'll text you the details. Thank you, Nichelle." Adrian ended the call and sighed. Was he taking this thing too far? Was he prepared to cross the line and ruin Solomon's family just because Elliot had abandoned him and his mother?

He closed his eyes, remembering the happiness of his childhood. Pamela loved him fiercely. They Rollerbladed together, hung out on the beach, discovered tofu and found out that it wasn't for them. His childhood friends thought he had the coolest mother ever, but they didn't see how lonely she was. When they'd get that weekly package from New York, Pamela would cry, all the while trying to hide her sadness and tears from Adrian. But he'd seen them and never knew why.

To hell with changing his mind; he wanted someone else to feel that pain.

Dana and Imani walked out of the spa feeling and looking spectacular. With her locks curled and retwisted, Dana was tempted not to ride her motorcycle to the movie premiere. Tempted, but not totally swayed. She loved that bike after just a few hours of owning it.

"I have to get fitted for my dress," Imani said, then turned to Dana. "Promise me two things."

"I'll think about it."

"No riding until after the premiere, and please, no more late-night visits with Adrian."

"Trust me, I'm done with him. And I'll think about the riding part. Where's Raymond?"

Imani smiled. "My wonderful husband is getting fitted for a tuxedo and hating every minute of it. He wanted to know why he couldn't just wear jeans and his favorite Hendrix T-shirt. Although he'd look very sexy in it, I told him this is the first time he's hitting the red carpet with me as the headliner in a movie."

"Still not used to the life of a movie star's husband?"

Imani nodded. "But he's always a good sport about it and that's why when we get back to New York, I'm going to talk to Broadway Cares about doing a fund-raiser for the clinic. I'll even do Alexander Roman's show and give my salary to Raymond and Keith. They work so hard with so little."

"Let me know. Hopefully I'll be done with this book and I can shoot the event for you guys."

Imani reached out and hugged her friend tightly. "You're wonderful and you deserve to be happy. I hope Ian is the man to make you happy."

"I'm not sad, Mani. I've gotten my head together and I know what I need. It's not Adrian."

"Hallelujah!"

Dana headed up to her room to pick out her

outfit for the premiere. As she walked toward the elevator, she felt her phone vibrate, indicating that she missed a call. She pulled the phone from her pocket and saw the number. Even without having his name saved in her cell, she knew it was Adrian. Pressing the UP button on the elevator, she deleted the missed call. She wasn't going to call him—ever. If Adrian wanted to deal with his mess alone, she'd let him. He'd done it before and he could do it again. As the elevator reached her floor, she found herself wondering if she should return his call, though. What if he needed her and this was a call for help?

"No," she whispered as she unlocked her room door. "Adrian wants you because he thinks you want Ian. He is playing a game that I don't want to be a participant in."

Perching on the edge of her bed, Dana ran her hand across the bedspread and memories of her night with Adrian flooded back. God, how she craved that man. Needed him as she needed the oxygen in her lungs. But he didn't trust her enough to let her into whatever was clouding his . . . *Why do I care?* she thought as she pounded the bed. Dana rose to her feet and crossed over to the closet to retrieve her outfit.

Dana had originally planned to wear a blue pantsuit with a pink tunic and silver strappy heels. Sucking her teeth, she glanced at the jumpsuit she'd packed on a whim. The black bandeau suit was a skin-hugging throwback to Foxy Brown, and

Dana had always been too afraid to wear it while shooting pictures. The last thing she needed was a Janet Jacksonesque wardrobe malfunction.

But she wasn't taking pictures tonight.

Dana grabbed the outfit and laid it across the bed. She was going to have a good time tonight and leave all thoughts of Adrian behind.

And at that moment, her cell phone rang. It was Adrian. As much as she wanted to ignore the call, she answered.

"What do you want?" she asked.

"You."

"Adrian, I'm not doing this dance with you anymore. What do you want me for? Is it because you—"

"I told you last night that I love you. Dana, I just want to see you. Can we at least meet for coffee?"

She looked at the clock. There was plenty of time for a cup of coffee, but what did she and Adrian have to say to each other? Maybe he wanted to talk about the troubles at his club. As much as she wanted to pretend she didn't give a damn, she did. Sighing, she finally agreed to the coffee. "I'll meet you at our Starbucks in twenty minutes."

"Thanks, Dana."

She ended the call and shook her head. *Weak sauce,* she thought as she disrobed and slipped into the jumpsuit. Dana crossed the room and stuffed her heels into her motorcycle bag and stepped into her boots. She laughed as she headed out the door. She'd broken both of the promises she'd made to her best friend and the lies she'd told herself. The trip to Starbucks wasn't going to take more than twenty minutes, depending on the traffic on Santa Monica Boulevard. She wasn't going to do more than talk to Adrian. She wasn't even going to give him a hug. *Keep it simple and quick,* Dana told herself as she climbed onto her Harley and headed down the street.

As Adrian walked into Starbucks, he wondered what he should say to Dana about why he had to see her. He couldn't stomach lying to her, but he also couldn't tell her that he was out to ruin the man who abandoned him as a child and broke his mother's heart. One of the reasons he loved Dana was because she reminded him of Pamela. Her spirit was as giving and loving as his mother had been. His mother had taken an instant liking to Dana when they'd met, telling her son that Dana was the kind of woman you held on to.

Adrian wished he'd listened. Maybe Dana's love was more important than revenge. But how was he going to convince her to give him another chance when he'd done such a great job of presenting himself as an asshole?

The roar of a motorcycle shook him out of his emotions. "I know she didn't," he muttered as he watched the cycle circle the parking lot. He didn't have to see her face to know that Dana was the rider. He knew those hips.

Turning toward the door, he headed outside to meet her. As he watched Dana pull her helmet off and shake her locks, he was transfixed by her curve-hugging outfit. His groin twitched and threatened to burst through his fly as she walked toward him. Adrian tried to calm his hormones, but he was standing there with his mouth slightly agape watching a goddess approach him. He'd nearly forgotten that he'd come outside to voice his umbrage at her choice of transportation. "Wow. You look amazing," he was able to say as his eyes roamed her body.

"Surely you don't want to talk about how I look."

"Dana, about this morning, I don't want you to think that spending the night with you had anything to do with that guy. I have a lot to make up for because I hurt you," he said.

"Adrian, we're not the same people we were two years ago. I'm not here to wiggle my way back into your life. I was hoping to never see you again. You've made it clear that you don't trust me enough to have a significant role in your life. You wouldn't even let me be there for you when your mother died and I know how her passing hurt you."

Adrian stepped closer to her, his lips inches from her face. She smelled like roses and jasmine. He stroked her cheek and felt her tremble slightly. "When my mother died, I found out some things that I needed to process alone. I was wrong to push you away, but I didn't know what else to do."

She shrugged away from him. "There you go with that 'I needed to be alone' crap again. If you need all of this solitude, then why pretend that you want to make up for what you did to me? You keep parts of yourself wrapped up and hidden away and I can't—won't—deal with that."

Adrian drew her into his arms and she didn't resist his embrace. That was a good sign, he surmised. "It's complicated and I don't want you to be a part of . . ."

"Of what? If you can't be open with me, then stop calling me. Stop playing with my heart when you know I—"

"Dana, I've never stopped loving you and if you'd give me another chance—"

"To hurt me again? I don't think so." She slapped his arms away. "All or nothing. That's how it has to be."

He squeezed his eyes shut. Would she want to stay if she knew it all? Would she want to have anything to do with him if she knew he'd spent the last two years planning the demise of the people she worked for? "I want to give you everything," he said. "But—"

"No buts," she snapped as she pushed him in his chest. "Why am I such a fool when it comes to you?"

"You're nobody's fool. Dana, my life changed when my mother died. She told me the man who I thought was my father wasn't. The man who donated his sperm ignored me all my life, ignored my mother, but when she took her last breath, he was on her mind."

"Adrian."

"My head hasn't been right since then." He dropped his head and Dana cupped his cheek. Her tender touch offered him the soft comfort that he'd missed since she'd been gone. The kind of gentleness he needed to keep his heart from turning into a block of ice.

"I'm sorry."

"So am I. It doesn't make up for how I treated you and what you saw that night. I knew I had to find this man and I know it isn't going to be pretty when I do. That's what I wanted to keep you away from." The half-truth burned his tongue. He didn't want to put her in the middle of this family war. That's why he'd been so over the top in their breakup. Too bad he'd done such a good job of making her hate him.

"Adrian, I wish I could—"

He brushed his lips against hers. "I need you. Need you to be that light in my life, something good."

"Adrian."

"Please. The biggest mistake I ever made was allowing you to walk out of my penthouse that night thinking I was some cold bastard. I thought I could do this and not look back, but seeing you here again and being with you, I know I can't live without you."

Dana leaned in and kissed him slow, deep, and long as if she was answering him with her hot tongue. If he was right, her answer was yes. Pulling her closer, he relished the feel of her body against his, though in the back of his mind, Adrian wondered if the truth would destroy not only the Crawford family, but also his tentative reunion with Dana.

Chapter 8

Dana stood there looking into Adrian's eyes, not knowing what she was seeing, but she knew there was still a struggle going on inside him.

He stroked her cheek gently and smiled. His eyes didn't match his lips, though, and Dana saw that. And when she started to call him on it, Adrian took her hand in his and kissed it. "You look worried."

"I am," she whispered. "Is there something you're not telling me?"

There was a lot Adrian wasn't telling her and he wished that he could tell her everything. But not until she finished her work with those people. He kissed the back of her hand. "No." Leaning in, Adrian gave her earlobe a quick nibble. "Do you have to go to that premiere?"

Dana looked at her watch and cursed under her breath. "I have to go," she said.

"Let me drive you because—"

"I got here on my own, didn't I? We're not starting that 'your bike is too dangerous' stuff again."

Adrian threw his hands up. "But let me just say this. It's an unnecessary risk when you had—"

"Somebody stole it."

"Not hard to do when someone left the keys in the car."

Dana stopped in her tracks. "You found the car?"

"I was looking for you. There was GPS on the car and I called the company. When I got the location, I thought something was wrong."

Dana snorted. "Oh, something was wrong."

"Besides that," he said. "I thought you were in danger, had been carjacked or something worse."

"I had a broken heart at the time. A carjacker wouldn't have stood a chance that night."

Adrian heard the pain behind her attempt at humor and wished that he could take that night back and tell her about the hell he'd been going through and the pain he'd been feeling at that moment . . . but he'd chosen revenge instead. Would his desire to ruin his father cost him the love of his life?

Adrian knew at that moment he should've told her everything. But how would she react to the underhanded things he had planned? Knowing Dana, she'd try to talk him out of it.

"That car is still yours, babe," he finally said.

She rolled her eyes, knowing where this conversation was going. "Adrian."

"I'm done. Ride your motorcycle. Just be safe. I don't want to lose you."

She smoothed her hand across his cheek. "If you play your cards right, maybe you'll have me again."

He drew her into his arms. "You're mine. As the song goes, once mine, always my—"

Dana placed her hand over his mouth. "And when's the last time anyone heard from Sam Salter? Remember that."

Adrian kissed her hand as her cell phone began to chime. "That's Imani. I have to get this." Dana clicked the ANSWER key and before she could say hello, she was bombarded with questions.

"Dana, where are you? I mean seriously, do you know what time it is? Ian is waiting for you. And thank God he's going to ride in the limo and not on that motorcycle that you love so much."

"Imani, I'm on my way."

"From where?"

"The longer I talk to you, the later I'm going to be."

"Okay. Just get here, safely."

Dana clicked the phone off and turned to Adrian. "I have to go."

"You know, I have passes for that screening as well. Why don't we go together?"

She shook her head no. Adrian furrowed his brow. "Why not?"

"Because," she said as she walked over to her bike. "I have a date."

As she hopped on her Harley and slapped her

helmet on her head, she heard him call out, "With Hollywood Ken?" Ignoring him, she started her bike and headed to the hotel.

As Adrian watched Dana ride away, he felt the old feelings of dread. His biggest fear about Dana on that or any other motorcycle had always been an accident. At least there was a little bit of protection in a car. Closing his eyes, he tried to shake the image of her broken body on the side of Santa Monica Boulevard. He didn't want to think about her being with Ian either. But he was pretty confident that she wasn't very serious about him. And if Ian Kelly had real feelings for Dana, then he'd better get ready to have his heartbroken. Adrian started for his car when his cell phone rang. Looking down at the number, he frowned, realizing that it was his father.

"What?"

"Adrian," Elliot said. "We need to talk, just you and me."

"Now is not a good time. I have plans."

"I won't take up too much of your time. I just happen to be inside the Starbucks you're standing in front of."

Adrian turned around and saw the older man sitting at a table. When their eyes met, Elliot lifted his paper cup in acknowledgment. Clicking his phone off and shoving it into his pocket, Adrian crossed over to the man he considered his sperm donor.

"Talk," he said as he stood in front of the table.

"Have a seat."

Adrian narrowed his eyes into snakelike slits.

"Please," Elliot said calmly. "There's a lot to say."

"You said you wouldn't take much of my time, so let's get it done." Adrian grabbed the chair, turned it backward, and straddled it.

"Please understand that I loved your mother."

"Bullsh—"

Elliot held up his hand and closed his eyes. "Pamela was the most beautiful woman I'd ever seen and she was tender, sweet, and creative. She was the woman I should've married."

"But you were married when you met her. It's not as if she had a choice. She couldn't be with you because you'd already chosen someone else."

He nodded. "And as cliché as it sounds, my marriage wasn't a happy one. We'd just opened our first hotel in New York and Pamela walked in applying for a job. She reminded me of Pam Grier, that big afro made her stand out in the crowd. She could've been a model. But when she opened her mouth and started talking, she was just as smart as she was she was beautiful."

"That was your thing, preying on young women looking for jobs because your wife wasn't giving you what you wanted?" Adrian snipped.

Elliot sipped his drink slowly. "It wasn't like that." He set his cup on the table and stared at Adrian. "Pamela was brilliant and treated me like a man. She was the backbone of that Harlem hotel. And she laid the framework for all of this—this Crawford empire. I wished for so many years that I could've shared this with her."

Adrian's jaw was so tight that he thought it would snap. "But you didn't have the balls to leave your perfect little family. Now you want the world to know how amazingly you mixed business and family?"

"I would've lost everything if I had."

"But it was okay for my mother to lose everything and raise me alone? Freaking father of the decade."

"If I was penniless, how was I going to take care of you and your mother? Cynthia knew I loved Pamela, but when she found out that she was having my baby, I had to make a decision."

"You made the wrong one." Adrian leaped from his seat. "And I'm going to ensure that you recognize that." He stormed out of the coffee shop, stronger in his resolve to destroy his father.

Dana pulled her motorcycle up beside the limo, which Imani and Raymond were going to head to the Dolby Theatre in. When Imani spotted her, she hopped out of the car and crossed over to her. "Thank God you have dreads, because you would have helmet hair on the red carpet. No one wants to see that. And God forbid you end up on *Fashion Police* with Joan Rivers. That woman is so vile."

"Hello to you too," Dana said to her friend. "I thought I was late."

Imani shrugged and batted her eyelashes. "I

figured if you thought you were late, you'd leave your—wherever you were—sooner. Where were you again?"

"At Starbucks. Where's Ian?"

Imani tilted her head toward the hotel. "Having a drink with Raymond in the bar. Now, I was telling the truth about Ian waiting for you."

Dana ran her hand across her forehead and sighed.

"What's that look?" Imani asked as they walked toward the entrance.

"I can't see Ian anymore," she whispered.

"Oh. My. God. You fell for Mr. Slick's shit!"

Dana glared at her friend. "Keep your voice down, and I didn't fall for anything. Adrian and I had to get some things out in the open. Now that we have, I'm not going to pretend that I don't still have feelings for him or even that I don't still love him."

Imani shook her head and walked into the hotel. "After what you told me about him, how can you even question whether you love him or not?"

Dana expelled a frustrated sigh. "If I knew the answer to that question, my life would be so much easier and I'd be able to walk into this bar happy about a date with Ian Kelly."

"Instead, you're walking in here thinking about the asshole who sent you back to New York with your heart shattered like glass," Imani finished. She draped her arm across Dana's shoulders. "At least you're going to look cute on the red carpet."

Dana glanced at Imani's canary minidress and nude heels. "I won't be the only one. Trying to get on the Best Dressed list?"

Imani fluffed her curls and beamed. "I have a secret. This is probably the last time I'll be able to wear a short and formfitting dress for a while."

Dana stopped. "Are you pregnant?" Her voice was barely above a whisper.

"I think so," she replied. "My period is two months late, that champagne from the other night made me so sick, and my husband and I have been—"

"Spare me the dirty bedroom details," Dana joked.

"I just hope I'll be able to finish my new movie without harming the baby."

"What movie? I feel so out of the loop with you these days."

Imani slapped her hand on her hip. "Because you are," she said. "Still, this is what we wanted. A great career and being busy all the time. We deserve it."

"What's this movie about?" Dana asked as they headed for the bar.

"The working title is *Flying Ace* and it's everything that *Fearless Diva* should've been. Look, enough about me. You have a serious dilemma on your hands."

Dana nodded and started to say something, but she locked eyes with Ian, who was smiling brightly at her. She liked him and in a different time and place, she'd be happy to get closer to him. But her stupid heart was in Adrian's hands. What in the hell was wrong with her?

"Hello, beautiful," he said as he crossed over to her. Ian enveloped her in a tight hug. "Have you been able to resist the call of the road?"

"Not at all," she replied with a forced smile. "That's why I'm running late now."

"It was well worth the wait. I have a surprise for you."

"What's that?"

Ian led her to the bar and handed her a black helmet. "We're not riding in a limo."

Raymond laughed when he heard his wife gasp. "Now you two are just getting on my nerves with this motorcycle-riding mess." Imani turned to Raymond as he sipped a whiskey sour. "If you even think about it . . ."

"I told you, I'm waiting until my midlife crisis," he joked. "Then I'm going to get one of them to teach me how to ride it."

"And I'll hurt whichever one of them teaches you." Imani waved for the bartender and ordered a virgin strawberry daiquiri, then winked at Dana.

"I'll teach you, Raymond," Dana exclaimed as she held up the helmet. "And Imani will just have to deal with it. As a matter of fact, once she sees the amazing riding outfits that go with motorcycles, she's going to be happy to hop on the back of the bike with you."

Ian and Raymond laughed as Imani pouted. "Are

you ready to go?" Ian asked. "We can take a spin for fun, then head to the theater."

"All right." Dana and Ian told their friends that they'd catch them on the red carpet. Once they were outside and Ian had gotten his motorcycle, Dana slid her helmet on.

"Well, let's get a move on, doll," he said as he gave her a smoldering look. "And I have to tell you one more time—you look amazing."

"Thank you," she said as they climbed on the bike. Holding on to Ian, Dana actually felt a little guilty for thinking about Adrian so much. But she felt extremely guilty when she wished that she was riding with Adrian and holding him tightly. They came to a stop and a pack of paparazzi started snapping their pictures. This was a new feeling for Dana, being on that side of the camera. Ian, however, handled it like a pro, flipping up the shield on his helmet and giving them his trademark smile. She held on to him tighter as Ian revved the bike and tore off from the intersection. Once they made it to the theater, Dana relaxed a bit. She and Ian hopped off the bike, removed their helmets, and were mobbed by reporters.

"Ian, who's the lovely young lady?"

"Are you two dating?"

"Were the rumors of fighting on the set with Heather Williams and Imani Gilliam true?"

"Guys, guys," Ian said, flashing that smile and emphasizing his Southern accent. "Let's just enjoy the movie."

A female reporter smiled at Ian. "How much of the movie includes you topless?"

Ian winked at her. "At least half of it."

"Then I'm going to enjoy this."

Ian smiled as he wrapped his arm around Dana's waist. "Ready?"

"Yes." She smiled as another photographer took their picture. Ian leaned in against her ear. "Having fun yet?"

"Are all of your dates this eventful?" Dana grinned as they approached the red carpet and she started to step back from him, but Ian wouldn't let her go.

"This is part of the deal. You have to pose and smile for the camera," he said.

"You know this is way out of my comfort zone," Dana said as they stood in front of the movie poster background. "I really like being on the other side of the red carpet." Dana never realized how hot it was underneath those lights and how annoying flashes were. *Keep smiling*, she told herself as she and Ian posed for another set of pictures. Dana had to admit, she wasn't the least bit disappointed when *Entertainment Tonight* pulled Ian away. One of the red carpet attendants was about to escort Dana over to the holding area when Imani called out her name.

"You and Ian have to take a picture with me and Raymond," she said as she crossed over to her friend, who pulled her in front of another group of photographers. Ian joined them and the cameras went wild. Reporters hollered out questions, asking Imani about her feud with Heather, asking her who she was wearing and if she was ready to tackle another action role. Then, in the same rapid-fire fashion, reporters started shooting off more questions about the movie, the motorcycle, and finally Dana.

"This is the fabulous Dana Singleton," Imani chimed in.

A few of the legitimate photographers knew who she was and smiled at her. The other paparazzi just shrugged and continued snapping pictures. Then Ian gave them the money shot when he leaned in and kissed Dana. She was caught off guard and she was sure that it would show in the photos.

"Your lips were simply irresistible," Ian whispered in her ear. She could smell alcohol on his breath, which gave her pause. She was not going to get on a bike with an intoxicated Ian.

"Well, that's going to get the rumor mill going," she replied with a smile as they headed inside to the screening. Dana had been to a few screenings before, but she had no idea that the stars got this kind of special treatment. Sushi, private seats, more alcohol than the law should allow, and those pesky reporters. Dana and Raymond ate and watched Imani and Ian work the press. "So, Dr. Thomas," Dana said, holding her fork up as if it were a microphone. "How do you feel about getting ignored for nearly two hours?"

"Ah, it's wonderful. I get to eat and not worry

about anyone caring that I got wasabi on my shirt."
They broke out in laughter. Raymond tilted his
head toward Ian. "You two getting serious?"

Dana shook her head. "Don't tell Imani, though.
Mrs. Matchmaker thinks she has hit it out of the
ball park with this one and I think Ian is buying
whatever your wife is selling."

"The club owner, you're still in love with him?"

"I really need to work on my mysterious side. Do
you think I'm crazy?"

Raymond shrugged and took another California
roll from the server's tray being passed around.
"Listen, if you believe he deserves a second chance
and you love him, then go for it. But Imani would
want me to tell you to watch yourself with that guy."

"Adrian isn't as bad as I led you guys to believe,"
she said. "He's had it rough since his mother died
and . . . I know what I'm doing."

"All right," he replied. "But I don't want to see
my wife's best friend heartbroken."

"Because your wife will keep you up at night
bitching about it?" she quipped.

Raymond polished off his roll and shook his
head. "Because I think you deserve better and I'd
hate to have to kick his ass on your behalf. Don't let
the smooth taste fool you. I'm from Harlem."

Dana gave Raymond a sisterly hug. "Thank you."

"Anytime. But don't break the news to Imani
yet," he joked as Dana grabbed a California roll of
her own.

When the movie started, Imani and Raymond

snuggled up together, watching in rapt attention, and Dana sat uncomfortably with Ian's arm around her. "Wow," she said when his image filled the screen—shirtless, carrying a really big gun. "You look great."

"Six hours a day in the gym just to get this scene right." The heat from his breath sent a tingle down her spine and she immediately felt guilty, as if she were cheating on Adrian. Ian could have any woman he wanted; he didn't have to have her. He could understand that, couldn't he?

He leaned closer to her, as if that was possible, and smiled as he watched his scenes. The movie was good and Dana enjoyed watching Imani make up for that abysmal *Fearless Diva* in this action flick, but Ian was becoming a little too touchy-feely.

"Ian," she whispered. "I want to watch this."

"I can get a director's copy later," he said, and for the first time, Dana noticed the slurring in his words.

"Are you drunk?"

He flashed his smile, which was a little toothier now. "Just a little."

"You need some coffee, especially since you didn't take a limo here."

Ian rested his head on Dana's shoulder. "I trust you to take me back to the hotel. Maybe even spend the night with me?"

She stroked his cheek. "I'll get you home safely, but you're sleeping alone."

"Are you sure about that?" He winked at her, then kissed her shoulder.

Dana smacked his thigh. "In the morning, you can blame it on the alcohol, but right now, you need to pull it together." She nodded in the direction of a couple of reporters. "We're being watched more than the movie."

Ian held his head up briefly and gave the reporters a passing glimpse. "All right, let me find some coffee."

Dana waved for one of the sushi girls and whispered for some coffee. "And keep it coming, discreetly."

"Yes, ma'am," she replied.

Ian kissed Dana's shoulder again. "I like you. That was really cool what you did."

Dana tapped his knee. "Calm down. I'm just doing what any good friend would do. Besides, there are too many cameras around for you to stumble around drunk."

"Again, I like you. Dana, you're a really cool chick," he whispered. "Most women wouldn't have come here on a motorcycle and you did. Now look at you taking care of me and trying to keep the reporters from knowing I'm shitfaced."

"You probably shouldn't," she mumbled, then focused on the screen. How was she going to deal with a drunk Hollywood Ken? She tried to quiet him down as the waitress returned with a cup of steaming coffee.

Chapter 9

The movie ended to thunderous applause. Imani, Ian, and even Heather looked happy with the response. She and Imani played nice in front of the media, but Dana could feel the underlying tension. Glancing at Ian, she was glad to see that he'd sobered up nicely. Still, she told him that he should ride back with Imani and Raymond in the limo. Ian agreed and allowed Dana to ride his Harley back to the hotel. And he made his intentions clear. "I hope you'll stay when you drop the bike off."

"I don't think so," she said as she patted him on the arm.

"I really blew it, huh?"

Dana shrugged. If she'd been honest with him, Dana would've told Ian that he'd never had a real chance anyway. She wanted Adrian, even though she knew he was bad for her and that she was probably setting herself up for another heartbreak. But just like the Four Tops, she couldn't help herself.

She gave Ian a fleeting kiss on the cheek, then headed outside to grab Ian's bike. She was surprised when she saw Adrian standing on the now-abandoned red carpet.

"What are you doing here?" she asked him.

"Waiting for you," he replied as he crossed over to her and wrapped his arms around her waist. "Did you and Hollywood Ken have a good time?"

Dana shrugged. "Eh. You know how these things are. Stars, booze, someone gets a little too drunk and—"

"If that son of a—"

"Calm down, cowboy. Ian was a perfect gentleman, despite his overindulgence. That's why I'm taking his motorcycle back to the hotel—to save him from a scandal."

Adrian shook his head. He was about to tell Dana to have the bike towed when Heather Williams called out his name. Dana looked at her and then back at Adrian. "Friend of yours?"

"This will only take a minute," he said as he dashed over to Heather.

What in the hell? she thought as she watched the two of them talk in hushed tones. The valet brought Ian's bike around to the curb and handed Dana the helmet. "Thanks," she said as she glanced over her shoulder at Heather and Adrian, assuming that Heather was his revenge or backup plan in case she and Ian were serious. She was about to start up the bike when Adrian ran over to her and hopped on the back of the Harley. He wrapped his arms around Dana's waist. "Are you going to give me ride or what?"

"I thought you were setting that up with Heather."

"That was strictly business. She's hosting an after-party at my club tonight," he said.

Dana paused and glanced over her shoulder. "But I thought you had—"

"It's been taken care of," he said. "So, are you going to take me for a ride or what?"

She flipped the visor down on her helmet and smiled before taking off from the curb, giving Adrian a jolt as they took off. He held her tightly, almost understanding why this dangerous hobby of hers was so thrilling. But he wasn't about to get one of these death machines and he wasn't going to make a hobby of riding with Dana, even though he'd asked for the ride.

When she brought the bike to a stop at the curb of the Beverly Hilton, Adrian was happy to hop off. "So, we'll take a cab from here?" Adrian asked.

"Or we can walk and you tell me all about your business with Heather Williams," she said as she locked Ian's helmet on the back of the bike.

"All right," he said. "And then you can tell me what was up with you and Hollywood Ken." Adrian folded his arms across his chest and raised his eyebrow at her. "I don't have anything to hide."

"And Ian and I are just friends. Imani introduced us because she thought . . . You know what, I'm not the one who has a history of lying."

"Touché. But if we're starting over, when are you going to let that go?"

Would she be able to let it go? Would she be able to truly trust Adrian and give herself to him freely? "That's going to take some time."

He took her chin in his hand, forcing her to look into his sparkling eyes. "You're going to give me the time to make it up to you? I've never loved anyone the way I love you and if I could—"

Dana placed a finger to his lips. "I don't need you to sell me on that," she said. "Just promise me that you won't keep things from me again."

Adrian kissed her to stop from telling her another lie. He held her close, nibbling at her bottom lip. "Let's get out of here. My car is actually two blocks away at my club. I want to show you something." Before she could say yes or no, Adrian scooped her up in his arms and they took off down the street laughing. Dana couldn't believe she was having such a good time with Adrian. He was relaxed, seemingly the man she fell in love with two years ago. Now, riding the motorcycle was new. She wondered if this could become a new habit?

"You can't keep me out too long," she said. "I have a photo shoot in the morning at the Sony studios and I have some pictures to edit."

Adrian gritted his teeth. "So, am I going to be denied the sight of your face in the morning?"

"Have you always been this corny or is it a new development?"

He nibbled at her chin and stroked her cheek. "And you've become a comedienne, huh?" Adrian placed Dana on the ground as they arrived at his club. As expected, the place was packed. Adrian scanned the crowd looking for Solomon or Heather. When he saw the two of them approaching each other, he couldn't wait for the explosion. He wasn't disappointed as he saw Heather haul off and slap Solomon. The camera phones flashed and Adrian was sure there was a video going as well. He could imagine more protests at the construction site, more headlines and more trouble for that "family values" book.

"Is that Solomon Crawford?" Dana asked as she took a glance over Adrian's shoulder. "This can't be good."

Adrian pretended not to care. "And why would that be? He probably hit on the wrong woman."

"That's Heather Williams and from what I heard, they have a history. The tabloids are going to be all over this. Aren't they building a hotel in Los Angeles?"

Adrian glanced at Dana, wondering how close she was to the Crawford family. "You know them pretty well or something?"

"Everyone in New York knows of them," Dana said, entranced by the scene going on below Adrian's glass encased office. "Seeing Solomon and Kandace together, you're reminded that real love exists. There was a big feature on NY One about them."

Adrian grabbed his chest and pretended he was having a heart attack. "Was that jab at me?"

"If the body blow hurts."

He drew her against his chest. "How many times and how many ways can I apologize?" His lips brushed against her forehead, sending a tingle down her spine that caused a rippling of desire between her thighs.

She smiled. "I can think of a few."

Seeing the passion in her eyes, Adrian slipped his hand inside the halter of her jumpsuit, teasing and massaging her breast until she moaned as her nipple hardened. Exposing her breast, he covered her nipple with his hot mouth. Dana closed her eyes, tossing her head back, forgetting that there was some drama going on behind the glass. Her knees quaked as the top of her suit fell down and Adrian's hands roamed her back while his mouth pleasured her breasts.

"Step out of this thing," he said, pulling back from her for a brief moment. Dana shifted her hips, allowing the suit to flutter to the floor, and mentally patted herself on the back for ditching her underwear.

Adrian let out an appreciative whistle. "Damn, woman, you look good enough to eat. As a matter of fact"—he spread her legs—"I think I will." He dropped to his knees, then coaxed her to straddle his face. His tongue sought out her throbbing bud, lapping the sweetness of her desire as she called out his name.

"Oh yes," she cried. He held her thighs tightly, kissing and licking her wet folds until she nearly collapsed on top of him. Adrian pointed to the plush sofa in the corner and silently told her to go there. On shaky legs, she crossed the room as he shed his clothes, then joined her on the sofa. Her eyes fell on his hardness and in the back of her mind, she decided she needed to make him moan as he'd done her just moments ago. Propping up on her knees, Dana reached out and grabbed Adrian around the waist. "Let me taste you now," she said huskily. Before Adrian could say a word, Dana's lips and tongue had him in her grasp and he loved it. She was so sensual and sexy. But when she locked eyes with him, she nearly brought him to climax. "Need. Inside. You. Now." He stepped back from her and she seductively licked her lips, which made him harder than a concrete column.

He grabbed his pants and fished a condom out of his wallet and slid the sheath in place. Crossing over to the sofa, he grabbed Dana's waist and pulled her against him. She wrapped her legs around his waist, giving him direct access to where she needed him most.

"Damn, damn, damn," he moaned as he plunged into her.

Dana gasped, moaned, and gripped his shoulders as he ground against her.

"Adrian. Adrian. Adrian." Her climax was near; she could feel the explosion building, and when he thrust forward, she let it go.

Adrian nibbled on her neck, slowing his pace, just following the rhythm of her moans, and finally, he came. Falling against each other, they rested on the sofa, breathing in sync and for that moment in time, all that mattered to Adrian was the woman he held in his arms.

"Too bad we can't spend the night here," he whispered against her ear as he stroked her bare back. "I don't think I want to let you put clothes on ever again."

"Mmm," she moaned. "Too bad I have to work tomorrow."

"Pictures of the stars?"

"That is why I'm here, though I'm sure you'd like to believe I'd come two thousand miles for you." Dana laughed.

"I'd go twenty-two thousand miles for you," he said, suddenly growing serious. "Dana, I never should've let you go. Never should've—"

She placed her index finger to his lips. "You've apologized enough. Let's move forward, together. But don't expect me to give up my motorcycle this time. You're going to have to deal with it."

"Can't get you to trade it for another Corvette? The new Mustang?"

Dana tweaked his nose, then kissed his cheek. "Nope. Maybe you should learn to ride."

Adrian shook his head furiously. "I'll leave that to you. Just promise me, no racing. And no long rides with Hollywood Ken."

"Give that a rest. Imani was just trying to hook up

every single person she knows, since that's her duty as a happily married woman."

Adrian sucked his teeth. "She doesn't care for me much, huh?"

Dana shrugged. "She doesn't know you. But that's neither here nor there. I like you."

"Just like?"

She brushed her lips against his. "You know it's more than that."

He held Dana's face between his palms, looking directly into her eyes. Adrian missed the days when they could freely say *I love you*. He missed the days when she was all that mattered. If his father had been worth a damn, Adrian wouldn't be on this quest for revenge. He would've never lost her in the first place if Elliot Crawford hadn't shirked his responsibilities as a father.

"What?" she asked.

"I've never stopped loving you."

"Will you tell me why you did what you did one day?" She bit her bottom lip. "I don't want to ruin this moment, but you're going to have to tell me at some point."

"You're right, let's not ruin the moment. Hungry?"

"A little. And I know just what I want."

"What's that?"

"One of your omelets, so let's go to your place."

Adrian smiled, remembering how she would devour his cheese and tomato omelets—the only dish he was able to cook.

"I guess we're going to have to stop by Albertsons on Venice, then," he said as he released her and they got dressed.

When Dana went into the bathroom, Adrian remembered the drama he'd set into motion and glanced out at the club while pulling his shirt over his head. Solomon and Heather were gone. He wondered if Solomon, like his father, had taken Heather away so that he could cheat on his wife.

"I'm ready," Dana said, breaking into his thoughts. "And you're still half naked. What's going on?"

"Nothing, just looking out there to see what's going on."

Dana nodded. "Did you ever get things straightened out?"

"What? Oh, yes."

She gave him a surreptitious glance but kept quiet. Adrian slipped his pants on, crossed over to Dana, and wrapped his arm around her waist. "Let's get out of here before you change your mind or remember how my omelets really taste."

Chapter 10

After a quick stop at the grocery store, Dana and Adrian arrived at his penthouse ravenous and ready to cook. Well, in Dana's case, watch Adrian work his magic with the eggs. She wasn't going to lift a finger to cook. As Adrian unloaded the groceries and Dana made herself comfortable on a bar stool in the kitchen, he wished this was an everyday occurrence, coming home and looking into her smiling face. Sure, they wouldn't eat omelets every day, but he would spend many days and nights doing whatever made her smile.

"What?" she asked when she caught his gaze.

"Nothing." He set the eggs on the counter and leaned into Dana. "How in love with New York are you?"

"That came out of nowhere." She grinned. "New York is a part of me—now. Why?"

"Because I want you to come back to me, back to LA."

Dana sucked in a deep breath. "Don't you think it's a little early for that?"

"I made the mistake of letting you go before, and I'm not going to let that happen again."

"Who says I'm ready to take that chance with you again?" Honestly, Dana wasn't sure how much she was willing to give up for love this time. "Why can't you move to New York?"

He gritted his teeth. Moving to New York would mean being in the place that caused his mother nothing but pain. He'd be within striking distance of his father and he wasn't sure that he could be that close to Elliot Crawford and not want to kill him.

"New York has never been one of my favorite places."

"And I hate LA. The traffic, the smog, and the air kisses. Ugh. Most of the people out here are plastic. New Yorkers are real."

Adrian reached for a mixing bowl from above the refrigerator. "Then I guess we're going to have to find some sort of midway point, huh? Chicago?"

"Are you serious?" she asked as he cracked the eggs in the bowl.

Adrian nodded and whisked the eggs. "These last two years without you have been hell and I don't want to lose another day."

"Then why?" she asked, her voice low and dripping with leftover hurt. "Why did you push me away when all I wanted was to be there for you? I know how much your mother meant to you. I was fond of her as well. You robbed me of my chance to grieve her too."

Adrian placed the bowl on the counter and crossed over to Dana. "I'm . . . Sorry isn't enough," he said as he drew her into his arms. Part of him knew he should come clean. He should tell her about his father, the secret his mother told him on her death bed. But still, he didn't want her involved in the ugliness that was about to envelope his life. "Dana."

"Don't 'Dana' me. I really feel like you're holding something back," she said.

"Why do you say that?" *Tell her the truth,* his conscience called out.

"I know you."

"Dana." He stroked her cheek and smiled. "There's nothing I need to confess other than I love you."

She eyed him suspiciously. Adrian kissed her softly, gently sucking on her bottom lip because he recognized that look she'd given him. "Let me start cooking," he said when he released her.

Dana wasn't convinced by his act. He was hiding something. While he cooked, Dana decided to make some mimosas. "I know you have some champagne in here." She crossed over to the refrigerator and fished out a bottle of Perrier-Jouët. She held the bottle up as Adrian sprinkled a handful of cheese over the eggs. "I see you still keep the good stuff."

"Yes, and you're the only one who I want to share this with," he said as she popped the cork. Dana shook her head at him.

"Laying it on a little thick, huh?" she asked as she crossed over to the cabinet and grabbed two champagne flutes.

Adrian flipped the eggs and added more cheese; then he turned the heat down and walked over to the edge of the bar where Dana stood, pouring orange juice into the glasses. He took the juice from her hands, pushed the glasses, juice, and champagne to the other end of the bar. "Let me show you how I lay it on thick." Adrian lifted Dana up onto the edge of the bar, then kissed her with a hot and smoldering desire that shook her to the core. When he untied the halter of her jumpsuit, Dana moaned in anticipation. Adrian massaged her breasts until her nipples were diamond hard. Just when he was about to take one of them into his mouth, the buzzing of his smoke alarm put the brakes on. "Shit," he muttered, realizing that he'd dropped a pot holder on the eye of the stove. He put out the small fire as Dana laughed hysterically.

"What were you thinking about?" she asked as she hopped off the counter.

Adrian tilted his head, focusing a stare on her bare breasts. "If you have to ask . . ."

Dana pretended to be scandalized and covered her chest with her arm. "Well, sir, I can't believe you're lusting after my body when I'm starving."

Adrian glanced at the omelets in the pan. Satisfied that they would be good, he plated them and asked, "So, how do you plan to earn your supper, ma'am?"

Dana shrugged out of her jumpsuit and placed her hands on her hips. "I guess we can work something out."

Adrian dropped the plates on the bar. "Hot damn," he exclaimed.

Dana sauntered over to him and took a plate off the counter. "Not until I eat," she said. "You're welcome to watch."

Adrian picked up his plate and the mimosas, then followed a naked Dana into the living room. He'd missed times like this. Missed watching the sway of her hips in front of him on quiet evenings at home. How many more moments like this would they have together?

"Let's toast," he said when he joined her on the sofa.

Dana took the glass he'd offered and smiled at him. "What are we toasting to?"

"Second chances."

Dana clanked her glass against his. "I'll drink to that."

Adrian watched as she sipped from the glass. Her lips were so enticing and he really didn't want to eat the omelet that he'd cooked. He had a taste for Dana. She set her glass on the coffee table and planted herself on Adrian's lap. "I'm suddenly not very hungry," she whispered as she thrust her hips forward.

"I could eat . . . something." He lifted her until he was facing her feminine mound of desire. Slowly, he kissed her thigh, licking her as if she were an ice cream cone as she spread her legs. She was so wet and ready for his mouth. Adrian felt her quiver as he brought her closer to his lips. His tongue split her wet slit and she moaned in delight.

Her passionate cries made him go deeper, suck harder until his erection ached, seemingly jealous of his tongue. He peeled his mouth away from her, ready to feel her warmth, needing to be inside her.

"I need you," he intoned as he unzipped his pants.

"You got me," she replied as she eased down his body to assist in removing his pants and boxers. Dana smiled at the sight of his erection, then stroked it gently.

"You're all I've ever needed," he whispered, his head thrown back in pleasure as her mouth replaced the stroke of her hand. The heat of her breath, the wetness of her mouth, and the lick of her tongue made Adrian's knees quake and bring him to the brink of an orgasm.

He placed his hand underneath her chin, silently telling her to stop. "Damn, baby," he moaned, then gripped her hips.

Dana licked her lips and smiled at him before planting herself on his lap. Adrian stroked her face before pulling her in for a kiss. Their tongues danced together as she spread her thighs. Without a thought of protection, he entered her valley, thrusting his hips against hers as she rode him. He grabbed her breasts, massaging them before sucking her erect nipples. She tightened her thighs around him, crying out as ripples of delight flowed through her body. Dana and Adrian locked eyes as she felt the waves of an orgasm wash over her. Adrian leaned her against the sofa cushions, diving deeper and intensifying her second orgasm.

The blissful look on her face took Adrian over the edge. As much as he wanted to, needed to, he couldn't pull out before spilling his seed inside her. A moment passed before either of them moved. Adrian glanced at her belly, wondering what kind of father he would be if she happened to get pregnant. Would he be a coward like his biological father and walk away, or would he be like the man who raised him—strong, responsible, and caring?

"What's that look?" she asked.

"We were reckless."

Dana nodded. "But I'm on the pill. I'm not trying to be a mother anytime soon and I'm sure you're not trying to give up your LA lifestyle for fatherhood."

"But I would."

Dana raised her eyebrow as if she didn't believe him. She had no cause to, especially since he never wanted kids when they were together. What had changed? she wondered as she caught him looking at her stomach again.

"Relax, Adrian," she said. "I'm STD free and—at this moment—not pregnant. Should I be worried about you?"

"No," he said. "Listen, I'm just . . . We've never been careless like this and I don't want—"

She placed her finger to his lips. "Can we cross that bridge if the time comes? Are you sure you don't have something you need to tell me?"

Adrian kissed her finger, smiling at her warmly. He had a lot he had to tell her. He had many things to say to her; he owed her the truth about his father and how he wanted to bring his family to their knees. But instead of answering her, he simply gave her a deep kiss.

"Adrian," she said when their lips parted.

"Umm . . ."

"The omelets are cold and I'm still hungry."

Smiling, he lifted off her and said, "Let's get dressed and go to Roscoe's. I don't think I can pull that off a second time." Adrian nodded to the oddly shaped omelets. "And"—he ran his index finger down her thigh—"I'm too distracted to cook."

"Well, Roscoe's it is," she said, then looked at the clock above the TV. "Damn. I can't. I have an early morning and my body still thinks it's on the East Coast."

"Thank God it isn't," Adrian ribbed. "I guess it's room service, then."

"Excuse me?"

"I don't care where we sleep as long as we do it together," he said as he reached for his pants.

Dana started to say something sarcastic, but she wanted to wake up in Adrian's arms and feel the warmth of his breath against her neck as they slept. So she just smiled. "Let's get dressed and go, then."

About thirty minutes later, they were headed to Dana's hotel. As he drove, Adrian glanced at her, wondering again if he should tell her the truth. Was he afraid that Dana would talk him out of his anger or was he afraid that she'd be angry with him?

When Dana caught one of his awkward looks, she shook her head. "I'm going to ask you for the last time, what's wrong?"

"Nothing. I can't look at you?"

"I guess," she quipped, then fingered her thick hair. "I hope you don't mind if I edit some pictures before bed. I want to stay ahead of my deadline."

"Not at all." But Adrian didn't want to see pictures of Ian Kelly and his ilk. The pictures he wanted to see would be plastered all over the papers tomorrow—protest at the Crawford construction site, Solomon getting smacked by Heather, and possibly Richmond's mug shot. He gripped the steering wheel tighter and forced himself to concentrate on the road and push the thoughts of his *family* out of his mind. He could hear Dana talking about the Crawfords, but he refused to allow the words to seep into his brain.

"I'm sorry," she said when she noticed the look on his face. "I'm going on and on about work and that scene in your club and you zoned out."

"It's okay."

"I get the feeling that you're not fond of the

Crawfords. Did your business with them not work out?"

"No." He wished she'd stop talking about those people. The more he answered her questions, the more he felt as if he were lying to her. He wanted to keep her away from his war. But how could he?

"I'm sorry to hear that," she said.

"Don't be. Shit happens."

"I guess you're right. I can't wait for this to be over. Maybe I'll take a vacation in Los Angeles."

Adrian smiled broadly, genuinely. "That sounds like a good plan. I know where we can go to avoid the smog you hate so much."

Dana smiled and stroked his arm. "I thought you'd like that. Then maybe you can come to New York and hang out in my territory for a while."

He gritted his teeth. "I don't understand why you love that dirty—"

"Hey!"

"You've been in LA long enough to know that this trumps New York."

Dana sucked her teeth. "It's all right."

Adrian exited off the highway and headed toward the hotel. "Be honest."

"Los Angeles hasn't always been good to me and you know that. You haven't even seen New York. Nor do you know the greatness of a hot dog from a street vendor."

Part of him wanted to pour his heart out to her as he pulled into the parking lot of the hotel. He wanted to tell her that his mother loved and lost so much to that city, and if he had his way, he'd never set foot there. But then he'd have to tell her the rest of the story. The way Elliot Crawford broke his mother's heart and banished them thousands of miles away.

"I have the best part of New York right here," he said, then stroked her knee.

"As much as I want to bask in the compliment, there's more to New York than me." She grinned.

"Not in my book." Adrian climbed out of the car and crossed over to the passenger side to open Dana's door. He took her hand in his and kissed it gently. "You know, I love you more than you know."

She paused and stared into his eyes. "Why do I feel like there's a *but* coming?"

Adrian tilted his head to the side and started to tell her what the *but* was, but he knew the main thing he needed to do was get her upstairs in that hotel room so he could kiss her without the prying eyes of security cameras or Imani.

Too late. "Dana," she called out. "Where have you been?"

Dana raised her eyebrow as Adrian wrapped his arm around her waist, as if he were bracing for Hurricane Imani.

Adrian glanced at the man standing beside her; he looked as if he wanted nothing more than to go upstairs and go to sleep. How in the hell did he deal with this woman? Actresses were his least favorite people in the world, because they always seemed to have to be on. Imani, he'd surmised, was no different.

Imani cut her eyes at Adrian and then sidled up to Dana. "You're kind of losing your mind. Ian was looking for you."

"Did he sober up any?"

Imani held her index fingers a few inches apart. "But how drunk are you?"

"We'll talk later," she said, glancing over her shoulder at Adrian. He kissed her on the back of her neck.

"In other words, we'll see you in the morning," Adrian said, then offered Imani a sly grin. Just as she was about to respond to him, the man Adrian assumed was her husband grasped her elbow.

"Good night, adults," he said, looking pointedly at Imani. "Let's go."

Imani glanced at Dana and Adrian, then turned to her husband. "Whatever," she whispered, and followed him inside without another word.

Adrian made a mental note to send that man a case of his favorite drink.

"We should go too," Adrian said to Dana. "Since you have work to do and I want to distract you."

She shook her head and gave him a quick peck on the cheek. "Let's go." They dashed inside and decided to take the stairs to her room rather than wait for the elevator. Adrian took the steps two at a time and Dana laughed while struggling to keep up.

"Slow down," she said, pretending to be out of breath. "I'm going to be so tired when I get to the room that I'm going straight to sleep."

He stopped, turned around, and scooped her up into his arms. "I don't think so."

With Dana in his arms, Adrian bounded up the remaining steps until they reached her floor.

"Whew," he said.

"Hey! No one told you to play Mr. Fireman."

"There's a hose joke in there but I'm going to let that go."

Dana burst out laughing as he lowered her to the floor so that she could open the door. "Remember, I need to do a little work."

"Fine, I'll order room service since we didn't get to eat at my place. Well, food anyway."

She glanced at him over her shoulder as she crossed to her laptop. "You are so bad," she said as he perused the menu. Booting her computer, Dana plugged the memory card from her camera in and Adrian took notice of a picture that had nothing to do with Hollywood or the movies. It was Elliot Crawford. She didn't notice Adrian glaring at the screen over her shoulder as she edited a picture of Elliot and his granddaughter standing in front of the construction site. He got a brief view of some of the protesters standing behind the grandfather and granddaughter. Elliot looked like he was pointing out points of architecture to the little girl.

As if she understands what the hell he's saying. I wonder if that baby understands that the man holding her is a lying asshole. Adrian turned away from the picture, feeling ridiculous because he was jealous of a baby. He crossed over to the balcony doors and opened them. Taking a deep breath, he questioned his plan to bring his father down. His mother's final wish hadn't been for war; she wanted him to know who his father was and possibly get to know him. Looking back at Dana as she plugged away on the computer, he smiled, then turned his eyes upward to the sky.

"You're behind this, aren't you," he whispered to the heavens. "She brings out the best in me. You've always said that." Adrian sighed. He'd been so angry that he had allowed his emotions to take him down a dark road. Now he was regretting what he'd done to Solomon. His brother wasn't his enemy and he shouldn't have set up that photo. Just as he was about to reach for his cell phone, he felt Dana's arms wrap around his waist.

"Room service just arrived. What are you doing out here?"

"Thinking, talking to Mom, and thanking God that you came back to me." He turned around and kissed Dana on the forehead.

"Adrian."

"Listen," he said, cutting her off. "I made the

biggest mistake of my life when I made you believe that I was with those women. I should've been open and honest with you about how I was feeling."

"Adrian, that's the past, but if we're going to have a future, you have to be honest with me about everything." She stroked his cheek. "Come on, let's eat and crawl into bed."

Chapter 11

The next morning, Dana woke up nestled in Adrian's arms and she didn't want to move an inch. The heat of his body felt so delicious and comfortable. *Just five more minutes,* she thought as she snuggled closer to him. He brushed his lips against her neck and she smiled. "I thought you were sleeping," she said as she felt the hard thickness of his erection against her bottom.

"Sleep is overrated," he whispered, then nibbled her ear.

Dana wanted to give in to the passion, to the heat and desire bubbling inside her belly, but she had to pull out of his embrace.

"I have to shower and get to work," she groaned. "I have to meet with Lois from the publicity department for breakfast."

"Lois can eat without you," he said, stroking her hip. "Take the day off."

"Says the man who works all night." She reluctantly moved his hand from her hip. "The sooner I finish with this meeting, the sooner we can link up and get right back into bed."

He gently bit her shoulder. "How much longer are you going to be working on this assignment?"

"Well, technically today is my last day. But I was going to start on a new project, something more personal to me."

Adrian propped up on his elbows. "What's that?"

"My photo book. I want to look at more than the glamour and glitz of Hollywood and Broadway."

"So this means you're going to be in LA for an extended period of time, huh? How much of that time do I get?"

She turned around and faced him, tilting her head to the side. "Well, I've been trying to figure that out myself. Do I have a reason to spend more time with you?"

Adrian chuckled as he took her right hand and placed it on his hardness. "Here's one reason." Then he took her hand and placed it against his chest. "But here's the main reason. You can't take my heart to New York and if you leave me again, it's going to break."

Dana shook her head. "Cute but corny, Mr. Bryant. I could stay, but I know I don't want to spend the next few weeks in a hotel."

"I know exactly where you can stay," he said.

"Will there be omelets?"

"Every day."

She kissed him and hopped out of bed. "Then I guess I'll be staying in LA. And I don't want to hear one word about my bike."

Adrian groaned and flipped over on his stomach. "I still don't think that thing is safe. Especially since you have this need for speed."

Dana grabbed her toiletries from the dresser and turned to Adrian. "Explain this to me—if you're so worried about my need for speed, what was the purpose of buying me a Corvette?"

"Four wheels instead of two," he said matter-of-factly. "I know motorcycles are your thing, so I'm going to try and accept it."

"I appreciate that because you don't have much choice in the matter, sweetheart." She dashed into the bathroom before Adrian could muster a reply.

Sitting up in the bed, he listened for the shower to start. When he heard the water going full blast, Adrian picked up his cell phone and called Elliot.

"Son," the older man said, forgoing a hello. "I have to say this is a surprise."

"Are you always so damned smug?" Adrian gritted out.

"I hope you didn't call me for an argument."

Adrian sighed. "No, I didn't. I want to meet with you. We should talk. Face-to-face."

"When would you like to meet, Adrian? We have a lot that we need to discuss and clear up."

"Yes, we do. I have some time this morning around eleven. Where would you like to meet?"

"There's a Japanese restaurant on Wilshire—

Takami Sushi and Robata. We can meet there at noon." Adrian wasn't going to allow Elliot to schedule what time they'd meet. He'd been waiting on his father for years, Elliot could wait for him now.

"That works for me," he said. "I'll see you there."

Adrian ended the call at the precise moment that Dana finished her shower. If he left when she did, he'd have time to go home, shower, and mentally prepare himself to forgive his father. Dana walked out of the bathroom wrapped in a white towel and all Adrian wanted to do was pull the towel from her body and make love to her for the rest of his life.

The rest of his life. That's how long he wanted to be with Dana. And in order for him to be with her and love her the way she deserved, he had to bury his anger and hatred toward his father. Maybe there would come a time when he'd think of Elliot as family. Maybe making peace with him today would be the first step in the right direction. He couldn't help but wonder if his father would apologize for what he did to his mother. That's what hurt Adrian the most, the fact that his mother died thinking of a man who seemingly didn't give a damn about her.

Thinking about Pamela's last day wasn't helping him.

"Adrian? Did you hear me?" Dana asked, snapping him back to reality.

"No, what did you say?"

Dana rolled her eyes. "I asked if you wanted to meet for dinner around seven."

"That's fine. Do you think you can meet me at the club? I have to go over my books, and since we're closed tonight, this is the best time."

"All right," she said. "I'll pick up some takeout and Starbucks."

Adrian climbed out of bed and crossed over to her. She had pulled on a pair of black lace boy shorts and a matching bra. Damn, how had he missed that? She looked delicious. Those hips were calling his hands. He heeded that call and pulled her into his arms. "Do you really have to put clothes on and leave?"

"Yes." She leaned back against his chest, not wanting to leave at all. "And if you don't let me go, it's going to be that much harder for me to leave."

He thrust his hips into her backside. "It's already hard, baby."

Dana pulled away from him. "Hold that thought until I get off work and I will make it worth your while."

He winked at her. "I know you will."

Dana quickly dressed, grabbed her camera, and gave Adrian a slow smoldering kiss, then dashed out the door. Once he was alone, Adrian started thinking about his father again. Would he get the answers his inner little boy needed? Did Elliot think Adrian wasn't good enough for him to love? Adrian pulled his clothes on, shaking his head. "I don't have time for this." He headed to his car and drove home so that he could shower and make it to the restaurant.

"I hope I'm doing the right thing, Mama," he said as he grabbed his jacket and walked out the door.

When Dana arrived at the studio, she was surprised to see Ian there. He was sporting a pair of dark shades and a New Orleans Saints hat.

"Hi," Dana said.

Ian nodded. "Thank you for last night. I got my bike this morning."

"Looks like you got more than that. A bad hangover as well, huh?"

Ian nodded. "Bradley Cooper made millions from pretending to feel as bad as I do."

"Why were you drinking so much on what should've been one of the best nights of your career?" Dana asked as they took a seat at the empty service table.

Ian removed his glasses, revealing his red-rimmed eyes. "Wasn't the smartest move I've ever made. But I'm glad you were there to keep me from making a total fool of myself."

"So were you looking for a date or a babysitter?"

Ian smirked. "I guess that's a fair question. Maybe I knew your heart wasn't in it," he said, then slid a copy of the *Times* across the table. Dana looked down at the paper and saw that photographers had captured her and Adrian leaving the movie premiere on Ian's motorcycle. Beside the picture of Dana and Adrian was the photo of Solomon

Crawford taking a slap from Heather Williams. Dana didn't bother to read the story; the headline said it all: MORE DRAMA THAN THE MOVIE.

Ian shrugged. "I guess he won."

"It was never a competition," she replied. "I think you're a nice guy and maybe in a different time and place we would've worked. But . . ."

"As the cliché goes, the heart wants what the heart wants. And if I'm honest, I shouldn't even try to bring anyone else into my mess of a life."

"So, last night wasn't an isolated incident?"

Ian shook his head. "Best-kept secret in Hollywood," he said with a wistful smile. "I thought about it when I woke up in a pile of my puke. This can't go on. So, since my next film doesn't start shooting for a while, I'm going to check into a program so that the next time the right woman comes along, I'll be ready for her."

"That's good for you," Dana said. "How are you going to keep this quiet?"

He smiled and shrugged. "I think that's what this meeting is about this morning. Do you realize the power you have on people?"

"What do you mean?"

"Dana, I've had this problem for a while and I've paid women off to keep it quiet and so far I've been lucky. No rumors, no stories leaked to the press. But last night, I saw something when you looked at me and I was ashamed of myself."

"Ian, we all have faults and I'm far from perfect. I hope you're doing this for you and not—"

"Oh, I am doing this for me. I'm finally ready to accept my faults and fix it."

Dana reached across the table and hugged him. "I'm happy for you and I'm going to be rooting for you."

"I'm guessing by the time I get my act together, you and the guy on the back of my bike will be off into the sunset." Ian stroked her arm as they parted.

"It just wasn't our time," she said.

He brushed his fingers across her smooth cheek as Lois approached them. "What does Erykah Badu say? Maybe next lifetime?"

Before Dana could respond to Ian, Lois jumped into the conversation. "Sorry for the delay, Dana," she said. "Because of Ian's decision to go into rehab, we need to show him in a better setting, you know. So people won't assume that he was drinking and riding."

Dana nodded. "I see some great photos with Ian in a suit."

"Hey," he said. "Do I get a say in this?"

Lois laughed. "Absolutely not. I love the idea. Maybe we can get a few with his shirt open as well?"

Ian turned toward Lois and shook his head with a sly smile. "That sounds even better."

"Then let's get started," Dana said as she reached for her camera bag.

* * *

Adrian arrived at the restaurant five minutes late. He spotted his father sitting at the bar sipping on what looked like water. Crossing over to him, Adrian felt like a little boy. He steeled himself when he reached the old man.

"Fa— Elliot."

"Good to see you, son," he said.

Adrian's body tensed when the older man called him son. *You're here to make peace. He is your father. At some point, you're going to accept that.* "Let's get a table," Adrian said.

Elliot rose to his feet and waved for a waiter. "We're ready," he told the man when he approached them.

"Very well, sir. Follow me." The waiter led them to a semiprivate table in the back of the restaurant. Adrian glanced out at the Los Angeles skyline. The sun bathed the city in gold and he took it as a sign that his mother was smiling, seeing the two men she loved together.

Once they'd ordered their drinks and Elliot waved the waiter away, Adrian looked directly into his father's face. He searched for more similarities between them. The eyes were the same. They had a similar complexion, and their lips were shaped the same.

"Do you have something you want to say?" Elliot picked up his glass and sipped his tonic water.

"My mother really loved you. She thought about you often, I've discovered."

"If circumstances had been different, your mother and I would've been happy together. Pamela was the light of my life."

Adrian narrowed his eyes at Elliot. "Then why didn't you marry her?"

"Things were very complicated. I didn't love Cynthia as a man should love his wife. She was a cold woman and I was a means to an end for her and she was for me as well. I'm ashamed to say that I married her for the money."

Adrian shook his head, wondering how his mother could love a man this heartless. "Once you had all the money you wanted, you could've left," Adrian replied, wishing he'd asked for something stronger than strawberry lemonade.

"Cynthia wanted children and she wanted a family. We had a contract. If I left, I'd lose everything and I wouldn't have been able to support you and your mother financially."

Adrian slammed his hand on the table. "Don't you think she needed more than some goddamned money? Don't you think I deserved a father?"

"I've regretted that decision for years. But Pamela decided that I shouldn't be a part of your life."

Adrian leaned back in his chair. "Think she was wrong? I see how you treat your sons."

"Make no mistake, I love my sons—all of you— but Solomon and Richmond were spoiled. They had everything handed to them. I can tell you know struggle and you have fight in you."

Adrian shook his head. Was this son of a bitch serious? He and his mother struggled because of him. His mother left the city she loved and had wanted to live in all of her life because of him. "You're full of it."

Elliot shrugged nonchalantly. "I can't change the past, but I was hoping that you called me here because you wanted to get to know me better. All of this controversy surrounding my other two sons got me thinking. Maybe it's time for me to get to know you better. Bring you into the business."

Adrian opened his mouth, itching to tell him that the more he talked the less he was interested in getting to know him. What he'd learned so far turned his stomach. "What was it like for you growing up?" he asked Elliot.

The older man snorted, took a sip of his drink, and glanced out the window. "I was poor. Smart, but poor. I was the first in the family to attend college and get out of the ghettos of Baltimore. I lost my brother to the drug trade, watched my father work himself to death, and my mama died without a cent to her name. That kind of life made me hungry. But I watched all of these people with their silver spoons depending on Mama and Daddy but not doing anything to make something of themselves. I could've been a hustler . . . tried it but I wanted more."

Adrian shook his head. Sadly he could recognize himself in his father's words. They were more alike than he wanted to admit. "I wanted more as well,"

Adrian said. "When my basketball teammates talked about their families, I always felt as if something were missing in my life. Paul never acted like a real father. Didn't care about what I did, whether I got in trouble or not."

"Paul?" Elliot asked, and had the nerve to sound jealous. "Who was Paul?"

"My mother's husband. He died when I was seven and for years, I thought he was my father."

Elliot tensed. "She was married?"

"Weren't you?" Adrian shot back. "You had your life. Was she supposed to stop living? It's your god-damned fault that we ended up here when my mama loved New York. She searched for happiness and never turned her back on me. Too bad you left both of us for the almighty dollar."

"But I sent you and your mother money faithfully so that you wouldn't have to struggle like I did when I was growing up."

"You think a few crumbs from your buffet make up for the emotional pain my mother and I endured?"

Elliot inhaled sharply. "I guess it doesn't. But I was hurting as well, separated from my true love and not knowing the fate of my son. I thought with your mother being three thousand miles away, I'd be able to love Cynthia, but I thought of her every day. Missed the times we shared. She made me feel like a real man, not someone who owed her anything. I could be myself with your mother."

"Shut up!" Adrian thundered. "If you had all of

these feelings and this deep love for my mother, you would've found a way to be with her. With me."

"You can't sit here with childish anger because Daddy didn't tuck you in at night. Build a bridge and get over it."

Adrian lunged across the table and grabbed Elliot by the lapels of his jacket, causing the other patrons in the restaurant to watch them in horror. "You piece of sh—"

A strong hand yanked Adrian back and Elliot fell into his seat. Looking up, Adrian nearly took a right hook from Solomon Crawford. Ducking, he pushed his brother backward into a waiter's cart. Solomon stumbled, then steadied himself. "What in the hell is going on here?"

"Why don't you ask our dear old dad?" Adrian spat.

Elliot looked from Adrian to Solomon. "What is he talking about?" Solomon asked.

"Mr. Family Values here didn't tell you about the son and woman he had tucked away in Los Angeles?" Adrian said.

Taking note of the phones and iPads pointed at them, Elliot turned to Solomon. "This isn't the place."

"Dad, what is this fool talking about?" Solomon asked as he looked from Adrian to Elliot.

Elliot shot a quick glance at Adrian, then shook his head. "I don't know. Obviously he wants to cause a scene."

Adrian's heart broke. He knew in that moment

that he would never accept this man as his father. Nothing had changed and Elliot Crawford was still about saving face and protecting his image of the perfect family. Having a bastard son and a dead mistress didn't go along with that image. "Son of a bitch. If you think this is a scene, you haven't seen nothing yet." Adrian pushed past Solomon and tore out of the restaurant. He sat in the parking deck, silently cursing himself for believing he could have anything other than contempt for the man who abandoned his mother. "Mama, you were better off without that slimy son of a bitch."

Starting his car, Adrian peeled out of the garage and drove to the house in Inglewood where his mother raised him. Parking on the street, he could almost feel her watching him from the bay window.

Smiling, he remembered how his mother used to ride her Schwinn alongside him, her hair pulled up in an Afro puff as they raced up and down the block. He was never embarrassed to hang around his mother and wore the term *mama's boy* like a badge of honor. What he couldn't understand was the story his father spun about loving his mother but not wanting to be with her. Didn't he understand what a jewel his mother had been and how lucky he was to have her in his life?

How many years had his mother wasted longing for a man who didn't want her? Adrian exited the car and walked over to the house. He could hear the echoes of his childhood and hoped whoever lived in there had the happiness that he did as a child. Just because, Adrian dropped a few hundred dollars in the mailbox. He didn't know the family who lived there or if they needed the money, but he hoped it would pay for something they wanted.

Walking back to his car, Adrian decided that he was going to take his story straight to the media and he wasn't holding back a detail. Going after his brothers had been wrong; it was Elliot who needed to suffer. Since the money and the image was so important to him, it was time to shine the spotlight on him that he didn't want.

Driving to his house, Adrian knew he had to find a picture of his mother with Elliot. He vowed to never call that man his father again. He sped down the street ready to pull his trump card.

Dana looked at her watch. It was seven-fifteen. Yes, she was late, but there was no sign of Adrian anywhere. "Great," she muttered as she leaned against her bike. "I'm hungry and he needs to come on."

She glanced at her watch again. Seven-twenty. Still no word from Adrian, no text, no call. She dialed his number and the phone went straight to voice mail. "Adrian, where are you? I'm at the club waiting on you and that Chinese takeout you promised me. Well, maybe you didn't promise me Chinese, but I'm yearning for some egg foo young and spring rolls. Hopefully I'll see you soon."

As soon as she ended the call, her phone rang again. "Well it's about time."

"Dana, where are you?" Imani asked.

"Waiting for Adrian. Why?"

"You need to get to a TV, quickly. Your boy is on there talking about the Crawfords."

"What?"

"Did you know that your man is Elliot Crawford's son?"

Dana stood on the street with her mouth agape. "Where is all of this taking place?"

"He's on KTLA in front of the Crawford Towers. I think the shot was live."

Dana hopped on her bike after clicking END on her call with Imani and headed for the construction site. Adrian had some explaining to do.

Chapter 12

Adrian shook hands with the reporter after the live shot ended. "This is some heavy stuff," the blonde said with a flip of her hair. "Would you—" Before she could finish her statement, her cell phone rang. "Yes," she said, keeping her eyes on Adrian. "I'm on my way." Smiling at him, she shrugged. "Looks like dear old dad was watching and he has a statement to make. Maybe after this news cycle is over, you and I can have a drink?" She winked at him and Adrian shook his head.

"I'll pass," he replied as he saw a Harley barreling toward him. Adrian hadn't thought about what his appearance on the news would mean for Dana. And he'd totally forgotten that they were supposed to meet at his club. "Shit," he muttered as he crossed over to her.

"What's going on, Adrian?"

"I'm sorry I didn't—"

Dana threw her hand up in his face. "This isn't

about that and you damned well know it. Elliot Crawford is your father? Is this the big secret you've been keeping from me and wanted to hide me away from? You think it's okay for me to find out on the news?"

"Dana, this has nothing to do with you, and this is why I wanted to keep you away from all of this."

"How could you just blindside me like that?" She shoved him against his shoulder. "How long have you known?"

"Dana, I don't want to do this out here right now."

She slapped her hands against her hips. "You don't have a choice."

"Let's get out of here and I'll explain everything."

Dana shook her head. "You know what, I'm not doing this with you anymore. I'm having déjà vu because this is the same bullshit you did to me two years ago. I asked you not to keep anything from me. I asked you to be honest with me no matter what, and once again, you've lied to me."

"How did I lie to you? I told you this isn't about you and if you want to wear your feelings on your shoulder because my father lied about his relationship with my mother and my paternity, have at it." He tore away from her and hopped into his car. Part of her wanted to follow him and demand that he talk to her and tell her everything. But she decided that she wasn't going to put herself through this again. She couldn't allow her heart to be smashed again.

Her phone rang and she knew it was Imani. She didn't have time to listen to her friend say *I told you so*. Pulling her helmet onto her head, Dana hopped on her bike and sped away. Though she tried to focus on the road, Dana couldn't help but berate herself for falling back into Adrian's life. Things began to make sense to her, the need to embarrass Solomon, why he wanted Richmond at his club and drunk. What kind of man did this to his family, no matter how estranged they were? Was this the kind of man she wanted to give her heart, love, and trust to?

Leaning right, Dana headed back to hotel, her mind racing as fast as her bike's engine. Maybe she should've gone back to New York immediately, but part of her wanted to find out what Adrian was up to and how finding out about his father really affected him.

When Dana arrived at the hotel, she wasn't at all surprised to find Imani waiting for her in the lobby.

"Did you find him?" Imani asked.

Dana rolled her eyes. "I did. And I don't want to talk about it."

Imani cocked her head to the side. "And you think that's going to stop me from asking questions?"

Before Dana could tell her friend to go find her husband, two fans rushed up to them and begged Imani for her autograph. She signed the notebooks they pushed in her face and Dana thought about dashing to the elevator, leaving Imani and her questions in the lobby. Instead, she waited for Imani to finish up with her fans.

"Still enjoying your fame?" Dana asked once they were alone.

Nodding, Imani pointed at her friend. "Don't try to change the subject. What are you going to do?"

Dana walked toward the elevator with Imani close on her heels. "What can I do? I still have a job to do and then there's this thing with Ian." She pressed the UP button and waited for the door to open.

"What thing with Ian?" Imani asked.

"He's going to rehab. I had to reshoot his publicity photos today. That's one of the reasons why I wasn't in front of a TV to see Adrian's bombshell. Part of me wants to stick around and be Ian's cheerleader. Did you know he had a drinking problem?"

Imani shook her head. "No idea at all. I'm really shocked. But why would you want to be his cheerleader when it's obvious where your heart lies."

"What are you talking about?"

"You made it seem as if you and this Adrian guy were going to start your failed relationship over . . ."

"Watch it," Dana gritted out.

Imani shrugged and placed her hand on her friend's shoulder as they stepped on the elevator. "I just want to make sure you're all right."

"I've done this before. I'll be fine."

"Well, you don't have to do it again. And if you're going to be Ian's cheerleader, who knows what might develop romantically?" Imani wiggled her eyebrows.

Dana rolled her eyes as the elevator stopped on her floor. "Ian is nice, but I'm not up for taking care of a drunk movie star. And wait, you're actually pushing me toward a man who's about to go to rehab for his alcohol addiction over Adrian?"

Imani shrugged. "Well, Ian hasn't broken your heart. But I guess you're right. Why trade one set of problems for another set? The best thing to do is toss them all away. Including the newest member of the Crawford family." They walked into Dana's room and Imani immediately picked up the room service menu.

"Imani, I want to be alone."

"After we eat, and I promise, no more questions about that asshole. If your gig here is done, you can go back to New York with me. Raymond left this morning because he's tired of living out of a suitcase and he said he needs to give Keith some time to spend with Celeste."

"You married a prince. I hope you realize that."

Imani smiled and stroked her stomach. "Yes, I do. And I want you to marry a prince too. You deserve nothing less."

Dana's thoughts drifted to Adrian. She couldn't deny that she still loved him and yearned for a future with him. Nor could she pretend that she didn't believe he wasn't trying to hurt her again. But she was still mad as hell. Still hurt that he felt he had to hide his pain from her. Imani picked up the phone and ordered food while Dana absent-mindedly flipped through the channels. She stopped when she saw Adrian's face on Headline News's *Showbiz Tonight*. The host set up the story, saying that Adrian Bryant, a successful Los Angeles nightclub owner, discovered his family roots and went public after his father, famed hotel mogul Elliot Crawford, denied that he's his father.

"Sounds like a case for Maury Povich," the reporter said. "But it's much deeper than the stories on the salacious talk show as the Crawford family is in the midst of producing a family book. Andrea Jackson is in LA with more on this story. Andrea."

The camera cut to a pretty, brown-skinned reporter with the Hollywood sign as her backdrop. "AJ, there's no lack of drama in Hollywood and this story is just adding to it. Most of us know about former womanizer Solomon Crawford and his connections with some of Hollywood's sexiest leading ladies. Now, he and his family are dealing with accusations that Elliot Crawford was living a double life and had another family on the West Coast."

Dana wanted to change the channel, but she was riveted. And still a little pissed that she had to watch HLN to find out the truth—or at least Adrian's version of it.

"That man," Adrian said, "decided that money was more important than being a father to me or having a relationship with my mother."

"When did you find out that Elliot Crawford was your father?"

"My mother told me with her last breath. Then I researched this man. He wants people to believe that he's all about family, but that couldn't be further from the truth."

"Why are you telling your story now?"

Adrian paused, then looked into the camera. "Because people need to know the truth."

His last statement incensed her and Dana snapped the TV off and tossed the remote across the room.

"Damn," Imani exclaimed.

"What?"

"In all of the years that I've known you, I've never seen you lose your cool like that."

Dana shook her head. "No, because you're the one who usually flies off the handle." She chuckled. "Remember when you threw a hot dog at that seventy-five-year-old man on Eleventh Avenue?"

"That dirty old man deserved it. Asking me if I wanted him to put mustard on my breasts. Ugh!"

"But he sold the best hot dogs ever," Dana said. "A hot dog would be amazing right now. Did you order room service yet?"

Imani shook her head. "They had me on hold and I hung up."

"Let's get out of here. We can go to Pink's."

"Sounds good to me," Imani said as she rose to her feet. "I've been dying for a good hot dog since we landed."

They headed out the door and Dana promised herself that she would not think about Adrian.

* * *

Adrian paced back and forth in his penthouse, wondering if he'd made a mistake. Not about going public with his family drama, but keeping it from Dana. What if he'd ruined his chances to reconcile with her and eventually marry her? The look on her face when they parted ways reminded him of that terrible day at his penthouse. He'd hurt her again and this time, he hadn't meant to.

"I have to go to her," he mumbled as he grabbed his keys. Adrian rushed to the elevator and waited for the doors to open. It was time to tell her everything. When the doors opened, Adrian was greeted with a right hook to the jaw.

"I hope you didn't think your media crusade didn't go unnoticed," Solomon snapped.

Adrian rubbed his jaw. "Dad send you to do his dirty work?"

"He's not your father! Where in the hell do you get off telling these lies?"

Adrian punched Solomon in the face, causing him to stumble backward. Solomon started to charge at him again, but stopped and shook his head. "I could beat you to a bloody pulp, but you'd just use it for more TV time."

"I don't give a damn about being on TV. Why don't you ask your father who Pamela Bryant is? Want me to get a DNA test?"

"What's your end game? How much money do you want?"

"Money? Is that a Crawford trait? Everything is about money? I don't give a damn about your money. You and Dad can keep your riches. It's obvious that I don't need a damned thing from you. But my mother's last breath was about that man. Do you know how I felt knowing that my mother left behind the city she loved because this slimy bastard wanted to stay with your mother for money?"

Solomon clenched his fists at the mention of his mother. As much as he didn't want to admit it, there was a ring of truth in what Adrian was saying. Los Angeles had always been a forbidden place to build a hotel while his mother was alive—even after they'd retired and he and Richmond were in charge.

"How did your mother know my father?" Solomon asked.

Adrian sighed and narrowed his eyes at his brother. "They met when she worked in the Crawford hotel in Harlem."

Solomon looked as if he was deep in thought for a moment. "That sorry bastard," he muttered.

"What was that?" Adrian asked with a smug smirk.

"Why now? Why did you decide to come out now?"

Adrian glanced at his watch. "I don't have to answer to you. I have to go."

"No, you have to answer my damned question," Solomon said as he blocked Adrian's exit.

Adrian slapped his hand away. "Keep your hands

to your fucking self," he growled. "You want answers, go talk to your father." Pushing past Solomon, Adrian pressed the elevator button and waited for the doors to open.

When they opened and he stepped on, he was none too pleased that Solomon followed him. "Look, if what you're saying is true . . ."

"What? If you don't shut the f— Look, I don't owe you a damned explanation. You need to get that from your father. All he'll ever be to me is a sperm donor."

Solomon leaned back against the mirrored wall and studied Adrian. He could see similarities. Strong ones. "Damn," he mumbled.

Adrian glanced at him. "What now?"

"You're not lying."

Adrian rolled his eyes and bit back a caustic comment. Lying was probably a family trait. He was sure his brother did his share of lying to all of the women he'd strung along. He knew for certain that Elliot Crawford was a liar. When the doors opened, Adrian bolted. He'd entertained his brother long enough.

"Hey," Solomon called after him. "We really need to talk about this."

"I'm done talking," Adrian said; then he got into his car. Dana was more important than family ties right now.

* * *

Imani's eyes rolled in the back of her head as she took the last bite of her hot dog. "God that was so good!"

Dana laughed, looking down at her half-eaten frank. It wasn't that it didn't taste good; her appetite just wasn't there. Imani caught the blank look in her friend's eye. "You're thinking about him, aren't you?"

"That obvious?"

Imani nodded. "You never let a good hot dog go to waste and that is a lot of hot dog on that tray. Why don't you just call him?"

Dana cocked her right eyebrow. "Seriously? You were just talking big shit about him."

"But you're my friend and I want you to get over this funk of yours. Besides, that fool owes you answers."

Dana nodded and picked at the bun on her hot dog. "You're right. He does owe me answers."

"And I'm going to get another chili dog," she said. "I'm pregnant and I can eat two hot dogs without worrying about what the press will say."

"I can't believe you're having a baby and still filming that spy movie."

Imani shrugged. "It's a great role and I have a wonderful stunt double."

"I'm sure Dr. Thomas has checked everything out for you and your bun in the oven," Dana said as she crumpled the rest of her uneaten hot dog.

Imani nodded and smiled brightly. "I hope this is a boy with eyes like his dad."

"As long as this boy or girl doesn't have an attitude like his or her mom, that kid will be perfect."

Imani thumped Dana on the shoulder. "I don't have an attitude."

Dana rolled her eyes and laughed as Imani headed back to the stand. Reaching into her pocket, she pulled out her cell phone and dialed Adrian's number.

"Dana," he said.

"We need to talk."

"I'm on my way to your hotel."

"I'm not there. I'm at Pink's."

"Wait for me. I'll be right there."

Dana clicked her phone off and crossed her legs. Was she ready to hear what Adrian was about to tell her? Imani sauntered back to the table, smiling for a few fans with camera phones before joining her friend.

"When is that going to get old?"

Imani shrugged. "Do you know how long I've waited for people to recognize me for something more than being 'flop diva'?"

"A long time," she replied.

"Well lookie here," Imani said. Dana glanced over her friend's shoulder and saw Adrian approaching their table. "Do you want me to—"

"Leave? Yes, I do."

"We rode together, remember?" Imani said incredulously.

"Yes, but Adrian and I need to have a conversation without your comments."

Imani stood up, taking her hot dog with her. "Just talk," she warned.

Dana nodded, then shooed her friend away. Adrian nodded at Imani, who greeted him with an eye roll as she walked away.

"She's still not a fan?" Adrian said as he took a seat across from Dana.

"At the moment, neither am I. How could you keep this from me?" she demanded, not bothering with small talk.

"I wanted to shield you from this. When I found out about my paternity and how my mother loved this man who didn't give a damn about her, I wanted to go to war. My plan was to bring them down to nothing. My mother loved New York and that bastard exiled her here. You've often asked me why I hate New York. Well, it's because I knew it was a source of pain for my mother."

Dana nodded, still not understanding why he kept this from her. "Why would you want to go to war with your family instead of getting to know them?"

"Did that bastard make any effort to get to know me? I needed a father and I got nothing." Tears welled up in Adrian's eyes. "And my mother loved a man who didn't give a damn about us."

"Did you at least talk to the man?" Dana asked softly.

Adrian snorted. "He's still denying me and his relationship with my mother. That's why I went to the media."

"What do you want from him, Adrian? Your mother raised you well without him and if he was stupid enough to allow you all to be his secret, he lost out. But you can't let this need to get even with him destroy you."

Adrian studied her face and started to tell her that she had no idea what it was like for him, always wishing for a father to show up and teach him how to throw a football, how to dunk the basketball like Michael Jordan, and how he could make his fast ball more effective. There had been nights when he prayed that Paul Wallace would take him to a Cub Scouts meeting and tell the other people in the troop how proud he was of his son. But how could he be proud of a child that wasn't his?

Dana lifted her hand to his cheek. "You can't change all the basketball games he missed. You can't make up for him not being there for you. But you can show him that you're a better man because he wasn't in your life."

"How did you know what I was thinking?" he asked as she took his hand.

"Because I understand how this has to hurt. What I don't understand is why you felt that I wouldn't have had your back."

"I don't know. This was something I needed to

do on my own. You were busy with your work for
Sony and—"

"I'm talking about two years ago, Adrian. Was
that ruse of yours necessary? What did you think I
would've done?"

"Exactly what you're doing now. Talk me out of
being bitter and tell me to be the bigger person,"
Adrian said. "That's why I wanted you far away from
this. I wanted to bring them down, and every time
I had a plan to do something, there you were."

"What do you mean?"

Adrian chuckled. "The first night I saw you with
Hollywood Ken, my plan had been to leak a story
about Richmond being with a hooker. Then the
night of the premiere, I had made sure Heather
and Solomon ran into each other, hoping for some
fireworks."

Dana frowned. "What would that accomplish?"

"Nothing, everything. The world needed to see
the headlines and know that this family isn't perfect, like they want the world to believe. I want
them to hurt."

"Again, what does that accomplish? What does
it change?"

Adrian dropped his head for a second as if he
was thinking about what Dana said. She had a
point. He hadn't changed a thing. Hadn't caused
them an eighth of the pain that he'd felt all of his
life. "I don't know. It's not as if they had anything to
do with what their father did."

"Precisely," Dana said, stroking the back of his hand. "You need to get past this."

"I wish I knew how."

"You need to have a real conversation with your family. Away from cameras and without the threat of going to the media."

Adrian sighed. He knew she was right, knew that the right and adult thing to do was just what she said. However, he still had the urge to get a pound of flesh. He still wanted Elliot Crawford to suffer and hurt as his mother had.

"What's that look?" she asked, taking note of his scowl and furrowed brows.

"What look?"

Dana tilted her head to the side and shook her head. "Can you stop acting as if I don't know you, Adrian? Even when you try to hide something, your eyes give everything away."

"Is that so?"

She nodded, silently telling herself that she should've looked into his eyes that night two years ago and maybe things would've been different. "Maybe I should let it go. After all, who wants to be a part of this family circus?" Adrian said.

"Don't deny that you actually want to get to know them. Maybe you can get the answers you're searching for."

He grinned and brought her hand to his lips. "When did you get so smart?" he asked before kissing the back of her hand.

"I've always been a genius. You just never took note of it."

"Did you ride that motorcycle of yours here?"

"Nope," she said. "Imani and I came together. I'm sure she's gone by now."

"Let me take you back to your hotel."

The couple stood and Adrian drew Dana into his arms. "I love you, Dana."

His admission caught her off guard and sent a shiver throughout her body. She wanted to bask in the glow of his love, but she still felt as if she had to look over her shoulder, waiting for the other shoe to drop. What if he didn't give up his quest for revenge, and what if he let it consume him again? She knew what was going on this time, but would it make a difference?

Adrian stroked her cheek. "I mean it," he said. "And I'm going to earn your love back."

"Adrian—"

He cut her off with a smoldering kiss, coaxing her tongue into his mouth, savoring her taste and making her purr. Dana gripped his shoulder, not sure if she should pull away or draw him closer. She wanted and needed him, but could she truly trust him? Finally, she pushed back.

"Let's go," she found the raspy voice to say. "I have some work that I need to finish up and I can't . . ."

Adrian chewed on his bottom lip. "You know, I . . ."

She threw her hand up. "What? Adrian? Are you

going to tell me that you didn't mean to lie to me again? Or are you finally going to tell me why you don't trust me enough to be a part of your life for real?"

"That's not it at all, Dana. You are more than just a part of my life, and honestly, I worried that this would scare you away."

Dana shook her head and fought back the urge to laugh. But she had to hold back because her phone rang. Pulling it from her pocket, she saw it was a New York number she didn't recognize. "This is Dana."

"Dana, it's Marion Lloyd from Wainwright Publishing."

"Hi, Mrs. Lloyd," Dana replied, her brows furrowed in confusion. She had queried the company about her photo book idea months ago and hadn't heard a word from them. This call was totally unexpected. "What can I do for you?"

"Well," the woman said, "I've been going over your proposal and I have to say I'm impressed. We had another photo project that was scheduled for next fall. However, due to recent developments, we're going to shelve that project and a space on our production calendar has opened up."

"Really?" she replied, feeling slightly guilty that the Crawford's misfortune might be the break she had been waiting for.

"I noticed that you didn't have an agent representing your work, and normally we don't take unsolicited proposals, but you came highly recommended and your work is very recognizable. Are you available to meet next Tuesday?"

"Well, I'm in Los Angeles right now. I should be back in New York by next Thursday. Would that work for you?"

"That works perfectly, if we can make it after two p.m."

"That will be even better. By then my body will be back on East Coast time." Dana laughed, then caught Adrian's eye. He looked as if he was thoroughly disappointed to hear her happily talking about returning to New York.

"I look forward to speaking with you and getting this project started."

"See you then," she said. Dana stopped herself from doing a fist pump and her own version of the happy dance. Looking at Adrian, she saw he had questions.

"What was that all about?" he asked.

"A publisher is interested in my book. My unfinished book. I can't believe it."

"Good for you," he said. "So that means you're going to be leaving soon?"

"I guess so. I have to call Edward Funderburke. Maybe he can act as my agent when I meet with the publisher."

"Who is Edward Funderburke?"

Dana smiled. "Hopefully the man who is going to get me the deal that I truly deserve."

Adrian raised his right eyebrow. Dana shook her

head and said, "He's an agent, silly. And dropping his name these days has a lot of clout in New York."

"Thought he was another Hollywood type I'd have to compete with. What happens when you go back to New York and start this project? I thought you wanted to shoot some more here."

"I do," she said. "But I have to get the deal first." Dana started dialing on her cell phone. "I have to talk to Edward now."

Nodding, Adrian headed toward the hot dog stand so that Dana could complete her call. He had mixed emotions about this project. He knew it was something that Dana wanted, but she'd have to leave and he wasn't ready to let her go. Maybe he needed to go back to New York with her. Glancing at her, he took note of the wide smile on her face and he knew that a trip to the Big Apple was in his future if he planned to make Dana a fixture in his life. Was he ready to go to the place where his mother's heartache began? Sighing, he knew the answer. He was going to have to take a trip east.

Dana listened to Edward as she watched Adrian at the counter. She was a little too excited to notice the pensive look on his face.

"Well, Dana, I don't generally represent literary works," Edward said. "But for you, I'll do it."

"Thank you, Edward."

"Now, you know I owe you. Will any of my clients make the book?"

"You know it," Dana said with a smile. "I'll give you a call when I get back to the city."

After hanging up, she walked over to Adrian, who'd gotten a hot dog and a lemonade. "Couldn't resist."

"Let's sit down while you eat. How are you going to handle this?"

"The hot dog?" he asked as they headed for a table.

"Adrian, be serious. You have to fix this with your family. I don't care how you feel about your father, but what about your brothers? They're innocent victims just like you."

"Yeah, right. They grew up with the money and a father."

"And were fooled just as you were. Maybe if things were—"

"That man said he stayed for the money. That must mean that it was his wife who held the purse strings. I can't help but think they all got a big laugh about it while my mother and I suffered."

"You really think that man laughed with his sons? They wouldn't have understood what was going on any more than you would've had your mother laid it out for you."

Adrian took a big bite of his hot dog as if he was trying to stop himself from responding to her.

Dana grabbed his lemonade and took a sip while he chewed. "Since you're done with the publicity shots for Sony, what are you going to do next?" he asked after swallowing.

"Go back to New York. I'm going to see if this

book deal is legit. This is something I've wanted for a long time."

"Or you could stay here with me."

Dana gulped. "Adrian, you know we aren't ready for that yet."

"Why not?"

She stared into his sparkling eyes, wishing they weren't so hypnotic, wishing she could tell him why she wasn't ready to risk her heart to him again. "I don't know."

"Then you can't say no. Dana, I love you and I know you love me too. We've allowed too much time to pass and I don't want to let any more slip away."

"Adrian, you hurt me. You hid things from me and made it seem as if you had a problem trusting me."

"I told you, it wasn't about you. I didn't want you to be caught up in my vendetta."

"So you wanted me to believe you were a cheating bastard? Where's the logic in that?"

Adrian smirked. "I never said my plan was fool-proof."

"Where's this plan now?"

He shrugged, then finished his hot dog. "Maybe it's time for me to take your advice and deal with this family of mine as an adult."

"And while you're doing all of this, where will that leave us? I think you need to focus on your family. This has been nice, but, Adrian, we can't get back together."

He took her hand in his and focused his emerald stare on her. "I know I don't deserve it," he said. "But I'm asking for a second chance. I love you more than you'll ever know and I have a lot to make up for. But you have to let me do that."

"I don't know if I can do that," she replied honestly. "Do you know how hard it was for me when I walked out of your penthouse that night? How many nights I cried because I thought you'd given in to that LA club promoter trap of easy sex with any woman willing to spread her legs? What's really changed?"

"I've never been that guy and I thought—"

"You're still the man who lied to me and is still lying! Why did I have to find out about your family secrets on the news? If you love me, that means you want to share things with me, good or bad."

He sighed, wishing she understood that in the midst of his war with the Crawfords he wanted her to be his salvation. He wanted her to be the one thing that hadn't been touched by it all. Adrian knew he could explain that to her until he was blue in the face, but he had to admit, if the shoe was on the other foot, he wouldn't be hot for a second chance either.

"How can we fix this? We've been together here and I thought we were working our way back to being us."

"Define *us*."

Adrian kissed her hand. "You know what it was

like when you were here. Late-night trips to the beach, looking toward our future and making love in the sand."

She crossed her legs tightly at the memory. Adrian leaned closer. "You make me want to be a better person."

"I wish I believed that," she replied. "It's time to go."

The duality of her words struck him like a fist enclosed in brass knuckles. "All right," he said. "So, I guess you're going back to New York soon."

She nodded as they walked to the car. "I'll probably leave in the next two days."

"I'm coming with you."

Dana's mouth dropped open. "Why . . . what?"

"If I'm going to win you back, I guess I have to do it on your turf."

"You're coming to New York?" she asked, trying not to smile.

He nodded and opened the passenger side door for Dana. "You're not going to get away from me again. If that means I have to go to New York to show you that you belong to me, then that's what I'll do."

"What about your family?"

He shrugged. "I'll get to that."

"You know that's important." She slid into the car and strapped her seat belt as he closed the door.

"Right now, there's nothing more important to me than you," he replied as he got behind the wheel. She turned her head and looked out the window. Though this was the Adrian she remembered and loved, his dark side still scared her. What would this trip to New York prove? How would he react to seeing all of the Crawford riches? Hell, Dana lived right up the street from a new boutique Crawford hotel. Would seeing that make him hop back on the revenge train?

They rode in an uncomfortable silence, and when they arrived at the hotel, Adrian turned to Dana as he put the car in park. "Let me know when you're flying out."

"I will," she replied, then leaned over and kissed his cheek.

Adrian cupped her face and captured her lips in a hot kiss that he hoped conveyed how deeply he needed her. Slipping his tongue between her lips, he heard her moan slightly. She tasted sweet like honey and it took everything in him not to rip her clothes off and make love to her in the car. When her hand dropped to his lap, Adrian nearly went weak. He pulled back from her, his eyes focused on her swollen lips.

"I'll come back later and help you pack."

"How about you come back later and help me out of my clothes?" she replied saucily.

"You don't have to ask me twice," he said with a wink.

Dana exited the car and waved good-bye to Adrian while her heart rate slowed to a normal beat. She had to be honest with herself and decide if she was willing to risk her heart and soul with Adrian again. Did she love him? Yes. Did she believe he loved her? Some days more than others. But if he was willing to come to New York, to be a part of her world, then she should look at this as an opportunity to start over. Yes, that's what she needed to do.

Chapter 13

Adrian drove to the Crawford Towers construction site. Part of him expected the place to crumble and for his family to be laughed out of Los Angeles. However, the work continued. The protesters lingered, but the numbers had dwindled since the story about Richmond and the hooker broke. It wasn't as if Los Angeles was the center of family values. After all, the scandal would probably put more people in the hotel when the doors opened. What would going to war with the Crawfords change?

"What in the hell are you doing here?" Richmond boomed when he spotted Adrian on the sidewalk. "Thinking about burning this place down? Or are you trying to come up with some more lies to spread about my father?"

"So, this is how it's going to be every time I run into one of my brothers?" Sarcasm dripped from his words like honey.

Richmond glared at him. "I'm not your damned

brother. My father was devoted to my mother and for you to spread these lies because your—"

Adrian grabbed Richmond by the lapels, causing a few of the workers to stop and look at the scene. "If your next words were going to be about my mother, you'd better consider how much you want your teeth."

Richmond snatched away. "But you can bad-mouth my family in the press and I'm supposed to keep silent about it?"

Adrian was about to unleash a torrent of profanity when he saw Solomon and Elliot walking toward them. "This is a family reunion for real now," he muttered.

Richmond turned toward his father and Solomon. "Is this a setup or something?" he shouted. "I hope you two are here to get this loser out of our lives."

Elliot held his hand up and shook his head. Solomon stood in a stoic silence. "This is a serendipitous event, having you all here."

Adrian gritted his teeth and shot daggers at his father. Solomon locked eyes with him and seemed to have a moment of recognition. Studying his brother, Adrian realized how much he and Solomon looked alike and how they shared similar mannerisms. Richmond really seemed to be the odd man out.

"Is what he's been telling the media true?" Richmond demanded.

"Let's go somewhere private and talk," Elliot said calmly.

Richmond tossed his thumb at Adrian. "What does it matter if we talk in private? He's probably going to run straight to the media when we're done."

Adrian rolled his eyes and groaned. "I don't want to sit in a room and hear you spew more lies." He focused his cold stare on Elliot. "After all, you denied being my father."

"And I was wrong." He looked back at Solomon. "He made me see that. I owe all of you the truth. I can't change the past, but I would like for the three of us to have a future."

Elliot's two sons exchanged confused glances. "This bullshit he said on TV was true?" Richmond asked incredulously.

"Let's take this inside." Elliot nodded toward the finished restaurant at the bottom of the towers and they followed him inside. The restaurant was almost completely furnished, hardwood tables arranged in a U shape facing the bar. Two seventy-five-inch flat-screen TVs were attached to the wall, looking as if it would be a great place for hotel guests to catch sporting events or presidential debates. The club owner in Adrian was impressed, realizing that the U-shape arrangement also opened up a small dance floor.

The men sat down. Elliot crossed his legs as he moved his chair back from the table a bit. Three pairs of eyes stared at Elliot, silently asking him a million questions while waiting for him to say one word.

Finally, Elliot spoke. "I've wronged all of you.

I've hurt your mothers and allowed money to change me."

"Meaning?" Solomon asked.

Elliot looked at his son. "Meaning that I didn't grow up in the lap of luxury like your mother. It's probably what brought us together. When we met in college, Cynthia was trying to be rebellious. Your grandparents sent her to Howard to find a suitable husband. But the freedom she experienced allowed her to make her own decisions. I'm not proud of this, but I allowed myself to become a kept man."

Adrian cringed, then glanced at the disappointed looks on his brothers' faces. Elliot continued. "I wanted to create Crawford Hotels, just one luxury hotel in New York. I needed money and your mother dangled it in my face. All she wanted was heirs, a suitable husband who would get your grandparents off her back and no divorce.

"I was young, wanted to take the easy way out, and I agreed. Cynthia molded me into what she thought a husband should be. Had me join the right organizations, helped me cover up my impoverished Maryland roots, and your grandparents bankrolled the first Crawford Hotel. Right after construction started, your mother got pregnant. But she suffered a miscarriage. When she got pregnant with you, Richmond, the hotel was opening. Seeing the pain and hurt Cynthia carried after the miscarriage, I put my foot down and told her that she was going to rest and be pampered for nine months. We started hiring staff at the hotel, even though we were so far in the red, the books looked as if they'd been attacked." Elliot chuckled at the memory, but no one else shared in his laughter.

"Anyway," he said, looking at Adrian, "Pamela Bryant walked in for an interview and when she opened her mouth, I heard that Southern accent. She was stunning." Elliot's sons twisted uncomfortably in their seats. Elliot cleared his throat. "And she was smart. Too smart to just be the front desk clerk. When I hired her, I knew that she'd be a great addition to the company. A month later, we were sitting in my office laying the groundwork for Crawford Hotels Inc. She was such a huge part of this company. She had so many great ideas. If it wasn't for Pamela, I—we—would've never moved into Manhattan, Coney Island, or rebuilt the Harlem hotel after that fire in 1972. At first, it was strictly professional. I wanted to be the family man your mother expected me to be. But she constantly reminded me that I'd be nothing but a poor country boy without her. But when I was with Pamela, she made me feel like a man. Made me feel like she needed me and valued what I had to say."

Adrian slammed his hand on the table. "You needed your fucking ego stroked because you married a woman for money and she wouldn't let you forget it?" Richmond shot Adrian an angry glance and Solomon smirked.

"He has a point," Solomon murmured.

Elliot, for the first time since he sat down, seemed to get a bit emotional. "This wasn't about my ego. I wanted to love my wife as much as I ended up loving Pamela. When I was with Pam, it was as if I'd entered another world. She was kind, gentle, and—"

"Then why didn't you just divorce my mother?!" Richmond blurted out. "Here's what you don't know—Mom cried many nights over you. I heard her and it tore me up because I didn't understand why my mother was sad all the time."

Elliot looked at his son, feeling as if he'd been sucker punched. "I . . . I didn't know."

"That seems to be your standard line when it comes to the women you've screwed over," Adrian retorted.

Solomon watched in silence, but his face expressed his anger and disappointment.

"I'm not perfect, but you all have to understand, I was stuck between a rock and a hard place. No matter what decision I made, someone was going to be hurt."

"So to hell with doing the right thing, huh?" Solomon said quietly. "You just shipped one family to Los Angeles and stayed in New York pretending to be father of the year?"

Elliot nervously tugged at his pant leg and looked away from his sons. Moments passed as a stifling silence enveloped them. Adrian broke the silence. "You didn't answer the question, *Dad.*"

"I never had any intentions to ship Pamela anywhere. Obviously, I wasn't honest with Pamela or Cynthia. I couldn't get a divorce and Cynthia wanted another child. Then she heard rumblings about what was going on with me and Pam. At the same time, Pam found out she was pregnant and so did Cynthia."

Richmond gasped and looked from Adrian to Solomon. "What kind of ghetto—"

Elliot held up his hand. "Cynthia, I learned later, confronted Pamela. She told her that I was never going to leave her and if she was smart, she'd leave New York."

"My mother wasn't the kind of woman to run away because someone told her to," Adrian exclaimed. "Don't keep the details secret. What role did you play in all of this?"

Elliot nervously cleared his throat. "Cynthia fired Pamela on the spot. She also told her that I'd have nothing to do with the child."

"She was right," Adrian snorted.

"That was Pamela's choice," Elliot replied defensively, and Adrian clenched his fists. He was so tempted to lean across the table and sock him in the face. "When Pamela left the company, she left her forwarding address, and after Cynthia and I had a big fight about her firing Pam, I came to California."

Richmond nodded. "It makes sense now. No wonder Mom never wanted us to build out here."

"She forbade it," Elliot said. "But it didn't matter because Pamela didn't want me to come back anyway. I'd messed up my relationship with her when I told her that if she got rid of the baby, she could come back to New York and things could go back to the way they were."

Adrian leaped from his seat. "You heartless son of a bitch!"

Solomon stood and touched his brother's shoulder. "I'm not going to tell you to calm down," he said. "But just think about this—at least your mother was smart enough not to listen to the bastard. Dad, I can't believe you hid this from us all of these years and still tried to hide your lies. I'm done with you and this company. I quit."

"Solomon!" Elliot said.

"No," he barked, rubbing his face. "All of those years you judged me for being a 'womanizer' and told me how I was ruining the family reputation. Shit, I was playing the game you created. At least I was smart enough not to make babies and hide them."

Adrian was torn between giving his brother a high five and punching him in the stomach. Instead, he decided it was time for him to leave. "I've had enough too."

Richmond stood as well, glaring at his father. "So have I."

"So, I tell y'all the truth that you wanted and now you're turning your back on me?"

Adrian glanced at him. "Why did you come to Los Angeles after all these years? Did you think you were going to come back here and right nearly forty years' worth of wrongs? Thought my mama would still be here and give you a second chance to hurt her? Or did you think I'd be so happy to meet you—you know, the son you never wanted—that we'd be best friends?"

Solomon nodded. "I'd like to know the answer to that as well."

Elliot rose to his feet, anger distorting his face. "You know what, the three of you are an ungrateful lot of bastards. Did any of you lack for anything? You grew up in the lap of luxury. I slept on a dirt floor. Am I sorry I let your bitch of a mother keep me in line with her money? No. I'm not. The only thing I regret is not being able to be with the woman I loved. So, walk out. I don't need any of you!"

The older man stormed out of the restaurant as his sons watched. When Solomon saw that Richmond was about to go after him, he grabbed his brother's arm. "Let him go."

"He's still our father," Richmond said as he snatched his arm away. "And you know Dad isn't well."

"Karma," Solomon said with a shrug. Adrian silently agreed. Once he and Solomon were alone, they looked at each other for a few moments.

"You knew all along, huh?" he asked Adrian.

"My mother told me on her deathbed. And honestly, I was going to do everything in my power to make you all suffer while you were here."

Solomon pursed his lips. "You're a Crawford all

right," he said with a sardonic laugh. "What stopped you?"

Dana flashed through his mind. Her smile. Her taste. Her touch. "A woman who means more to me than revenge."

"Must be a hell of a woman because I don't think I would've stopped. Listen," Solomon said. "I don't expect us to be best friends overnight—hell, Richmond and I grew up together and I can barely stand him—but I'd like to get to know you."

"Hell, we're practically twins," Adrian retorted.

Solomon released a loud guffaw. "What do they call us? Irish twins."

"Something like that."

Solomon reached into his pocket and handed Adrian his business card. "If you're ever in New York, look me up and bring that phenomenal woman with you."

Adrian took the card and nodded. "I just might do that."

Solomon nodded, then left the restaurant. Adrian jogged to catch up with him. "Hey," he called after his brother.

"What's up?"

"What did Richmond mean when he said D—Elliot—isn't well?"

Solomon shrugged. "Dad has been battling a cough for a while, but when I asked him about it, he said he was fine. I don't know and right now I don't give a damn about that man."

"How can you say that? I'm supposed to feel like that. At least you grew up with him."

Solomon shook his head. "Knowing what else was going on, I have to wonder if he was so hard on me because he couldn't be a part of your life. Dad and I weren't close and if you ask me, you were probably lucky that he wasn't a part of your life."

Adrian was taken aback. He'd envisioned Solomon and Richmond growing up with a doting mother and father. He thought that Elliot did all the things he assumed fathers did, attending basketball games, helping with science fair projects, and giving Bill Cosby–like advice.

"It was like that for real?"

"Let me just say that everything I've learned about being a father, I learned from my wife."

Solomon stalked away and Adrian felt like a fool for so many reasons. He rushed back to his car. He needed to see Dana right now.

Chapter 14

Dana sat on the phone with the airline ready to punch a hole through the wall. Why was it so difficult to use her airline miles to get home?

"Listen," she snapped, "forget the miles. I just need a flight to New York and I'm not trying to take the damned red-eye."

"Ma'am, I'm trying to accommodate your request but—"

"How about I just call another airline?!" She pressed END on the phone, fell backward on the bed, and groaned. "This sucks." When the phone rang again, Dana expected it to be the airline calling back, but it was Imani.

"What's up?"

"You tell me. Did you and that guy—"

"His name is Adrian."

"Did you and Adrian work things out? And if you did, please tell me why?"

Dana sighed. "I really don't have time to deal

with you right now. Don't you have a movie to film?"

"Yeah, but I'm on a break."

"Well, I'm trying to get a flight back to New York and between you and the airlines, I have a throbbing headache."

"I can get you back to New York. Just take my ticket."

"Imani, you are a lifesaver."

"Think of it as payment for all of those hot dogs you paid for in the lean years. So, does this return to New York mean that you've come to your senses about that— Adrian?"

"There you go making my headache come back."

"Then I guess I shouldn't tell you that Ian has been asking about you."

"No, you shouldn't. And I thought he was gone to rehab?"

"But I am anyway. He said something about riding the PCH with you on those horribly dangerous motorcycles before he goes to the center."

"It sounds like he is stalling getting the help that he needs. Right now, I want to see the Brooklyn Bridge and the inside of my house," Dana replied. "I can't thank you enough for this ticket."

"Just promise me that you're not going to be tooling around New York on a motorcycle."

"I'd tell you that I'm not going to do that, but I don't want to lie to you. As a matter of fact, I need to call someone to handle shipping my bike to the city."

"You need to leave that and a number of other things right here in Los Angeles," she retorted.

"For your information, Adrian is coming to New York as well."

"Oh God! Why are you taking the additional baggage with you? I can only imagine how this story is playing in New York. And if you think the Los Angeles media is bad, just imagine how the reporters in New York are going to stalk you and the newest member of the Crawford family. You think Raymond and I had it bad after we came back from Hawaii, imagine how you and Adrian are going to be treated when you show up at JFK?"

"It's really not Adrian's fault that his father lied to the world and presented this image of being father of the year. I'm sure no one is going to alert the press that we're coming, right?"

"Dana Singleton, I'd hang up on you and never speak to you again if I didn't already know you'd lost your mind."

"I know you, Mani, and sometimes you will act before you think."

"You know I wouldn't do that to you. Now, if he was coming into town alone, then I might call someone. However, you don't deserve that. But seriously, you don't think he could've handled it a bit better? Talking to his dad before hitting the airwaves?"

"Imani, you don't know the whole story and you need to stop being so damned judgmental when it comes to Adrian."

"Let me just say this—I don't like him because he hurt you. I'm not convinced he won't do it again, but it's your life."

"Thank you," Dana said.

"But if he hurts you again and it happens to happen in New York, he's going to have to deal with me! And remember I live in Harlem. I know people."

Dana broke out into laughter. "Yes, those old ladies who come to Raymond's clinic."

"Those ladies are tough. Don't sleep on them. Adrian wouldn't know what hit him."

"Well, it's not going down like that. The fact that he's willing to come to New York proves that he's changing."

"Really? A trip to New York proves that? How?"

Sighing, Dana really didn't want to get into Adrian's New York baggage. She made an excuse to get off the phone with her friend and started searching for a shipper.

Moments after she had secured shipping for her bike, Dana's phone rang again. "Imani," she snapped.

"Sorry, wrong person," Adrian said.

"Oh, hi."

"Come to the lobby," he said.

"What if I'm doing something important?"

"I'm going to ask you to put it on hold because I want to wrap my arms around your waist and have you take me down the PCH on that motorcycle of yours so that we can go somewhere private and talk."

"Wait a minute, who are you and what have you done with Adrian Bryant?"

"Listen, I just want to get away with you," he said. "Before we head to New York where there's wall-to-wall people."

"All right, let me change."

"How about I come upstairs and help you do that?" he quipped.

"Ah, you got me all excited about riding now."

"We can do that upstairs too."

"I'm grabbing my helmet and I'll see you in a few." Dana hung up the phone, changed into her motorcycle boots, and grabbed both of her helmets. When she arrived in the lobby, Adrian was leaning against the wall by the elevator, dressed in a pair of jeans, Timberland boots, and a white tank top. He took one of the helmets from Dana's hands and kissed her cheek gently while giving her a slow once-over, drinking in her image clad in liquid leggings, black motorcycle boots, and a formfitting T-shirt.

"Wow," he whispered. "I don't know if I want to share this view with the world."

"Put your helmet on. There's no way I'm going to let you weasel your way out of this. You do realize that you said you would never ever get on a motorcycle again?"

"I'm learning to never say *never* these days." He

slipped the helmet on his head and flipped the visor up.

"Did you talk to your family?"

"Let's talk about that when we get to our secret location."

"Where are we going?"

"I'll give you directions," he said.

Dana raised her eyebrow at him as she put her gloves and helmet on. "From behind?"

A slow smile spread across his lips. "It's not as if I haven't done it before." She gave him a playful smack on the shoulder.

"Whatever. Let's go before you change your mind."

The couple headed to the hotel's parking garage where Dana had parked her bike. Adrian couldn't help but notice her excitement as she mounted the bike. Watching her as he slid on behind her, he smiled thinking about how good it felt when she rode him the way she handled this machine. She revved the engine and took off down the narrow pathway. Adrian fought the urge to scream as she leaned left to avoid an extended cab of a pickup truck that was parked in a spot too small for its width. Once they made it onto the street, Adrian could've sworn she sped up and was pretending she was Batman from *The Dark Knight*. Finally, she slowed a bit and called out, "Where to?"

"Hang a left," he said into the helmet's built-in microphone.

She nodded and took the turn. They glided down

the road, and much to Adrian's glee, she slowed down a lot. Finally, they arrived at Will Rogers Park. When Dana stopped the bike, Adrian released a sigh of relief and said a quiet prayer of thanks. He and Dana climbed off the bike and she smiled as she removed her helmet. "That was a rush, right?" The excitement in her voice nearly made him double over in laughter.

"It was something."

"Says the man who drives a hundred miles an hour in a sports car."

"Yes," he said as he took off his helmet and set it on the back of the bike. "A car, closed in, surrounded by metal and glass with four tires."

She held her hand up and shook her head. "We've been down this road before."

"Yeah, we have and here we are on your motorcycle." Adrian held his hand out to her and pulled her against his chest. "But I did enjoy holding you."

"And you were holding me very tightly," she quipped. "I wasn't going to let you fall."

"There were a few moments when I wasn't too sure about that." He slid his hands down her sides and cupped her bottom. "So, I had a conversation with my family and I use that term very loosely."

"What happened?" she asked, wondering if he was going to tell her the trip to New York was off.

"That man is an asshole. He didn't just hurt my mother. The way he treated the woman he was married to . . . Solomon quit his job."

"What? He is Crawford Hotels."

Adrian dropped his hands and shrugged. "He's also my Irish twin. There's a four-month age difference and when that man found out my mother was pregnant, he tried to talk her into getting an abortion. Hearing that he never wanted me, it hurt."

Dana stroked his cheek, unable to think of something to say. "Are you all right?"

"No and yes. All of those years I thought he'd been dad of the year, and I hated his other sons because they had the luxury of growing up with him in their lives. We all experienced our own sort of hell, them with him and me without him."

"I feel bad that I encouraged you to talk to him now," Dana said, her voice filled with guilt.

Adrian shook his head. "It's not your fault that he used women in his life like chess pieces. One woman gave him money but treated him like the hired help. My mother stroked his ego and made him feel like a real man. He dropped sperm in them both and had sons he didn't give a fuck about." The pain in his voice was palpable.

Dana melted and wanted to comfort him. "I'm sorry," she whispered.

Adrian shook his head. "No need to be sorry. At the end of the day, it looks as if I got the better deal."

Dana stroked his cheek again. "What happens now?"

Adrian released a snort. "Not a damned thing. I know my mother wanted me to have a relationship with that man, but there's no way in hell that I'm going to do that."

"What about your brothers?"

He shrugged his broad shoulders. "Solomon seems cool and all, but I don't know about Richmond. He has misguided loyalties. Said something about that man being sick or something."

"Adrian, you can't be this cold and unfeeling. He's still your fa—"

"He is not my father. He's a sperm donor. My mother would've been better off going to a sperm bank and having the very first test tube baby for all the good it did having Elliot Crawford as my father."

"You're angry and you have every right to be," Dana said. "But I thought you weren't going to allow it to consume you."

"I tell you what, when one of your parents tells you that they wanted to get rid of you before you were born, talk to me about anger then."

Dana sighed, feeling that he was right but not appreciating his tone with her. "I understand that. Look, let's just walk awhile."

Adrian squeezed the bridge of his nose. "I'm sorry. I'm not trying to take this out on you, but this was not what I expected today."

"I imagine not. Just think, in a few days you'll be in the city that never sleeps . . ."

"Surrounded by the empire that my mother

helped build but never got to profit from," he lamented.

"What do you mean?"

"Elliot said my mother gave him the idea to expand the hotel chain and of course when his wife found out that my mother was pregnant and had moved out here, she forbade the company from expanding to the West Coast. I guess Elliot was flexing his power by building Crawford Towers here now that she's dead."

Dana remained silent, knowing that anything she said would more than likely send Adrian into another fit of rage. "Do you want to cancel the trip?"

"No, not at all. I promised you that I was going to New York with you and I'm not breaking that promise. You're the most important thing in my life."

She wrapped her arms around him and hugged him tightly. "Imani gave me her open ticket back to the city. It's first class, but maybe we can cash it in for two coach seats."

Adrian shook his head. "No, ma'am! When do we leave? I'll just get a last-minute ticket because I am not flying three thousand miles in coach."

She smiled and fought the urge to fist pump like the kids from *Jersey Shore*. "Thank goodness, because I really didn't want to ride in coach either."

Adrian lifted her in his arms and spun her around. "Remember how I was supposed to help you out of your clothes?" he whispered.

"Mmm-hmm."

"Let's get on that bike and go back to the hotel and make that happen."

"Sounds good to me," she said as he lowered her to the ground.

"But drive or ride—or whatever you call it—slowly."

Dana offered him a mock salute and a big smile. "I make no promises!"

Chapter 15

Dana followed Adrian's request and eased off the speed on the way back to the hotel. She even took the turns at a slower pace. But once the bike was parked, speed was the name of the game to get through the lobby. They sped through the lobby, into the elevator, and into Dana's room.

Before Dana could retrieve the key card from her pocket, Adrian pressed her against the door and covered her mouth with his, kissing her until her knees turned to jelly. She gripped his shoulders, pulling him even closer as their tongues danced a dirty lambada. It took every ounce of self-control Adrian had to keep himself from peeling those leggings off Dana and thrusting his throbbing erection inside her right then and there. He ached for her, needed and wanted her immediately.

A passerby caused the couple to break their kiss and give Dana a chance to locate her room key. Once inside the room, Adrian was able to get her out of those skintight pants, slowly easing them down her hips while he stroked her thighs. Dana melted, her desire pooling between her legs as Adrian's fingers danced across her thighs. He dropped to his knees as he pressed her against the wall and spread her legs. He covered her throbbing bud with his lips and sucked until she cried his name and his face was moist with her desire. Watching her reach the apex of pleasure made him harder than a brick. Licking. Sucking. Growing. Adrian knew he was torturing Dana as much as he was torturing himself. God, she was beautiful when she came. Ethereal. Glowing. He wanted to continue her pleasure and give her more. Darting his tongue in and out of her wet slit, he made her cry out in delight.

"Please!" she cried. "Adrian. Need. You."

He pulled his mouth from her and smiled at her as he lifted her shirt over her head, exposing her heaving breasts. "And I had no idea you weren't wearing a bra all day." He palmed her breasts, teasing her nipples with his thumbs before he pulled her onto his lap, wrapping her legs around his waist as he suckled her hardened nubs. Dana clawed at his shirt, needing him to end his delicious torture and inflict some of her own. With one hand, he held her at bay. "This is for all that speeding on the way to Inglewood," he said before popping her nipple back into his mouth.

Dana groaned, feeling as if electricity flowed through her veins. Adrian lifted her over his shoulders and carried her to the bed. Once he laid her against the soft comforter, he stripped and smirked at his squirming partner. She opened her arms to him, licking her lips as he slowly crawled up beside her. Rolling over on his back, he held a condom out to her. "I want you to handle me like you handled that Harley. I want your thighs locked around me while you ride me," he moaned as she opened the condom package and rolled it down his erection. She mounted him, much like she did the motorcycle. Legs opened wide as she guided him to her wet valley. Adrian plunged inside as Dana ground against him slowly. She gripped his shoulders as if they were the handlebars of her Fat Bob while she bounced up and down, head thrown back in ecstasy. He cupped her ass and ran his tongue across her bottom lip.

"Look at me," he moaned as he stroked her cheek. She opened her eyes, locking her stare with his intense gaze as they rocked to and fro. Adrian mirrored her movements, tilting his hips, thrusting forward and holding back his urge to climax. As he looked into her eyes, all Adrian could think about was how much he loved this woman, how she challenged everything he'd ever believed in, and how he could not live another day without Dana in his life. He pulled her against his chest, slowing the pace of their lovemaking. He wanted her to savor every moment, wanted to increase her pleasure. He gripped her hips and rolled over so that he was on top of her. "I love you," he whispered as he pressed deeper into her. "I love you."

Dana opened her mouth, wanting to tell him the same thing. But a slow, cold bit of doubt crept up her spine. Did she love him? Without a doubt, but his dark side still left her feeling some kind of way. She covered his mouth with hers, hoping to keep a flood of emotions from spilling out. As she reached her climax, her thoughts of his dark side ebbed for the moment. The man who'd tenderly made love to her just moments ago was the man she truly believed Adrian was.

"Baby," he whispered as he held her. "Now, that was a ride I can handle."

Dana chuckled and nestled closer to him. "Mmm," she replied.

"Mmm what?"

"I have no words. You have me speechless."

"Is that so?" he asked, then kissed her on the forehead. "I guess I deserve a pat on the back, huh?"

She gave him a soft pat on the shoulder. "There you go. Is that enough of an ego stroke for you?"

He took her hand and placed it on his growing erection. "I have something for you to stroke," he quipped.

"You're so bad, Mr. Bryant." She stroked him back and forth until Adrian felt as if he were about to explode. Smiling, he realized that no one could handle his body the way Dana did. She had skillful hands and lips. She put those lips to work as she eased down his body and took his thick shaft into her mouth. Adrian gripped the sheets as her tongue danced up and down his shaft. As she licked and sucked him, Adrian threw his head back, moaning in delight. He watched Dana's head bob up and down and saw the look of pleasure on her face as she pleased him. Though he wanted to hold back and save his climax for the moment when he was deep inside her wetness, when Dana took him so far down her throat that he cried as if he were a schoolgirl, he released it all.

Dana looked up at him as she licked his essence from her bottom lip and Adrian moaned again. There was something sexy and wicked about it and he was turned on again—just too spent to do anything about it right then.

"Damn, baby," he whispered. "You keep amazing me."

Dana grinned. "Is it my turn for a pat on the back and an ego stroke?"

"If I could move, it certainly would be."

"I guess it's a good thing that I'm nothing like you and I'm good without it," she quipped. "Are you hungry?"

"Starving."

"Let's order room service so that we don't have to leave this bed until it's time to go to New York."

She saw him cringe slightly when she mentioned New York. "What?" Dana asked.

"Nothing," he replied quietly. "Listen, I'm still going but I will never have the same feeling about that city as you do, especially after what my father revealed today."

"New York is more than Crawford Hotels," she said. "I promise you when we get to the city, you and I will have so many other things to do that we won't even have to think about your family."

Adrian sighed. As much as he wished that he didn't have to think about his family, he couldn't help but wonder if Elliot was ill. Even though he never knew the man and he was having a hard time considering him his father, he didn't want the bastard to die. Or did he want to watch him suffer the way his mother had in her final days? Did he need to hear Elliot's dying declaration as he'd heard his mother's?

"What?" she asked, stroking his cheek.

"I was just thinking about dinner," he lied.

Dana shot him a suspicious glance, then narrowed her eyes at him. "So, we're going to do this— again?"

"What are you talking about?"

"You lying to me. If there's something wrong, then you'd better tell me now."

"Nothing's wrong, Dana. Am I apprehensive about going to New York? Yes. But there is nothing for you to worry about."

She shook her head. "I swear—"

"Dana," he snapped. "Everything is fine."

She hopped out of bed, fished the room service menu from the nest of papers on the nightstand, and tossed it at Adrian. He ducked as the binder sailed his way.

"Hey! What in the hell is wrong with you?"

"The question is what's wrong with you because I know you're lying to me right now. And if you plan on using this trip to New York as another way—"

Adrian leaped out of bed and gripped Dana's shoulders. "All right, you want the truth? Something could be wrong with Elliot. And honestly, I don't know how I feel about it. Part of me hopes he is dying and then that little boy who wanted his father is hurting because he was never given the chance to understand what having a father—even a shitty one—was like."

"I'm sorry," Dana said. "I'm sorry that I—"

Adrian waved her off. "There's nothing I can do about it right now and I honestly don't know if I want to do anything about it at all."

"Adrian, you . . . Never mind. You're going to have to make your own decision about how you deal with your father."

"Or, I don't have to deal with him at all," he mumbled.

Dana shrugged and shook her head. "I hate to say this, but that is not an option."

He narrowed his eyes at her, wanting to say something but holding back because he didn't want to start an argument. Still, Adrian knew that he had the option of pretending his father didn't exist, even if it had been his mother's wish for him to get to know the man. Letting him die—provided that he was sick—would be poetic justice.

"Adrian," she said. "I'm sorry."

"Why are you apologizing? You're just being who you are—loving. Looking for the best in everyone and sometimes you just have to realize not everyone has a good side."

"Funny, Imani feels the same way about you."

Adrian laughed. "I'm not surprised. After all, she wants Hollywood Ken to be your boyfriend."

Dana narrowed her eyes at him. "When are you going to let that go? If I wanted Ian Kelly, I'd be with him. But I'm here with you."

"And I'm thankful for that. More than you'll ever realize. Dana, you make me a better man."

His words warmed her heart and she almost fell into his arms. "Prove it."

"Prove it?"

"Find out what's going on with your father."

He shook his head. "Please don't call him that. And don't expect me to change in a day. Solomon and I exchanged information. If there's something wrong with Elliot, I'm sure he'll contact me."

Dana bit her bottom lip, then sighed. She knew she could talk until she was blue in the face, but he was going to have to decide if he wanted a relationship with Elliot. "Let's order dinner."

He stroked her cheek. "You order dinner. I have to get my ticket to the Big Apple."

As she picked up the menu, she couldn't ignore how excited she was about going back to New York and taking Adrian along for the ride.

Dana may have been dreaming of seeing the Empire State Building while holding hands with

Adrian, but he wasn't sure what he'd expect to find in the city. The city where his mother lost her heart. The one place where he knew his mother wanted to be but couldn't because Elliot allowed money and his wife to banish her from the city she loved.

"Is that cool with you?" Dana said, breaking into his thoughts.

"Yeah, umm, what?"

"Dinner, I was asking if fish tacos were cool."

"That works for me," he said. "Why don't we spend our last night in LA by the pool. I bet you have a hell of a two-piece in that suitcase over there."

Dana tilted her head and grinned. "Actually, it's a strapless one piece and it is quite amazing."

Adrian glanced down at his watch. "You order the food and I'm going to the shop in the lobby to grab some trunks."

"Speedos," she called out as she dialed room service.

When Adrian made it downstairs, he pulled his phone out and called Solomon.

"Solomon Crawford."

"Solomon, it's Adrian."

"What's going on?"

Adrian sighed, looked over his shoulder as if he was expecting to see someone standing there. He chided himself for being paranoid about doing the right thing. "Have you talked to Richmond about what's going on with Elliot?"

"We're going to talk to him later and ask him what's going on. I'm surprised you care."

"That makes two of us."

"Listen, after all of that shit you heard, I can't blame you if you don't give a . . . I can't blame you if you don't want be bothered with this or us."

Adrian saw the opening and part of him—more than fifty percent of him—wanted to take it. "Keep me posted on what's going on."

"All right," he said.

Adrian hung up and placed his phone in his pocket, then headed into the gift shop. As he selected a pair of swimming trunks, Adrian promised to focus on his time with Dana and nothing else.

The knock on the hotel room door came at the same time that her phone rang and Dana was ready to ignore the call because she knew it was her nosy friend. Still, she grabbed the phone as she opened the door for room service. "Imani," she said as she motioned for the waiter to wheel the cart in. "I can't talk right now."

"It's Ian, not Imani."

"Oh, hi."

"I take it this is a bad time. I was calling because the studio wanted to reshoot some shots and I just wanted to be sure that we're still going to be able to work together."

"Ian, what are you talking about? We just reshot those photos and I thought you were off to your program?"

"Yeah, we did shoot those photos. I don't know where my head is."

"Ian, have you been drinking?"

He laughed. "One last hurrah. I was hoping that, uh, I could see you and maybe we could—"

"Ian, where are you?"

"At The Standard. I needed to get away and think."

"Are you all right?" she asked.

"No. I'm a damned Hollywood cliché," he bemoaned. "It makes no sense that I have all of this success, but I can't trust anyone to share it with me. Do you know how lonely I am?"

"Ian." Dana felt sorry for him, but she knew there was nothing she could do for him.

"Yeah," he whispered. "I don't know why I'm laying this on you. I'm sorry I bothered you."

Dana could hear ice tinkling in a glass as Ian sighed. "You need to put the alcohol down," she said, knowing it would fall on deaf ears.

"Can I put this drink down and hold you?"

He sounded so pitiful and dejected. Dana's heart broke for him and wondered if his life might be in danger.

"What would that really change? Why don't you put the drink down and go to the center. You have too much to lose by climbing into that bottle."

She heard heavy breathing and wondered if Ian

had passed out; then he said, "Will you still be my cheerleader?"

"Yes."

"The next time you hear from me, I'll be sober," he said.

"I look forward to that, Ian," she said as she locked eyes with Adrian. "Look, Ian, I have to go. Are you going to be all right?"

"Yes," he said. "Dana. Thank you."

"You don't have to thank me. But, please, call me when you get settled."

"All right."

Adrian shook his head as Dana ended the call. "Hollywood Ken. Should I be worried?"

"I need you to let it go. Show me the shorts," she quipped.

He opened the plastic bag and pulled out a pair of powder-blue swim trunks. "Your turn," he said.

"Pack up the food and I'll get changed." Adrian walked into the room and closed the door. He pulled Dana into his arms and kissed her hard and deep. Her knees shuddered and she gripped his back. Pulling back from her, Adrian smiled.

"Whoa," she said. "What was that for?"

"Because, just because." He stroked her cheek. "I talked to Solomon while I was at the hotel shop."

"Really?"

He nodded. "I wanted to know if he had an idea of what's going on with Elliot and he doesn't know. When we get to New York, I don't want to be bothered with them. I want to focus on you. Find out what my baby does in the Big Apple."

She smiled, but it didn't reach her eyes. Though she wanted to ask him if he would get over this animosity and try to find peace, Dana just turned toward the closet. "Let me get my suit."

He tugged at her waist. "Go on and say what's on your mind."

"I don't have anything to say," she replied. "But I need you to really think about how you're going to deal with your family going forward."

"Are we going to ruin our last night in LA talking about this?"

"No. Because the Adrian I love is going to do the right thing. I know this."

"What was that call with Ian about?" Adrian asked.

"He's having some issues and thought I could help him."

"Saving everybody, huh?" he said. "Do you need to go see him?"

Dana raised her right eyebrow at him. "Seriously?"

He nodded. "Of course, I'd go with you. But if your friend needs you . . ."

She took his face in her hands and kissed him softly. "And this is why I know you're going to do the right thing when it comes to your family."

He kissed her forehead, thinking that she had more faith in him than he probably deserved. "Let me get these tacos. If you need to go, let me know."

Dana's phone rang again; she hoped it wasn't bad news. But she had a cold feeling in the pit of her stomach as she looked at the unrecognized number. Had Ian been caught by a TMZ photographer stumbling around drunk in the streets or, worse, harmed himself?

"Hello?"

"Dana, it's Lois. I just got a rambling call from Ian. He wouldn't tell me where he was but said you could tell us how to reach him. What in the hell is going on?"

"He called me from The Standard and he's been drinking."

"Damn it. This is the last thing we need right now. Between Heather and her feuds with Imani and now Solomon Crawford, the movie is getting buzz for all of the wrong reasons."

"I'm sorry but Ian is in trouble and you're talking to me about publicity surrounding a movie?"

"Sorry, but that is my job. Damn it, I have to send a car to get him, but obviously he can't come out the front door on the Sunset Strip. Thanks for telling me where he is."

"Lois, will you let me know if he's all right when you find him?"

"Sure, sure. I'm going to call the hotel and see if they can tell me what room he's in—unless you know."

"I don't."

"All right, let me make some calls."

Dana ended the call and groaned. "I'm so glad I'm behind the camera and not in front of it."

"What are you going to do about Ian?" Adrian asked.

She shrugged. "Lois is worried about the movie buzz and not what Ian's going through."

He stroked her arm. "Do you want to go check on him?"

She was about to say yes when her phone rang again. Looking at the screen, she saw it was Lois calling back.

"Yeah?"

"I'm on my way to get him," she said. "I just talked to Ian and he sounds a lot less incoherent. He's willing to let me drive him to the center and he told me to tell you he's going to be fine."

"That's great," Dana replied.

"And I trust that I don't have to ask for your discretion in this matter," Lois said.

Dana rolled her eyes and sighed. "Lois, I . . . No, you don't." Dana ended the call and turned to Adrian. "I can't wait to get back to the city."

He drew her into his arms and kissed her forehead again. "Come on, babe, let's go relax."

Chapter 16

Adrian watched Dana dip under the water and marveled at the way her bathing suit clung to her lithe body. Sitting in the lounge chair next to the pool's edge, he struggled to hide his erection. "Damn," he muttered as she emerged from the pool, putting every Bond girl in the world to shame.

"What was that?" she asked as she twisted her hair to drain the water from her locks.

"You sure you want to go to New York? I know it's going to be hard to find a pool and I won't get to see this anytime soon."

She plopped down in the chair next to his. "You're wrong. My building has a rooftop pool that no one ever uses. And it gets hot at night, so I might even engage you in some skinny-dipping."

"Then let's get going," he quipped.

"As soon as I get the final word on Ian, we're New York bound."

Adrian attempted to muster up some excitement, but in the back of his mind all he could think about was the empire his mother helped to build but never saw realized. He didn't want his issues to cast a deep shadow over his trip with Dana, because this was all about her.

"You're not going to be traveling around New York on the motorcycle, are you?"

She frowned. "Well, *Imani*, I'm a grown woman and if I don't want to take the subway or sit in the back of a smelly cab, then yes."

"I can't believe Imani and I actually agree on something."

"Yeah, but she still thinks you're a jackass."

Adrian laughed. "There's a long list of people who would agree with her. But all that matters is what you think of me."

"I think you have the right touch of asshole," she said, then kissed him on the cheek. "I do love you, Adrian."

"I know. And I'm going to show you that your heart is safe with me."

Dana stared into his eyes and wanted to tell him the truth, that she wasn't sure her heart was safe with him because she'd seen his dark side and she didn't know when and where it stopped.

"What?" he asked.

"What do you mean?"

"You're the only woman I know who says more with silence than a room full of talking people."

"My mind is just on a few other things."

"Hollywo— Ian?"

She nodded, unable to be totally honest with him right then.

"Were you two together long?"

"We were never together at all. But Ian is a nice guy with demons. Just like somebody else I know."

"Ouch," Adrian said.

"I'm starting to see a pattern here," Dana replied.

He shook his head. "Nah, because the buck stops here." Adrian pulled her onto his lap. Dana stared into his eyes, searching for something but not quite sure if she knew what she was looking for. He misread her silence, thinking that her mind was on Ian as he leaned in and toyed with a lock resting against her forehead.

"Adrian," she whispered.

"I'm not jealous that you're sitting in my arms thinking about another man," he said.

"Honestly," she began, "I was thinking about you."

"Is that so?"

"How are you going to work through this anger and aggression you feel toward your father?"

He cleared his throat and closed his eyes. "I don't know. Can't say that I want to. And I know you want to see the best in everyone. You think there's always a silver lining."

"Because there is . . ."

"But this man doesn't deserve my forgiveness

and I can't be sure that I want to give it to him. I don't expect you to understand it, but you have to let me work through this on my own."

She nodded.

Adrian smirked. "I don't think you're going to do that," he said.

"All I can do is try, babe."

He kissed her chin softly and pushed her hair back. "So, are we going to go for another swim?"

"I think we should probably get packed. New York awaits."

Adrian wished he could be excited. But an uneasiness settled in the pit of his stomach the closer the trip to New York came. He smiled and tapped Dana's thigh. "Let's go inside," he said. Dana rose from his lap and wrapped her arms around his neck when he stood up.

"You're going to love New York. I promise."

He rested his hands on her bottom, gently squeezing her cheeks. "As long as I'm with you, I'm sure I will."

Dana brushed her lips against his. "I have to meet the shipper in an hour so that I can get my bike packed and shipped to the city."

"If I distract you, then you won't be able to send that motorcycle back to the city with you."

She narrowed her eyes at him as he slipped his hand between her thighs. "That is not fair."

He slowly stroked her inner thigh until her legs

felt like melting rubber. "I don't always play fair and when I do cheat, I cheat to win."

Dana moaned as his finger entered her suit. Leaning into her, he whispered, "Don't move."

"Then stop touching me right . . . there." Her voice left her and Dana could only moan and whimper as Adrian's finger twirled around inside her. Then he found that one spot that made her weak. She fell forward into his arms.

"My goodness," she said. "You win."

"Win what?" he said with a smirk.

"Anything you want. Other than me leaving my motorcycle here."

Adrian frowned. "Then I didn't win. We're going to have to work on that."

Dana winked at him and thrust her hips forward. "Let's go. We have to get to the airport," she said as he dropped his hands.

"And I need to go home and pack. So get your bike loaded up and we'll meet at the airport."

Part of her wondered if Adrian would show up if they didn't ride together. She decided to trust that he wasn't going to break her heart again. Shortly after she returned to the hotel room, showered, packed, and dressed, the shippers called her to tell her they were ready to pack the Fat Bob for shipment.

"I'll meet you in the garage," she told the man. "I have two helmets that need to be packed as well."

"Yes, ma'am. This is a nice machine, I have to say. I don't know why I was expecting a Vespa."

Dana laughed and ended the call. She thought about calling Adrian to see if he was on his way to the airport. Glancing at her watch, she saw that both of them needed to get a move on. New York was going to change everything. But would it be a good change?

Adrian's bags were packed. He'd printed his flight itinerary and tucked his boarding pass in his jeans pocket. So why was he standing at the door as if he had a five-minute drive to the airport?

"Damn it," he gritted as he opened the door and headed for his car. "This trip isn't about that man and I don't give a shit if he is sick. He has his sons to look after him. I never existed to him before, so we can continue that."

Adrian tossed his bags on the passenger seat, then crossed over to the driver's side and got into the car. Of course, as soon as he got onto the highway, there was gridlock. Banging his hand against the steering wheel, he swore under his breath. "This is what I get for wasting time thinking about a family that doesn't give a damn about me."

The clock on the car radio seemed to tease him as the minutes ticked away and traffic didn't move. Cursing again, he couldn't pull his cell phone out and call Dana because he'd left his Bluetooth and there was a CHP in the lane beside him.

"Damn it," he groaned as he inched forward in the traffic jam. Just as he reached for his phone, he saw another highway patrol in his rearview mirror. Deciding that a traffic stop would only delay him further, he just stewed and crept along the highway.

Dana rushed through the airport to make it to her gate. Luckily she'd made it through the TSA pat-down without a problem, but when she realized that she was on the other side of the airport from where her gate was, she had to skip the Starbucks and make a run for it. When she arrived at the gate, sweaty and out of breath, she expected to see Adrian standing there looking all calm, cool, and collected. But he wasn't there at all. "I'll be damned," she muttered, then glanced at her watch. Their flight was scheduled to leave in two hours.

"I know he didn't do this to me," she said as she took an empty seat and pulled out her cell phone. She dialed his number and waited for him to answer. Five rings and then voice mail. She was tempted to toss her phone, but why cause a scene in the airport when in the back of her mind she'd known this was going to happen? Now she was going to be subjected to choruses of *I told you so* from Imani. She pulled out the same paperback she'd been carrying around since her first flight to Los

Angeles. Maybe this time she'd finish the mystery novel. It would be a lot easier to get into the story this time; she would simply make Adrian the bad guy or the dead guy on every page. Gritting her teeth, she tried to focus on the pages and lose herself in the story. That worked for about ten minutes. She closed the book and picked up her cell phone. When she was about to dial Adrian's number again, she received an incoming call from Imani.

Deciding that she wasn't ready to tell her friend about her latest drama with Adrian, she hit the IGNORE button and tossed her phone in her purse. When she looked up, she saw Adrian barreling her way. Dana's smile lit her face like a candle.

"Traffic," he said as he approached her and drew her into his arms.

She gently slapped his chest. "And it didn't cross your mind to call?"

"It did, but I left my Bluetooth at home and I was surrounded by the man. I'm sure you had a lot of nasty thoughts running through that pretty little mind of yours."

"Were they unfounded?" she asked, then immediately regretted it. "You know what, you're here and they haven't started boarding yet."

Adrian shook his head and stroked her cheek with the back of his hand. "I'd be lying if I said it didn't cross my mind to skip this trip."

Dana's smile faded. She knew he had qualms

about going to the city, and while she knew it had nothing to do with her, it still stung.

"You were going to do it again?"

"Yes. For a moment, I was going to be a coward. Just like before. But I know I'd be the biggest fool ever to allow a second chance with you slip through my fingers."

Dana clutched his hand just as the boarding call began. "Thank you for being honest about this," she whispered.

Adrian smiled and leaned closer to her and saucily asked, "Do we get to join the mile-high club between here and New York?"

She jabbed him in his side with her elbow. "Incorrigible."

"But that's not an answer," he replied with a wink.

"Well, I'm not saying no."

Adrian tapped her bottom. "That's what I'm talking about."

Once their line began moving and they were seated on the plane, Dana was able to expel a relieved sigh. Clicking her seat belt, Dana rested her head on Adrian's broad shoulder. Before the plane reached its cruising altitude, they were both sleeping.

A jolt of turbulence woke Adrian, who was shocked to see that Dana was editing pictures on her MacBook Pro. After a month in LA, she had taken a lot of pictures. "So, you were just going to let me sleep all the way to New York?" he asked.

"Nope. I just wanted to get some work done before we started on our other adventure." She winked at him, then returned to the picture she'd been editing. Adrian looked at the picture and saw that it was Kandace Crawford holding a shoe with a broken heel.

"You two are friends?"

"No, she was just walking into Starbucks and I thought this would be a cool shot for my book." Dana sucked her bottom lip in, realizing that she was looking at his sister-in-law. "Seems like there's no escaping your family, huh?"

"Yeah," he said, looking away from the computer screen. A quick beat later, Dana had closed her laptop and tucked it away underneath her seat.

"Come here," she whispered.

Adrian lifted the armrest and eased closer to her, wrapping his arms around her waist. "Here I am, baby," he sang off-key.

She brushed her lips against his, then locked eyes with him. "I'm glad you really decided to be brave. And," she said as she took his hand and placed it between her thighs, "I'm going to reward your good decision."

"Is that so?" he asked as he stroked her crotch, happy to see that she wasn't wearing panties underneath her cotton leggings.

"Mmm-huh," she said with her eyes closed as

he slipped his hand inside the waistband of her leggings. The brush of his fingers against her bare skin made Dana shiver. Ripples of anticipation flowed through her body. Adrian smiled, nodding toward the bathroom as he removed his hand.

"Meet me in two minutes," he said as he got out of his seat. Dana's anticipation would have to wait longer than two minutes because seconds later, Adrian was returning to his seat and an announcement came through the intercom for all passengers to return to their seats and fasten their seat belts.

"Damn," Adrian muttered as he took his seat and buckled up. "I guess this gives us something to look forward to on the return trip."

"Oh yes," she purred, then leaned her head on his shoulder.

They bumped along for another two hours before the plane entered stable air. Dana felt sick and when she rushed to the restroom, she wasn't thinking about joining the mile-high club.

"Are you all right?" Adrian asked when Dana returned to her seat. He took note of how pale she looked.

"I guess the turbulence got to me," she replied as he wrapped his arms around her.

"We only have an hour to go, so why don't you rest." He stroked her hair as she snuggled against him.

"That's the plan."

The next time Dana opened her eyes, the announcement of the plane's final descent into JFK was coming through the speakers. Adrian, who was still concerned about how Dana was feeling, buckled her seat belt and adjusted her seat. Since his mother's death, Adrian hated seeing anyone he cared about in distress. His mind would go to the worst-case scenario. Looking at Dana as she wiped her forehead with a napkin, he forced the negative thoughts away. It was turbulence. He even talked himself into believing that he was a bit queasy himself.

The plane landed and right away Dana's face brightened. "Let's hear it for New York!" she said as she rose to her feet.

"Feeling better, huh?" he replied with a smile.

"Yes, and thank goodness because I have a date with Gray's."

"What's that?" he asked as he unloaded their bags from the overhead compartment.

"Gray's Papaya, the best place to experience a hot dog in the world. No offense to Pink's, but I want a real hot dog without the trappings of Hollywood."

Shifting the bags on his shoulder, he shook his head. "Pink's is legendary. This *Grey's Anatomy* joint had better live up to the standard that I've grown accustomed to."

"You're going to eat those words and the best hot dog ever." Dana's smile made him believe she was telling the gospel truth.

"Well, let's hear it for the second best thing I'm

going to eat today." His eyes sparkled devilishly and Dana didn't have to ask what the best thing was he planned to eat.

"Again," she said. "Incorrigible."

"You're going to love every minute of it," he replied with a wink as they began to deplane.

Chapter 17

Adrian and Dana climbed into a cab and she smiled as they pulled away from JFK. Once they got into traffic leading to Brooklyn, her smile faded. Bumper to bumper.

"Well, this is one thing that reminds me of LA," Adrian quipped.

"Oh, hush."

"And you're going to ride a motorcycle in all of this?"

She nodded. "If I was on my Fat Bob, I'd go right down the center lane."

"Like that's not dangerous. How did you get into motorcycles?"

Dana shrugged. "It was just something that looked fun and as it turns out, it was more amazing than I thought it would be."

Adrian glanced out the window and gritted his teeth as the cab slowly crept down Pennsylvania

Avenue and he saw the Crawford Motor Lodge. He couldn't help but wonder when it was built and if his mother had been the catalyst for its being built. Dana's hand forced him to return his focus to her.

"You're good?" she asked.

"I'll be fine. I just have to get used to the fact that those people have their names on a lot of buildings because of my mother."

"And are you going to reach out to them while you're here?"

"Can we at least get to your place before we start talking about them?"

Dana chewed her bottom lip, then agreed. He kissed her cheek. "As a matter of fact," Adrian continued, "until I get that famous hot dog and that other delectable treat, I don't want to talk about anything."

"And what do you want first?" she whispered. "Because Gray's is open all night."

"Good, then I can get seconds and thirds before we go for those famous hot dogs."

Dana placed her hand in the center of his chest as he leaned forward to kiss her. "One quick note— we're taking the subway."

He shrugged, then captured her lips in a sweeping move that made her shiver with desire. While she hated that they didn't join the mile-high club, she would certainly make up for it when they arrived at her home.

Whatever caused the traffic backup cleared up or the driver knew a shortcut to Park Slope, the neighborhood Dana called home. The driver pulled up in front of Dana's brownstone and Adrian was impressed with the neighborhood.

"This isn't what I expected Brooklyn to look like," he said.

"Watch a lot of Spike Lee movies and thought the whole borough was like Red Hook?"

"Ha," he said as he unloaded the bags from the trunk. "You keep forgetting, all of my images of New York come from television and movies."

Even the cabdriver snorted at that comment. Dana tilted her head toward the driver and said, "You have to excuse him. He's been on the West Coast since forever."

The trio laughed and Adrian paid the driver, tipping him handsomely. "Hey," the man said as he counted his money. "I like you Los Angeles guys."

When the taxi pulled away, Dana looked at Adrian. "Must have been a hell of a tip."

He winked at her and lifted the bags. "Yes," he said. "It was."

Dana led him to her front door. "Welcome to my home," she said.

Adrian stepped inside and looked around the spacious brownstone. It was beautiful, decorated with black and white pictures from Central Park, the Brooklyn Botanic Garden, and some color shots from Los Angeles. For the first time in a long time, Adrian recognized the artistic skill his woman had. Those pictures had a museum quality to them.

"Wow," he said as he stood in the middle of her living room as if he were in the Guggenheim.

"What?" she asked as she followed his eyes to the pictures.

"You're talented beyond measure. So, this is what you do in your spare time?"

Dana's cheeks heated underneath his adoration. "You could say that."

He pointed to an empty space above her fireplace. "What do I have to do to get a picture on this wall? Like the dude said in *Do the Right Thing*, can a brother get on the wall?"

She wrapped her arms around his neck and brushed her lips against his. "I'm sure a brother can get on the wall. He just needs to play his cards right."

He rubbed his hands down her hips. "I got a full house for you right now." In a swift motion, he scooped Dana into his arms and asked, "Where's the bedroom? I want to go all in right now."

Dana nodded toward the stairs. Crossing over to the staircase, Adrian took them two at a time to get into her bedroom. Once in the bedroom, he laid her on the bed and stripped out of his jeans and T-shirt.

She started to strip, but Adrian crossed over to her and held her wrist. "I want to do this," he said, his voice a deep whisper. "Just lean back."

Dana followed his instructions as he unbuttoned her tunic. Each piece of skin he exposed, Adrian kissed and licked. She moaned and writhed with desire under his touch. And when he peeled her leggings from her body and buried his face in the wetness between her thighs, Dana lost it, screaming out in pleasure. Adrian held her hips to his lips, making good on his promise to eat a delectable treat. Licking, sucking, and gently biting her as she thrust her hips forward. Dana grasped his head and he plunged his tongue deeper inside her and she howled in pleasure. As she exploded from the inside out, Adrian pulled back and smiled at her.

"Told you that I was going to eat something delicious," he said. "And, baby, you taste amazing."

Dana inhaled deeply and shivered as the aftershocks of her orgasm attacked her senses. "You know," she said, "it's amazing what you can do with that tongue of yours."

"You think so?" He took her hand and placed it on his erection. "Wait until you feel what I plan to do next."

She draped her legs across his shoulders. "Well, I think it's my turn to show you what I can do."

"I'm ready, baby."

Dana unwound herself from his body and turned him over on his back. She started at his neck, kissing and sucking him while she stroked his hardness. She flicked her tongue across his nipples, then moved down his washboard abs until she was face-to-face with his thick erection. Adrian held his next breath as he felt the heat from her mouth envelop him. She licked, sucked, ran her tongue up and down the length of him as he howled her name. He needed to be inside her to end the pleasurable torture. But Dana wasn't about to stop. She took him deeper into her mouth and Adrian exploded.

Pulling back, she offered him a shy smile as he threw his head back in delight. "Oh, baby," he cried. "Damn." He drew her into his arms and she rested her head against his chest. "That was amazing."

"One good turn deserved another," she replied.

"Uh-huh. I have to say, so far, I love New York."

Moments later the couple drifted off to sleep, wrapped in each other's arms. About an hour later, they woke up feeling refreshed and a lot less jet lagged. Dana reached for the remote to her TV while Adrian yawned and stretched his arms above his head. As she flipped through the channels, she stopped on NY1 when she saw a video of Solomon Crawford. Adrian sat up and watched with rapt attention.

"Crawford Hotels is facing some big changes on the heels of a West Coast expansion," said the anchor. "Sources tell us that CEO Solomon Crawford has resigned and there are reports that Elliot Crawford, the founder and owner of the hotel chain, has fallen ill in Los Angeles and will be flown back to New York."

"Wow," Dana mumbled.

Adrian rolled his eyes and held his tongue as the report continued. "Richmond Crawford will take over as CEO. The company has been steeped in controversy as of late. Richmond Crawford was pictured with a Los Angeles call girl, a man claimed that he's the love child of Elliot Crawford, and Solomon Crawford is allegedly feuding with actress Heather Williams, who he dated before marrying Kandace Crawford."

Part of him wanted to smile; the Crawfords were exposed. But he couldn't help feeling some kind of way about finding out that Elliot was seriously ill. However, what if he was faking the illness to take the media focus off the scandals surrounding his family? It's not as if the son of a bitch wasn't above lying.

"Sources say Elliot Crawford will be flown into an area hospital where he will be treated for an unknown illness."

"Turn it off," Adrian said.

Dana pressed the power button and eased out of bed. From the slowness of her steps, Adrian knew she had something to say.

"What?" he asked.

Dana turned around and shrugged. "We said we weren't going to talk about your family."

"But I know you and you're not going to stop thinking about this until you've had your say. Let's get it out of the way now so that I can digest my hot dog later."

"I think you should call Solomon and find out what's going on with your fa—Elliot."

"That's not going to happen," he said. "Do you know how many illnesses he's missed?"

"How long are you going to let the past cloud

your future? And how do you go from being the man who can be so gentle and loving with me to being so cold toward his family?" Dana felt her stomach lurch and bile rush to her throat. She ran out of the room and into the bathroom. Adrian followed and knocked on the door. "Are you all right?" He could hear her throwing up and this time they couldn't blame it on turbulence.

Then he heard water running. Finally, Dana replied, "I'm fine."

"Hurling in the bathroom doesn't seem fine to me," he said.

Seconds later, she opened the door and walked into Adrian's awaiting arms. "I'm going to blame this on the airplane food and pray that it isn't going to keep me from my meeting in a few days."

"Maybe we should skip the hot dogs and get back into bed. You got some soup in the kitchen?"

"All I have in the kitchen is baking soda. I haven't been here long enough to go to the market."

"I'm sure there's a Chinese restaurant that delivers. But should you really have egg drop soup?"

"Adrian," she said, stroking his cheek. "Baby, I'm good and I'm a New Yorker. Hot dogs calm all stomach ailments."

He narrowed his eyes at her. "Dana . . ."

"Adrian, if I thought something was seriously wrong, I'd be the first to go to the doctor. A little stomach virus will be gone tomorrow."

"Let's hope so or our next excursion will be to your doctor's office."

She offered him a mock salute. "Yes, sir. Now, why don't we get showered and changed so that I can watch you eat your words."

A slow smile crept across Adrian's face. "Well . . ."

"Stop!" Dana broke out laughing. "You shower first and I'll get the bags from downstairs."

"Let's reverse that. You shower and I'll get the bags." He kissed her on the cheek. "I still say we should stay in for the rest of the night."

"Not in the city that never sleeps," she replied, then returned to the bathroom. While she showered, Dana began to wonder about her nausea. *There's no way I'm pregnant,* she thought as the warm spray beat down on her.

Adrian picked up their luggage and took them into the bedroom. He set her bags near the closet and tossed his bag on the bed. He fished out a pair of jeans and an ombré shirt. As much as he wanted to ignore the news about the Crawfords, he turned the TV on again to see if there was an update on Elliot or the calamity in California. NY1 just played a loop of the earlier story.

Turning the TV off, Adrian fished his cell phone out of his discarded jeans and turned it on. Of course there were a few missed calls and text messages from his associates and club managers. After all, he hadn't left instructions when he left. But those calls could wait. He needed to call Solomon.

He was about to dial his brother when Dana walked into the room, wrapped in a short pink towel, her body damp and glistening from her shower. Thoughts of calling Solomon fled from his mind like air from a busted balloon.

"Are you sure we have to leave?" he asked as he crossed over to her and tugged at the top of her towel.

"Yes," she said, playfully slapping his hand away. "I left plenty of hot water in the shower for you."

"Having to walk away from you looking like that, I probably need a cold shower."

"Funny," she said as she crossed over to her closet and flipped through her clothes. Looking over her shoulder, she saw Adrian was standing in the doorway watching her. "Get going, Mr. Bryant."

"But you said we can score hot dogs all night. I like this show better."

Dana shooed him away and started to get dressed. She decided to wear a dress for a change and some shoes that she would normally admonish Imani for wearing. However, the black minidress she'd pulled out of the closet called for the red five-inch heels. She turned the TV on to check the weather and saw that it was going to be a balmy evening. As she was about the turn the set off, Adrian's cell phone rang. She looked at the screen and saw Solomon's name flash in the display.

Grabbing the phone, she rushed down the hall and met Adrian as he was exiting the bathroom.

"It's Solomon," she said as she handed him the phone.

Adrian pressed the TALK button. "Yeah? I'm not in LA . . . Saw that on the news . . . What? I'll have to call you back." He ended the call and then walked into the bedroom as if nothing happened. Dana was teeming with questions as she followed him.

"What did Solomon say?" she asked as she watched him drop his towel and cross over to the bed.

"Nothing important," Adrian said as he pulled out a pair of boxers and stepped into them.

"Oh, so you guys are BFFs now and he's just calling to say hi?"

"He just wanted to let me know that his father is back in New York. He has cancer and they checked him into a hospital for tests."

The calmness in his voice made Dana pause. "And that doesn't bother you at all?"

Adrian stepped into his jeans and looked at her. "Why should it?"

"Because I'm sure if Solomon called you that it was serious."

Adrian buttoned and zipped his jeans. "Let's deal with that later."

"Adrian, you can't—"

He pointed to the clock on her nightstand. "Do you see what time it is? Visiting hours at the hospital are over. And let's be real—Elliot and I aren't the typical father and son. I'll call Solomon in the morning and get further details. Tonight is all about you and me."

Dana nodded, but if she had her druthers, they'd go to whatever hospital Elliot Crawford was in. She wondered if Adrian could really handle losing his father without making peace with him. She slipped into her heels and crossed over to Adrian as he rubbed cologne on his neck. The scent was intoxicating, but she couldn't stop thinking about the way he was handling the news of his father's illness.

"Baby," he said, snapping her out of her thoughts.

"Huh?"

"I was saying that you look amazing. Why do I get the feeling that this isn't going to be the night we'd planned now?"

She tilted her head to the side and looked into his eyes. "I made a promise and I'm going to keep it," she replied.

"But you're going to be thinking about another man dressed like that and I already don't like that."

Dana slipped her arms around his waist and hugged him. "Can I just say one thing?"

"Go ahead."

"Biologically, he's your father and it doesn't seem as if there is a lot of time left for you to get to know him and make peace with him. If you don't do it for yourself, think about what your mother wanted."

He glanced down at her. "That was below the belt. You know that, right?"

"But it's the truth."

Casting his eyes upward, Adrian could almost feel his mother smiling and nodding in agreement with Dana. "All right. I'll call Solomon back once we're out and find out where Elliot is."

Dana smiled and took his hand. "Let's go."

Chapter 18

Before they made it to the Bergen Street station, Dana's cell phone rang. It was Imani.

"Hell—"

"Thanks for letting me know you made it back. I hope I'm interrupting something."

"Actually, you're not."

"Damn," she quipped. "Anyway, I assume you and Adrian are safe in the city."

"We are."

"Avoiding the paparazzi, I hope."

"So far so good."

"Well," Imani began, "I don't expect that to last. I just saw on the news that the Los Angeles County DA is looking into charging Richmond Crawford with engaging in prostitution."

"What?" Dana said, and looked up at Adrian.

"What's wrong?" he asked.

"Imani said the DA is considering charging Richmond for engaging in prostitution."

Adrian shrugged. "That's going to be hard for them to explain to stockholders since Solomon is no longer CEO and Elliot's dying."

"Imani," Dana said. "Let me call you back." When she ended the call, she stopped on the sidewalk. "What do you know about this?"

"Nothing."

"That's bullshit."

"Have you seen me at the district attorney's office? I don't have that kind of pull."

"Adrian. I know you'd been doing some underhanded things, but this is too much."

He held his hands up. "What exactly are you accusing me of?"

"I'm asking if you had anything to do with these charges against your brother. Did you set him up?"

"What if I did?"

Dana eyed him incredulously. "I don't believe you. How can you be so underhanded? Did you think about his family and how this would affect them?"

"Do you honestly think I cared about that at the time? I'm not going to apologize for how angry I was watching this family pretend they were the damned Cosbys when I knew the truth. I wanted the world to know and I had to engage in some underhanded tactics—then I was going to do it."

"When are you going to make it right, Adrian? At the end of the day, that's your brother. He's as much of a victim of your father's lies as you are."

He pounded his thighs and shook his head. "I'm

sure Elliot didn't tell his mother to have an abortion. I'm sure he never went to sleep wishing the man he thought was his father would spend time with him. So don't tell me that he's a victim. Don't tell me that he knows what I went through because neither he nor Solomon will ever understand."

"And your answer to that is to ruin their lives? What will that change? And if making their lives hell is how you deal with things when you're hurting, then how can you expect us to have a future?"

He dropped his head and released a heavy sigh. "How many times do I have to tell you that this doesn't have anything to do with you?"

"That's a lie. It has everything to do with me and us. You said you staged that ruse two years ago to keep me away from this. What happens when something else doesn't go your way? Do I get to be collateral damage again?"

"Dana . . ."

"Don't Dana me! Answer me."

"What do you want me to say?"

"The truth. I want you to tell me the truth."

"Fine, I hate them. All of them. I don't give a damn about Elliot dying. I don't care if the company crumbles or if Richmond goes to jail. Happy? I'm not a good guy in this situation."

Dana inhaled sharply. "So, anger is what you go with?"

Adrian chewed the inside of his cheek. "I don't want to go there all the time, but this is a lifetime of hurt. My mother—"

"Would be ashamed of you. The woman I knew wouldn't want you seeking revenge and you should be ashamed." She stomped off from him, dashing back to her brownstone.

Standing on the street, Adrian was pissed—at himself. Why had he opened his big mouth, and why had he confessed his sins to Dana? He'd known she wouldn't be behind him and his revenge plot; that's why he'd tried to shield her from this. Something about being in the city, surrounded by what he now knew was his mother's legacy, made him angrier. But Dana was right—how much longer could he hold on to the anger?

Pulling his cell phone from his pocket, he decided to call Solomon and get more details about their father's condition.

"Solomon Crawford."

"Hey, listen, I'm in Park Slope. How do I get to Mount Sinai?"

"Did you fly here for Dad?" Solomon asked, his voice expressing his surprise.

"No, I was here when you called earlier."

"And it just slipped your mind to tell me that? Dad needs a bone marrow transplant. Richmond knew this and was tested last month. He's not a match. I'm waiting on the results from my test and hoping there's a match on the registry. But now that you're here. Maybe you could get tested and see if you're a match."

"When you called earlier, you were going to ask me to get tested for that man? Are you serious?"

"You have every right to hate him, but are you so black-hearted that you won't even get tested?"

"If I am, then I take after the old man," he snapped.

"Cut the crap. If you didn't give a damn, I doubt you'd be calling me to find out how to get to him. Give me the address where you are and I'll have a car come get you."

There was a huge part of him that wanted to tell Solomon what pocket of hell he could send that car to, but he rattled off Dana's address and headed back to the brownstone. He had no idea if he'd be welcomed inside, so he did the New York thing and sat on the stoop.

About ten minutes passed and the front door opened. Dana, now dressed in a pair of distressed jeans and a Van Halen tank top, walked out onto the stoop.

"Were you going to sit out here all night?" she asked as she sat down beside him.

"No." He reached for her hand, but Dana didn't take his. "I thought about what you said."

"And?"

"I called Solomon. He's sending a car so that I can go see Elliot."

Dana nodded and accepted his hand. "Is that so?"

He brought her hand to his lips and kissed it gently. "I'm not going to pretend that I've had some sort of epiphany and I suddenly want to have this deep relationship with him and all is forgiven."

"I didn't think so," she said. "But I'm glad you changed your mind somewhat."

"Yeah," he replied. "Obviously Richmond knew of his father's illness and he was tested to see if he could donate bone marrow."

"Is he a match and can't come back to New York because of the charges you're behind?"

"No," Adrian said. "He's not a match. Solomon is waiting for the results of his tests and I guess the next thing is for me to get tested."

Dana pushed her locks behind her ear. "Are you going to do it?"

Before he could respond, a black Lincoln Town Car pulled up to the curb. "Will you come with me?" he asked as he rose to his feet.

"Yes. Let me grab my purse and keys," she said, and stood up.

Adrian drew her into his arms and kissed her gently on the lips. "Thank you," he replied. He turned to the driver and told him they'd be ready in a moment. Seconds later, Dana was locking up the brownstone and hopping into the car with Adrian. They rode in silence. Dana wished she knew what was going on in Adrian's mind. She wondered if he would really get tested. Moreover, she wondered if he held the key to saving his father's life, would he use it?

Adrian had the same thoughts as Dana. He would've given anything to save his mother, even if it was for one more day. Doing the same for his sperm donor? He couldn't say that he was enthusiastic about being his savior.

"Are you all right?" Dana asked as the car crawled to a stop at a traffic light.

"I'm fine," he said quietly. "I wonder how sick this man really is?"

"If he's in the hospital, I imagine that he's pretty sick."

"Or," he said, clearing his throat, "he's trying to take the heat off what's going on with his sons by pretending."

Dana dropped her head. "You can't seriously believe that."

He shrugged. "What can I say? His track record isn't the best when it comes to honesty."

Dana couldn't argue that fact, but she hated that Adrian was so cynical. She simply touched his hand and kept silent. The last thing she wanted was to have another argument with him. Dana needed to believe that Adrian wouldn't give in to the darkness inside him.

When they arrived at the hospital, there were a few news trucks parked in the hospital's main lot and twenty photographers milling around the front entrance. Adrian swore under his breath.

"This is just what I need," he muttered.

"Sir," the driver said. "Mr. Crawford gave me instructions on how to avoid the media circus."

"Good," Dana said when she noticed Adrian's

attention was still focused on the media at the front of the hospital.

The driver circled the hospital and the pulled onto a side street. They sat in the car while the driver exited and walked over to a building that resembled a hotel. "Amazing, the rich don't even have the same kind of hospitals that the rest of us have to deal with," Adrian mumbled. "What is this place?"

"Eleven West. I guess this is one way for Elliot to avoid the media snapping pictures."

The driver opened the door and told Dana and Adrian that everything was all clear. "Mr. Crawford's waiting for you to take you inside."

"Thanks," Adrian said to the driver once he and Dana exited the car.

Solomon ushered his brother inside and gave Dana a quizzical look. "Who is she and why is she here?" he asked.

Adrian flashed a frosty look at his brother. "She's the reason I'm here, so I'd advise you to watch your tone."

"Guys," Dana said. "This isn't the time or the place. I can wait in the waiting room or go take a walk."

"A walk?" Solomon said. "So you can lead the paparazzi directly to us?"

"She wouldn't do that," Adrian said with attitude in his voice. "And she isn't going anywhere."

Dana saw Kandace, Solomon's wife, approaching

them. "Solomon," she called out. "The lab results are back."

"Is the technician still in Dad's room? He needs to run another test if—"

Kandace placed her hand on her husband's shoulder. "You're going to be a match," she said, then shot Adrian a contemptuous glance. "What is he doing here?"

"Just in case," Solomon said.

"And he has some explaining to do before he dies," Adrian snapped, then stomped down the hall as if he knew which suite he was going to. Solomon caught up with him. Kandace turned to Dana with a suspicious gaze.

"What?" Dana asked.

"I hope you don't have some kind of game or role in what's been happening to my family as of late."

"I'm here for Adrian. I don't care about your family—I care about him," Dana shot back.

"But what does he care about? I know he's Solomon's brother, but I don't trust him and I know he has something to do with the craziness that was going on in Los Angeles."

Dana wanted to say something, but she kept silent. It was Adrian's mess to confess. "Let's just be there for them. All of that other stuff isn't important right now."

Kandace nodded in agreement. "You're right."

* * *

Adrian stood at the foot of Elliot's bed. The old man was sleeping, hooked up to IVs and oxygen. His mind flashed back to the last moments he spent at his mother's bedside. A wave of sadness washed over him. Despite knowing the cruel things his father said about him before he was born, seeing him this way made him feel very sad. Even a little hurt. The technician and a doctor walked into the room, causing Adrian to glance away from Elliot.

The solemn look on the faces of the health professionals took Adrian back to the days when he waited to hear about his mother's condition and how every time someone walked into her hospital room the news was all bad.

"Mr. Crawford," the doctor said in a hushed tone. "I'm sorry, but you're not a viable candidate for the bone marrow transplant."

Solomon chewed his bottom lip. "What's the next step?"

"You said there was another family member. We can do the blood test as soon as that person is available."

Solomon nodded toward Adrian. "That's him."

Adrian looked up and saw the technician coming his way. "Sir, are you ready to take the blood test?"

He locked eyes with Solomon, part of him wondering when in the hell he'd agreed to this, then nodded.

"Let's go," he said, and followed the technician out of the room. As they walked down the hall, Adrian wondered if he'd get to have that last conversation with his father. Would Elliot apologize for missing out on his entire life?

"Are you all right?" the technician asked.

"What?"

"I've been asking you a question for the last five minutes and you're zoned out."

"What's the question?"

"How are you related to the patient?"

Adrian cleared his throat and said, "I'm his son."

The woman brought her hand to her mouth, then muttered, "Oh. Well, the lab is right through here."

Adrian followed her into the tiny room and took a seat in a small chair. The technician handed him a red rubber ball. "Make a fist," she said.

He closed his hand around the ball and shut his eyes. Adrian forced himself not to ask questions like: What if he was a match for his father? Would he go through with the procedure? What was exactly wrong with Elliot? Here he was sitting in a chair to get his blood drawn and he hadn't even asked why.

"We're all done," the woman said.

Adrian had been so deep in his thoughts that he hadn't felt the prick of the needle. As the technician placed a gauze bandage on his arm, she smiled at him.

"You look a lot better in person than on TV," she said. "I hope things work out."

Adrian rose to his feet. "Thanks." Leaving the room, he sought Dana out. He needed to leave. Before he found his woman, Solomon stopped him.

"Thank you for doing this. I know it can't be easy."

"It isn't. What's wrong with him?"

"Acute lymphoblastic leukemia. He's been on a drug treatment, but it's not working."

"And he kept this from you?" Adrian shook his head.

"Keeping secrets seems to be his specialty."

"Do you think him coming to LA was because he knew the end was near?" Adrian asked as he and Solomon headed back to their father's suite.

Solomon shrugged. "I don't know what he was thinking. Maybe he was trying to connect with you. Maybe he was trying to give my mother a post-mortem middle finger."

"Or that finger could've been aimed at my mother."

"No doubt about it, he was—is—a son of a bitch."

Adrian looked in the room and saw a motionless Elliot Crawford in his bed. He felt like a child and fought the urge to ask Solomon what growing up with their father was like. Solomon followed his brother's gaze. "Listen," Solomon began, "what he did, we can't change. But we're family and we should probably get to know each other."

"Before you say that, I have a confession to make," Adrian said.

Solomon faced him. "What?"

Adrian cleared his throat and folded his arms across his chest. "I wanted to destroy you all. Him, you, Richmond. My mother suffered a lot and kept a record of it in her diary. When she died and I read it, all I could think about was this silver-spoon life you and Richmond had while my mother and I lived in exile."

"What did you do?"

"I set Richmond up with the hooker, fed the protesters the story about the call girl's arrest and Richmond's skate on the charges. I set up your fight with Heather Williams in my club—"

Solomon hauled off and punched Adrian in the face just as Dana and Kandace approached the men with cups of coffee.

"What in the hell is going on?" Dana asked, rushing to Adrian's side.

Chapter 19

Dana looked from Solomon to Adrian as Kandace struggled to hold her husband back.

"I deserved that," Adrian replied while holding his bloody nose.

"You deserve more than that, you punk mother— your beef is with him!" Solomon nodded toward Elliot's suite. "But you chose to put my marriage in jeopardy. Now my brother is facing jail because of your bitch ass."

"What are you talking about?" Kandace asked, dropping her hand from Solomon's arm.

"Everything that's happened in LA." Solomon flung his finger at Adrian. "He's been behind it."

Dana felt proud of Adrian, happy that he'd told the truth, but brother or not, if Solomon touched him again, she was going to jump in.

"Leave him alone," Dana said. "Do you know how hard it is for him to be here right now and to get tested to see if he can save a man who never gave a damn about him?" Dana looked at Kandace. "And if he tried to ruin your marriage, it looks like it didn't work."

"You should stay out of this," Solomon admonished.

Adrian shrugged Dana's touch off and stood face-to-face with his brother. "Don't you dare talk to her like that."

"Oh, you can disrespect my marriage and I'm supposed to give a—"

"Solomon!" Kandace exclaimed. A nurse and security guard rushed toward the group.

"Excuse me, but you all are going to have to take this outside or be quiet," the nurse said. "This isn't some street corner in the Bronx." She looked at the blood on Adrian's face and shirt. "Sir, do you need medical attention?"

"No," Adrian said as he glanced at the security guard, who had his hand on top of his weapon.

"Babe, let's go," Dana whispered. He nodded and they started down the hall, ignoring Solomon's ranting. Dana looked over her shoulder and saw his wife offering him calming words as they walked into Elliot's suite. Turning her attention to Adrian, she wrapped her arm around his waist.

"Despite that fight back there, I'm glad you told him the truth."

Adrian ran his finger across his nose. "I guess it's a fact, the truth hurts."

Dana dug a tissue out of her purse and wiped the

remaining bit of blood from his face. "Are you sure you don't want to get your nose looked at?"

"Nah, I've had a bloody nose before. I'm sure it won't be the last."

"I hope it is. Don't you think you're a little old to be a brawler?"

Adrian shrugged. "I'm sure Richmond is going to want his shot when he returns to New York."

Dana felt warm on the inside. Adrian was actually making long-term plans to stay in the city. They walked out of the main entrance, forgetting to look for the media. Immediately it was a decision they regretted. A group of photographers bum-rushed them, snapping pictures and yelling out questions.

"Is Elliot Crawford dead?"

"Are you the reason he's in the hospital?"

"Were you here to take a DNA test to prove Elliot Crawford is your father?"

"What happened to your face?"

"Is it true that you and Solomon Crawford were fighting over the Crawford family fortune?"

Dana held her purse up as they pushed through the crush of cameras and bodies. A few of the paparazzi gave chase, and Adrian, who was used to controlling what pictures were released and not being on the other side of this stampede, stopped.

"What are you doing?" Dana asked.

"Maybe if I give them a statement, they'll go away."

"Yeah, if this was LA," she whispered as Adrian faced the photographers.

"Are you really Elliot Crawford's son?" one of the photographers called out.

"Listen," Adrian said. "I'm here on a family matter and I'd appreciate privacy and time to deal with it."

"Then why did you put your business out there for CNN?" another photographer snapped.

"Yeah," another said. "You can't ask for privacy now. What happened to your nose?"

"I don't have anything else to say."

"Did Elliot Crawford die tonight?" a photographer called to Adrian's retreating figure.

Dana grabbed his arm when she saw that he was about to charge at the photographer. "Don't. Let's just go home and relax."

"Yeah," he replied. "Besides, I need to make some calls."

She raised her eyebrow; then she remembered—it wasn't that late in Los Angeles. "While you do that, I'll order takeout. And let's take the subway so your new friends won't follow us. The last thing I need is a pack of media hounds parking their asses on my stoop."

"I'm sorry about this," Adrian said.

"For once, you don't owe me an apology. You're actually doing the right thing and I'm proud of you."

Adrian kissed Dana's cheek. "I wouldn't offer that endorsement yet."

Dana cast her eyes upward at him. "You didn't take the blood test?" she asked.

"I did," he replied as they walked into the subway station. "But what if I'm a match? How ironic is it that I couldn't do anything to save the parent who loved me unconditionally, but now I have the chance to save the one who never gave a damn about me?"

"So, he has leukemia?"

Adrian nodded. "Neither Solomon nor Richmond are matches for a bone marrow transplant."

"And your results aren't back?"

"Nope."

Dana sighed as she swiped her Metro card, then passed it back to Adrian. He slid the card through the machine and joined Dana through the turnstile. They held hands and headed for the subway platform, falling in line with other riders who didn't give a damn who they were. Adrian couldn't have been happier.

"Does what happened in the hospital change what you're going to do in regards to your father?"

Adrian groaned. "I wish I could be pissed off at Solomon, but I stand by the fact that I deserved that. You know, when I started all of this stuff, I had no intentions to be around watching the aftermath."

"I'm sure you didn't."

Adrian grinned. "I blame you for this."

"Excuse me?"

"You showed me the error of my ways and I have a bloody nose to show for it." He smiled and gave her a slight nudge. "Maybe I'll get that on a T-shirt."

Before Dana could offer him a smart-aleck reply, the train arrived. "I guess that means I need to clean your nose and feed you so that you'll have a different message for your T-shirt."

He pulled her onto his lap as they took a seat. "Isn't it a little late for hot dogs?"

"I'm starving," she said. "And I put you on the train to take us directly to Gray's."

"Looking like this?" He pointed to the bloodstain on his shirt.

Dana fanned her hand. "This time of night, if you aren't drunk or don't have a little blood on you, people are going to wonder why you're there."

"Sounds classy."

Dana leaned her head against his chest. "Well, I'll make sure I purchase some eggs so that you can make some omelets tomorrow."

"Oh no, Miss Singleton. I want you to cook that one dish you're famous for."

She raised her eyebrow, then broke out laughing. "Bow-tie pasta and shrimp."

He nodded with a smile on his lips. "Yeah, between my omelets and your pasta, we're going to need new clothes."

"Whatever. This is our stop," she said.

She and Adrian exited the train and headed up Broadway, finally making it to the hot dog shop. Dana realized how hungry she was when she smelled the chili and the grilled dogs.

"Oh my goodness, I've missed this place."

They stood in line waiting to order and Dana recounted the many nights she and Imani had come here to eat hot dogs and stalk Broadway producers.

"Your girl was on a mission, huh?"

"Yes, she was." Dana laughed. "I'm surprised she hasn't snagged an endorsement deal."

"Ha. That would go over well with the bean-curd crowd in Hollywood."

"Well, that carnivore will never join that set."

Adrian shrugged as they reached the counter. "I've seen stranger things happen."

Dana ordered her signature hot dog with extra mustard and sauerkraut. "If that happens to Imani, then the Mayans were right."

Once Adrian ordered his dog, they headed outside and started for the subway station. As soon as Dana lifted her hot dog to her mouth, she felt a wave of nausea wash over her. She shrugged it off as being hungry and having jet lag. Still, she tried to take a bite of the food. Big mistake. Moments later, she was dropping her hot dog and vomiting on the street. Adrian tossed his hot dog in the trash can and placed his hand on Dana's shoulder. "If that's what a good hot dog does to you, I don't want to know what a bad one does. Are you sure everything is all right?"

Dana wiped her mouth with a paper napkin and shook her head. "I don't know what's going on," she said.

"Should we go to the ER?" he asked, then scooped Dana up into his arms.

"Just take me home," she said. Instead of waiting

for the subway or taking her underground, Adrian hailed a cab like a native. A yellow cab stopped on the corner and Adrian hopped in as Dana rattled off her address to the driver.

"Brooklyn? I don't go to Brooklyn this late," the driver said.

Adrian handed him a fifty-dollar bill. "Listen, she's sick and we need to get home fast."

The driver took the cash and nodded. He pulled into traffic and Dana's stomach lurched. She struggled not to throw up again. Adrian rubbed her head and wondered what was going on with Dana. Part of him feared that he'd lose her—to death. He felt as if the universe would spare Elliot but take Dana because he was supposed to learn some kind of lesson. Looking down at her as she rested in his lap, a lightbulb went off in his head. Was she pregnant? He thought about the times they'd been careless with protection. Was he ready to be a father? Was Dana ready for motherhood? More importantly, would she give up that motorcycle for a sensible car with room for a car seat and a trunk to hold a stroller? Where would she want to raise their child? Los Angeles? New York?

"Excuse me," Dana said. "Can you drop us off at the Duane Reade on Flatbush Avenue?"

"Okay," the driver replied.

Dana looked up at Adrian and said, "It's a drug-store."

"I kind of figured that."

She grinned and shook her head. "I guess we both figured out what might be wrong."

"Or what could be right."

Dana didn't respond, but she wanted to ask him how in the world the two of them would raise a child when she lived in New York and had no plans to move to Los Angeles. And as selfish as it seemed, Dana wasn't sure she wanted to make such a big change in her life and career. With a baby, she couldn't fly to Paris, LA, and Tokyo for shoots and no more late night trips for hot dogs.

"What are you thinking?" he asked.

"I'm scared."

He stroked her forehead until she sat up. "Are we ready for this?"

"We don't know anything yet, but know this— nothing will keep me from my child."

"If there is a child."

"Do you want this baby?" he asked. As the words left his mouth, he felt ill, wondering if this was the kind of conversation his mother and Elliot had had. Dana sighed and stroked the back of her neck.

"I don't know," she whispered. Adrian nearly stopped breathing.

"So, if you are pregnant . . ."

"I don't know that either."

"All right," the driver said, "here's your stop."

Adrian paid the driver as Dana climbed out of the cab. He looked at her standing on the curb and couldn't help imagining her with her belly full of his son or daughter. But did she want that? Would he be doing the opposite of what his father did all those years ago and have to talk Dana into being a family with him?

"Who would want to be a part of this circus?" Adrian mumbled as he crossed over to Dana.

"Let's get this test and go. Some chips too," she said as they walked into the store.

"Maybe you should get some crackers. That's what they eat on TV."

Dana laughed. "We're so clueless." They headed to the aisle with the pregnancy tests and condoms. Adrian remarked on how ironic it was that drugstores grouped those items together.

"If someone had used one, they wouldn't need the other," he said as Dana picked up a test.

"I guess we'll find out soon if we're the poster child for this section." She pointed to a box of Trojans. "We should stock up."

Adrian reached for a twelve-pack of Trojan Magnums. "You know those other ones are too small."

"Ha! You're right, though," she said with a wink.

"What if we don't need them anymore?" he asked, growing serious. "If you're having my baby, I want you to know that I'm behind you one hundred percent."

Dana turned away from him, sucking on her bottom lip. "That's the least of my worries," she said. "I know you will be a great father. But . . ."

"You don't want a baby?"

"I don't know. I've always dreamed of the traditional family. I never wanted to be someone's baby's mother. And then there's my career."

"Is this a New York thing?" he snapped. "Money before children?"

"Don't do that to me!"

"What about what you want to do to me? If you are pregnant, you didn't make that baby alone."

"But if I am and I have this child, I'll be raising it alone. You live in LA and I'm not moving because you have daddy issues and want to transfer your bullshit to me."

A couple of customers glanced their way and Dana stormed to the register. Adrian followed her but kept silent. Before Dana could pull out the cash to pay for the test, Adrian slid his credit card to the cashier. He thought it was a wise decision to leave the condoms on the shelf, since he was sure there would be no sex going on between the two of them anytime soon.

"I didn't need you to do that," she gritted out.

"I don't want to fight with you right now," he replied.

Dana took her bag and rolled her eyes at him as she headed for the door. They walked the four blocks to Dana's brownstone in an uncomfortable silence. When they reached the front stoop, she turned to him and sighed. "I have to say this and you can understand or you can let the past cloud your judgment. There was a time when I wanted nothing more than to have a baby with you. We were planning a future, remember? Then you left me. Fast forward two years and I've changed and you have your demons, so tell me why would I be excited about this situation?"

"Do you think I want to pass my demons on to my child?"

Dana felt two inches small. She'd been so worried about Adrian's so-called dark side that she hadn't allowed herself to realize he would never let those issues hurt his child. "I'm sorry," she said.

"Pregnant or not, I want a future with you. I need what we should've had two years ago. I messed up and allowed anger and the need for vengeance to take over my life. The truth is, we wouldn't be standing in this cloud of confusion if I had listened to my mother. Life is too short for me to stay angry. Nothing can change the past and what I did to my brothers was wrong. Hurting you was the worst thing that I've ever done, but I want you to know how much I love you. I need you, Dana. Whatever that test says, nothing is going to change the fact that I'm going to make you my wife."

Dana burst into tears and fell into his arms. Adrian cooed how much he loved her in her ear as he stroked her back. She looked into his eyes and he wiped a tear away from her cheek. "Let's go inside," she said. "And I love you."

Once the couple made it inside, Dana rushed to the bathroom and opened the test. Her mind was still muddled with thoughts of motherhood. Was she ready? Even knowing that Adrian was all in, she wasn't sure if she was ready. Reading the instructions, she sighed and sat on the toilet.

"I can do this," she whispered. "I can take this test and live with the results."

Adrian paced back and forth in Dana's bedroom. He started to turn the television on when his cell phone rang. He started to ignore the call, but he thought it might be business—until he saw the New York exchange. It had to be the lab.

"Hello?"

"Mr. Bryant, this is Lydia Guthrie from Mount Sinai Medical Center."

"Yes?"

"We got the results back from your blood test and, unfortunately, you are not a viable match for a bone marrow transplant for Mr. Crawford."

Adrian sighed, feeling a little bit of relief. "Okay. So, what does this mean for him?" he asked as he locked eyes with Dana, who'd just walked into the room holding the Clearblue Easy test stick.

"We're going to search the National Bone Marrow registry for a match, unless there is another family member who meets the criteria."

"I wouldn't know about that," Adrian said as he studied Dana's face. She was smiling, but was she happy with a negative result? Was she happy because she was pregnant? All he knew was he needed to get off the phone and find out what was going on.

Chapter 20

Dana had questions about the tail end of that phone call, but she knew Adrian wanted an answer.

"So?" he asked.

"Yes, we're going to be parents." She held the stick out to him. Adrian dropped his phone and drew Dana into his arms, spinning her around.

She placed her hand on his chest. "Hold up. Was that about your father?"

His excitement dimmed. "Yeah."

"Are you—"

"I'm not a match and I'm not upset about it."

Dana placed her hand to her mouth. "Adrian."

"I'd be less than honest if I said I'm upset. I hope the hospital finds a donor for Elliot. I don't want Solomon and Richmond to lose the last parent they have. But I couldn't save my mother."

Dana hugged him and his hurt resonated. "You should talk to him before it's too late."

"You know what," he said, "I don't want to think about that right now. I want to kiss my future wife and the mother of my child."

He captured her mouth in a hot kiss that made her shiver and her knees quake. Then in the worst moment ever, she felt nauseous. Pulling back, she rushed into the bathroom and wondered if this was going to be the next nine months of her life.

Adrian had no idea what to do to ease Dana's nausea, so he walked into the kitchen and brewed her a cup of tea. Though she didn't have any saltine crackers, Adrian found a box of Ritz. He placed a few on a saucer with the lemon tea and headed into the bedroom. Dana was sitting on the edge of the bed rubbing the back of her neck.

"All right, Princess Kate, here's some tea and crackers."

Dana offered him a sheepish grin. "Thank you. I have to get it together for my meeting in a few days."

Adrian joined her on the bed as she sipped her tea. He took her feet onto his lap and massaged them. Dana moaned in pleasure and she felt her stomach settling down. "I hope this isn't going to last nine months."

"If it does, we're going to have to buy more crackers."

Dana set her cup and saucer on the nightstand and gave in to the blissfulness of the foot massage.

She leaned back on the bed and drifted off to sleep. Adrian dropped her feet and pulled her jeans off and tucked her in. As much as he wanted to push his father out of his mind, Adrian couldn't shut his mind down and join Dana in a restful sleep.

The next morning, Dana woke up with no morning sickness and in bed alone. She was low-key pissed off until Adrian walked into the bedroom with a tray of fresh fruit, tea, and orange juice.

"Morning," he said as he walked over to the side of her bed and set the tray on the nightstand.

Dana smiled and wrapped her arms around his neck. "I could get used to this," she said.

"Breakfast in bed is my specialty," he joked. "I also stocked the kitchen with food. No hot dogs, though."

"Discovered Key Food, huh?" she asked.

He nodded. "I wasn't sure that I was going to find a grocery store around here, but walking a few miles, you can find anything."

Dana sipped her tea and nodded. "It was only a few blocks."

"Whatever. And this was left for you at the door," he said when he handed her a slip from a delivery company. "I guess your bike is in the city."

Dana's eyes twinkled.

"Umm," Adrian began. "You know there's no way in hell you're getting back on that bike."

"Are we starting this again? I am going to ride until the doctor tells me that I can't and after the baby is born—"

He shook his head and took her face into his hands. "You don't get it, do you? I worried about you when you were riding the motorcycle in Los Angeles. Riding with you, I worried about us. Now if you think I'm going to watch you—while you're carrying my baby—then you're out of your mind."

Dana tilted her head to the side and picked a pineapple from her plate. Now, she had no plans to ride the motorcycle and Adrian's concern made her want to laugh. She had to wonder, though, did he think she was going to strap a car seat to the back of the bike and take the baby around the city?

"This is going to be a long nine months if you try to micromanage my pregnancy," she said.

"I'm not trying to do that but . . . okay, I am trying to do that." Adrian shrugged. "I'm not going to lie, I'm scared."

"And so am I, but we can't live in a bubble. And I have to make an appointment with my OB to confirm the pregnancy. Maybe I should ride the motorcycle over there."

He narrowed his eyes at her. "I'll let the air out of your tires."

"You would do something like that," she said with a laugh.

He nodded and swiped a blueberry from her plate. "But I'm sure you won't force my hand."

"So, when I make this appointment with my OB, are we going to go to the hospital so you can see your fa—Elliot?"

Adrian stroked the back of his neck. "I thought

about that when I was searching for a supermarket. Maybe going back to the hospital isn't a good idea. If Solomon is still angry, we're going to fight again and this time, I will hit him back. Then there's the media."

Dana placed her hand on his shoulder. "Stop making excuses. You need to talk to him and at least get whatever you have on your chest off. I'll go with you and distract your brother so that you can have a fight-free visit with your—"

"Elliot."

"Yeah. Elliot."

Adrian placed his hand on Dana's still-flat belly. "This baby will never have to wonder what to call me or who I am to him."

"She is going to be a daddy's girl because she's already giving me hell," Dana quipped.

"I guess we'll see."

"You know," she said in between sips of tea, "when a man has a daughter after living a life of . . . uh—"

"It's called karma," he finished. "God punishes players, heartbreakers, and pimps with beautiful little girls and surrounds them with knucklehead little boys."

"I wouldn't be surprised if we have twin girls," she said.

"I wasn't that bad," Adrian said with a laugh.

"That's highly debatable." Dana picked up her phone and dialed her doctor's office. Adrian headed to the bathroom and took a quick shower. Dana was right; he did need to visit Elliot and have that final talk with him. He needed to make peace with his family because he didn't want his child—who he hoped would be a little girl with a smile like her mother's—to grow up in the middle of his one-man war.

After his shower, he returned to the bedroom and found Dana snuggled in bed, sound asleep. He dressed quietly, trying not to wake her. He failed.

"How long have I been sleeping?" she asked with a yawn.

"Not long. You rest, though. I'm going to the hospital to see Elliot."

Dana nodded. "My appointment with the OB is at three. Call me if you can't make it or if you and Solomon end up acting like MMA fighters again."

Adrian put his hands together and bowed at the waist. "I go in peace."

She eased up in the bed on her elbows. "Do you want me to go with you? I don't mind."

Smiling, he crossed over to her and kissed her forehead. "I'll be back before your doctor's appointment."

"Okay."

Once she was alone in her brownstone, Dana found herself unable to go back to sleep. She tossed and turned for a few moments before she got out of bed and took a soothing bath. After sinking into the warm water, Dana's cell phone rang and she groaned.

Slowly, she pulled herself out of the tub and grabbed her phone from the bedroom. "Yes?" she snapped when she answered without looking at the display.

"So, you two have come up for air," Imani quipped.

"I was going to call you."

"When? After two or three kids?"

Dana broke out laughing. "Are you having me followed?"

"No, but you two did make the *LA Weekly*. There is a story about the Crawford family, the call girl, who by the way says your man paid her to get in the car with Richmond."

"I know the story about that," she replied.

"And that's who you love?"

Dana sighed. "You need to give it a rest. I'm sure your godson or goddaughter will want you to get along with his or her father."

"What are you . . . Dana! You're pregnant?"

"Yes, maybe. I'm going to the doctor later to find out."

She could hear Imani sighing and imagined her friend struggling to find the right words to say with her lips twisted. "I can't believe this. At least our babies will grow up together. Wait, are you going to leave New York?"

"I don't know," she said. "We haven't talked about it. But Adrian's business is on the West Coast and—"

"But you are so New York. You're like Jay-Z. And I'd miss you too much if you left."

"So, this is about you?" Dana laughed.

"Partly. But what else is new? Seriously, if you're in LA and he turns out to be an asshole, how will me and my Brooklyn hoods get to put our paws on him?" Imani burst out laughing. "I'm sorry, I've been watching too much reality TV and reading this script too much. So, are you thinking of moving? Has he stepped up to do the right thing and marry you?"

"Adrian and I have talked about marriage. And you know what, I'm going to marry him. You're going to stand up for me as my matron of honor with a smile on your face."

"If this is what you want, then I have no choice but to support you."

"That's a ringing endorsement."

"Okay, I need to get to know this guy, all right?"

"I get that, but what you need to know is I love him and I want you to be happy for me."

"I am happy for you and I'm serious—I'll support this union but I'm keeping my eye on this guy."

"Yes, you and your imaginary Brooklyn gangsters will come after him and beat him down."

"Keep thinking they're imaginary," Imani laughed. "As long as Mr. Slick doesn't hurt you again, you guys will never meet them."

"How's the filming going?"

"Eh, it's a lot better since the recast."

"Ooh, who go fired?"

"Whiny old Heather. I don't know what your future brother-in-law did to her but since they were in the papers, that is all she could talk about. It got so bad that she called a character Solomon. The producers and the director tried to work with her, but she was more annoying than ever. I say good riddance. You know, she had the nerve to call me fat."

"What?"

"Yes, evil cow. I'm not even showing yet, but somehow she made a big fuss about me calling her out for the fact that she was still holding on to ten of the fifteen pounds she gained for that Oscar-nominated role."

"Mani! That was mean."

"Well, I'm pregnant. She has no excuse and I'm not sorry I hurt her feelings. Heather is a grade A bitch. If she was smart, she'd check into rehab like Demi Lovato and get some help."

"You know it doesn't work that way for us in Hollywood. If she goes to get help, Heather will forever be the crazy girl who studios won't work with. So you know what this means for you."

"What?"

"You'd better keep your crazy under wraps."

"Anyway!" Imani said. "Speaking of under wraps, you're going to have to keep that horrible motorcycle in storage now. That's a silver lining when it comes to Adrian."

"I see that both of you have the same idiotic thoughts about my Fat Bob."

"Oh, you think tooling around New York on a

motorcycle while carrying my godchild is a good idea?"

"I'm sure my godchild is loving jumping off fake buildings on a soundstage," Dana shot back.

"I have great stunt doubles. One chick looks so much like me, I think I need to ask my father if he has something he needs to share with the rest of the class."

Dana wanted to laugh, but thinking of the situation with Adrian and the Crawfords, she couldn't. Imani recognized her joke was in poor taste as well and offered her friend an apology.

"I can't imagine what Adrian is going through right now. Between the media, his fight with Solomon and now about to lose his father."

"He never calls him his father. It's just sad." Dana touched her stomach. "But when he found out about the baby, he was so excited."

"I bet he wants to give your baby the life he never had. Are you sure he asked you to marry him because he loves you and not because he's trying to make up for the life he didn't have?"

Dana was glad Imani tapped into what she'd been thinking. She sighed and said, "I don't know. I hope that it's not a sense of obligation. You know what, I know it's not that."

"I'm sure it isn't. People don't really do the shotgun-wedding thing anymore," Imani said in an attempt to reassure her friend. "After all, he asked you to marry him. You didn't make it a condition of having the baby."

"No, I didn't."

"But your doctor is going to make you stop riding that bike. I can't tell you how excited that makes me."

"Well, if I have to stop riding, at least I know a doctor in Harlem who would love to purchase my Harley."

"And if you're talking about my husband, I'm going to hurt you."

"I am talking about your husband and you'll just deal with it. Speaking of dealing with things, how are you handling morning sickness?"

"Oh, I don't have morning sickness. I have wake-you-up-in-the-middle-of-the-night sickness. Then when morning comes, I'm too tired to get up and throw up."

"Well, I knew something was wrong when I threw up while eating a hot dog from Gray's."

"Stop it! Is that an alien baby in there? I wish I could get to Gray's right now."

"When does filming wrap on this movie?" Dana asked. "And I thought you were coming to New York to do a Broadway show?"

"Raymond told me that I could do the movie or the show but not both because a pregnant woman needs rest. Since he's a doctor and my baby daddy, I had to listen. Actually, I'm glad I did because I've learned something."

"What's that?"

"I can play Superwoman on screen, but I am really human. This baby is sapping my energy."

"Wow. The most interesting part of this conversation is the fact that you thought you were a superhero."

"Oh, please. You ride a motorcycle because you think you're Batgirl, so hush. I have to go. They need me on set."

"All right, I will give you a call later. After Raymond and I agree on a price for the bike."

"Don't you dare," she laughed.

When Dana hung up with Imani, she really felt as if she had her friend's support. Now she prayed that Adrian would find some peace and acceptance with his family.

Chapter 21

Adrian looked over his shoulder, hoping that he'd lost the photographer who'd been tailing him all morning. The man, dressed in a faded black T-shirt and a pair of cargo shorts, was still a few feet away from him. "Damn it," he muttered. Adrian stopped and waited for the man to catch up with him. "What do you want?"

"I'm just trying to do my job. A picture of you and the Crawfords would pay my rent for a year."

Adrian clenched his fists and fought the urge to punch the man in the face and smash his camera on the concrete. "You know what, you slimy piece of—"

"Listen, you went to the media first and now you want to act as if you want privacy? Get over yourself," the photographer spat.

Adrian was about to deck him when he felt a hand on his shoulder.

"It's not even worth it," Solomon said. Adrian turned and looked at his brother. "This guy has been following the family since we came back to New York."

"Why don't you let me get this picture and then I'll leave you alone."

"You're going to leave us alone anyway," Adrian snapped. "Now get the hell away from here."

"That's right!" Solomon said. "And don't even think about snapping a picture."

"Come on," the photographer pleaded, holding his camera up. Solomon, who had made avoiding the tabloids and paparazzi a sport, held up a copy of the *New York Times* and spread it wide so that his face wasn't visible. He passed another section of the paper to Adrian so that he could follow suit.

"Nice trick," Adrian said as they walked into the hospital.

"What are you doing here?" Solomon snapped. "It's your fault that they know Dad's here."

"And how's that? Because you sent me out in the street with a bloody nose?"

"I hope you aren't expecting an apology, because I'm not giving you one."

Adrian shook his head. "Have I ever asked you people for anything?"

"No, you just wanted to seek and destroy."

"I had every right to be angry and I'd like you to deny that you wouldn't have done the same thing."

Solomon stopped and turned to Adrian. "Okay, you're right. I probably would've done something similar, but it would have been directed at the right person."

"At the time," he said, "I painted all of you with the same brush."

"Listen, I don't know how we're supposed to do this thing here, being brothers or whatever. I already have a brother I don't care for."

Adrian shrugged and glanced at his brother as they entered the wing where Elliot was being housed. "I guess this is the part where we promise to keep in touch and keep our hands to ourselves."

"I must be getting soft," Solomon remarked as he looked at Adrian's nose. "The bridge is still intact, not much of a bruise either."

"Come on, pretty boy, you know you're not much of a bruiser."

Solomon laughed. "Not these days. I have a wife who frowns on that kind of behavior."

Adrian's smile revealed a lot and Solomon pounced. "That woman who was with you, you're serious about her?"

"I'm going to marry her," Adrian said. "And her name is Dana."

"Dana Singleton? The photographer?"

"Yeah, how do you know her?" Dread crept up his neck. Knowing Solomon's reputation with women, he couldn't help but wonder if there was something . . .

"Dad wanted her to take the pictures for the book, but she had another assignment."

Adrian rolled his eyes. Luckily, that assignment brought her to Los Angeles and thank God she wasn't able to work with the Crawfords on that book.

"So, were you behind that as well?" Solomon asked.

"No. She was working with Sony and Universal for the new movie that your . . . that Heather Williams and Imani Thomas were in."

Solomon rolled his eyes. "I almost want to punch you again."

"What happened with you and Heather? If you don't mind me asking."

Solomon shrugged. "She wasn't the one. Plain and simple. At the time, I had some ideas about screenwriting, leaving the family business, and doing what I really loved. I dated her and she took it more seriously than she should have. I never told her I was in love with her. She just assumed that I would give her a chance because she was supposed to introduce me to some of the same producers I already knew."

"So, you used to use women?"

"I wouldn't say I was using her, but I wasn't trying to be her man either. If I really wanted a movie deal, I could've purchased one or a studio. But that was a different time in my life and other things were important to me back then."

"Whoa," Adrian replied. "I would've never expected you to be that guy."

Solomon furrowed his eyebrows. "That guy? What do you mean?"

"Someone who would want to go into show business."

"Believe it or not, I wanted to get as far away from the Crawford name and everything it stood for. Then I got my heart broken and decided to get some payback and break some hearts."

"That's a story I'd like to hear one day," Adrian said with a laugh.

"Nah, I believe in leaving the past in the past, especially when I have a bright future like I do now."

Adrian glanced at Solomon and nodded. He had a future and he couldn't wait until he was able to call Dana his wife. "Listen, I have to genuinely apologize for trying to come between you and your wife."

"That was low and I was tempted to do something more than punching you in the face."

"Yeah, it was. I've come to realize that love is a beautiful thing and it should be cherished."

"She has you wide open, huh?" Solomon chuckled softly. "It's amazing that any man with Elliot's DNA understands what it means to love someone else."

Adrian glanced at Elliot, who looked to be sleeping. "I got the results back from the blood test."

"What's the result?" Solomon asked, peering at his father.

"I wasn't a match. The nurse said something about continuing to search for a donor on the national registry."

"Yeah, at least Richmond will be here in the morning. Hopefully it won't be too late. I can't believe he kept this from me."

"What was it like, growing up with him? I know what you said in LA about him, but there has to be something there."

"He's my father and I can't say that he was Bill Cosby, but he was there. Distance at times, especially when I was around seven and started writing stories and wanted to share them with him. I wonder, now, if he was simply longing to see what his other son was doing. Dad and I didn't become close until I showed a real interest in the business. Once he saw that I inherited his desire to make money and had ideas that didn't mirror everything my mother had drilled into Richmond's head, I became his favorite son."

"Umm," Adrian replied. "But here you are . . ."

"Here we are. No matter what, he gave us life and I don't want to see him suffer if I could've helped him."

Adrian didn't say a word; he just watched Solomon's face fall as he continued to look at his father. "I need to talk to him, in private," Adrian said. He held up his hand as Solomon started to protest. "Look, I'm not going to pull the plug."

"I don't know if—"

"Dana said I need to make peace with him and she's right. I'm past the anger and disappointment because I have to get myself together for my son or daughter."

"What?"

"I'm going to marry Dana and we're starting a family. She's pregnant . . . at least we think she is." Adrian glanced at his watch. "And I have to get back to Brooklyn before her doctor's appointment."

"The moment I hear something getting out of hand in this room, I'm coming in."

Adrian gave his brother a salute and walked into his father's room. Adrian took a seat next to Elliot's bed. He watched the older man's chest rise and fall. For a brief moment, it was as if he were looking at his mother all over again. A ripple of emotions tore through him as he reached for Elliot's hand.

The old man's eyes fluttered open. "Adrian," he whispered.

"Yeah, it's me."

"What are you doing here? I thought—"

"When I came to New York, I had no idea how sick you were."

"I wasn't sure you'd give a damn," he replied, then coughed. His entire body shook. "I can't blame you if you're here to gloat."

"I don't get down like that. Life is precious."

"I know. Maybe I found out too late. Everything I've ever taken for granted has turned out to be what I needed to focus on. I wish I had been able to know you. To be part of your life and more than just a check."

"Well," Adrian began, then stopped. He couldn't tell him that he was too late, especially since he was dying. "We can't change the past."

Elliot laughed. "Are you sure you don't have some political aspirations? That was the most politically correct statement I've ever heard."

"What can I say?" Adrian asked. "We can't change

anything and there isn't much time left for me to be angry. Besides, I'm going to have a family of my own soon."

"That's good, son." Elliot broke into another fit of coughing. "I look at Solomon and his family. I see he's making all of the choices I should've made. If I had followed my heart, things would have been different. I tried to justify what I did by saying I was building a legacy for all of my children. I'd hoped you'd be able to take part in that as well but—"

"Look," Adrian said, "you can't keep making excuses for the choice you made. You wanted money and got it at my mother's expense." He struggled to keep his voice down.

"That's true. I tried to—"

"Look, we can't live our lives in should ofs, would haves, and could ofs—we have to take what we did and make peace with it or live with it. I made choices that I'm not proud of as well. I wanted—or at least I thought I wanted—to see you and your family suffer."

"I can't blame you for that," Elliot whispered.

"But I blame myself. I nearly forgot what love was and what it meant to give love and be with that one person who means more to me than anything else. I almost allowed myself to make hate a way of life. Sort of the way you allowed money to take over your life." Adrian placed his hand on Elliot's shoulder and nodded. "I have to forgive you."

"I don't deserve your forgiveness."

"Yes, you do."

The door to Elliot's room swung open and Richmond stormed inside. "You have some nerve showing your face here. Are you trying to get Dad to change his will or are you just here to make sure he dies?"

"This isn't the place," Adrian said.

Elliot was too weak to address his sons. He pressed the button on his IV for more pain medication. Richmond glared at Adrian and didn't hide his disgust when Solomon walked into the room.

"You're in on this too," Richmond demanded.

"You want to take all of this noise outside?" Solomon asked through clenched teeth. He nodded toward Elliot. "Do you think he needs this right now?"

"But he needed a visit from this guy?" Richmond retorted.

Adrian shook his head. "I'm going to let you argue alone," he said to Richmond. "Being that you grew up with him and had more of a relationship with him than I did, it seems as if you'd know better."

Adrian started for the door with Richmond on his heels. "What do you want? Money? A place in the company? No one owes you anything and—"

"I'm sorry that you think money is the only thing people want out of life. Money kept your parents together. Money forced me to grow up without knowing who my father was. I don't give a damn about money and I don't need it. If you haven't noticed, I've done well for myself without Crawford dollars. I wanted to know this man and why things happened the way they did. I wanted to make all of you suffer and I was wrong. I was being the ass-hole I accused him of being. What I'm not going to tolerate is facing an accusation every time I'm in your presence."

Solomon stopped Richmond from replying. "Dad's not breathing."

The three men rushed to Elliot's bed as alarms began sounding and a team of doctors and nurses burst through the door.

"We need room," the head nurse said. "You three have to go."

Dana glanced at her watch and wondered what was keeping Adrian. He knew her appointment was at three. She called him for a second time and the call went straight to voice mail.

She didn't have time to wait for him anymore. Dana grabbed her keys and her purse, then headed out the door. As soon as she started for the subway station, her phone chimed. Plucking it from her pocket, she saw that it was Adrian.

"You'd better have a good excuse."

He sighed and said, "He's gone."

"What?"

"Elliot died."

"Are you okay?" she asked.

"I don't know. I didn't expect to feel anything."

"Should I—"

"I'm going to meet you at the doctor's office. Just text me the address and Solomon said he'd put me in a car so that I can get to you and get away from Richmond."

Dana stifled a laugh, imagining that Richmond wanted to punch his brother as well. "I will send you the address and I'll see you there."

Hanging up with him, Dana liked what she heard. Emotion. Maybe his father's death had spurred him into thinking about his family and hopefully he made peace with his father before it was too late.

She inhaled sharply and texted the address to Adrian and entered the subway station. To her surprise and happiness, the train was on time and not as packed as she had expected it to be.

"Thank God for small miracles," she whispered as she took an empty seat and stuck her earbuds in her ears. As she rocked out to The Roots' latest, she nearly missed her stop. When Dana arrived at the doctor's office, Adrian was standing outside waiting for her.

"I'm going to need you to stop taking the subway as your main mode of transportation."

"Is that an endorsement for my motorcycle?" she asked with a wide grin.

"Absolutely not!" Adrian nearly shouted. "We're going to have to get a minivan or—"

"Now, I'm not going to drive a minivan—ever!"

Adrian drew her into his arms. "Where are we going to put the other five kids if we don't get a van or at the least an SUV?"

"Carbon footprint," she said. "Wait a minute, did you say other five kids?"

"Yes, I want a big family. So big we're going to have to move out of the city and get a ranch."

"I'd like to see that, you living on a ranch and me pushing out six babies," Dana said. She stroked Adrian's cheek. "Are you all right?"

He shrugged. "I'm fine, I guess."

"Were you able to talk to him before he . . . you know?"

Adrian nodded but left out the part about his brother coming into the room and starting an argument with him moments before Elliot died. "I don't have all the answers and I doubt I will ever get them. But I've made my peace with that. Maybe my mother had the right idea."

"Which was?"

"Getting to know the family," he said. "I wish I hadn't immediately jumped on my father's case and not started this war that no one would ever win."

Dana stood on her tiptoes and kissed him. "Now you can focus on the love instead of the war." She placed his hand on her stomach. "It starts here."

Adrian rubbed her belly. "That's right," he said.

"Let's get inside and find out when this bundle of joy will bless us with his presence."

"Her presence. This baby is your karma and she's going to be the prettiest little girl you've ever seen."

"Of course, look at her mother," Adrian said with a wink. Once they entered the doctor's office, they didn't have a long wait to see Dr. Angela Kendall.

She confirmed the home pregnancy test result after taking a blood sample from Dana. Adrian felt as if he could fly when the doctor gave them the results. Smiling, he turned to Dr. Kendall and said, "I have a question."

Dana rolled her eyes, knowing exactly where he was going with this.

"Okay, what is it?" the doctor asked.

"A pregnant woman shouldn't ride a motorcycle, right?"

"Lord," Dana groaned. "Can we please settle this now because I don't want to keep hearing about this."

Dr. Kendall looked from Dana to Adrian. "So, Dana, you're the rider?"

"Yes."

"It's dangerous for the baby, right? Because she said if you told her it was, she'd give up the bike."

"Well," Dr. Kendall began. "Dana is in great shape. I'm sure she's a safe rider. While there isn't an immediate danger to the baby and Dana could ride the bike until she stops feeling comfortable, I don't recommend that be your main mode of transportation. The jarring motion of the motorcycle could cause discomfort for you." Dr. Kendall folded her hands underneath her chin. "I'm guessing that Daddy doesn't want you to ride, period."

"That would be correct," Adrian said.

"Well, this is going to be an argument you two will have to solve on your own."

"And," Dana said, "please tell him that a sports car is not a safer alternative."

Dr. Kendall threw her hands up. "I get the feeling that this was going on way before you guys started a family."

The couple nodded and Dr. Kendall laughed. "Soon enough, the baby will make the decision about the motorcycle and the sports car."

Dana rolled her eyes at Adrian as if she were telling him that she told him so. "Don't worry, Doc, I'm not going to do anything to put my baby in danger. And if I have to give up the motorcycle— for a while—then I will."

"We'll work on making that a forever thing," Adrian said with a laugh.

Dana nudged him in his side. "Whatever."

"I'm going to leave you two alone with this argument. I will say this—there aren't baby seats for Harleys. And I know I'd have a hard time giving mine up."

Adrian shook his head and as he and Dana left the office, he turned to her with a grin. "You would pick a doctor who shared your inane love of motorcycles."

"I didn't even know she had a motorcycle. Honest!"

"And you have a bridge in Brooklyn you want to sell me as well, huh?"

"No, but we do have to get something to eat."

"Well, we've been invited to dinner," he said.

"Really?"

Adrian nodded. "Solomon and I are trying to see how this being brothers thing works."

Dana hugged him tightly. "I'm really proud of you for doing this."

"I never turn down free food," he joked. "Let's get a cab. I will never get used to riding underground."

Dana grinned and squeezed his hand. "Sounds like you plan on sticking around."

"You know it."

Chapter 22

Later that evening, Dana and Adrian were walking into Solomon's penthouse on the Upper East Side. She watched him to see if he had a reaction to the luxurious life his brother was living. She saw none. Maybe he had changed. Maybe he was going to have a relationship with his brother. But Dana couldn't help wondering how he'd make things right with Richmond? After all, he had gotten the man arrested and possibly cost him his marriage. Pressing the doorbell, Adrian kissed Dana's cheek.

"I'm pretty sure there won't be any hot dogs on the menu," he said.

"What a pity," she replied as the door opened and Kandace greeted them.

"Hi," she said. "And what's a pity?"

Adrian tossed his thumb at Dana. "She's a hot dog addict."

"Show me a New Yorker who isn't," she replied as she ushered the couple inside. Dana smiled at

Kandace and complimented her on what a lovely home she had. Kandace leaned in to her and whispered, "The Southerner in me needs a yard."

"I bet you do," she said. "But you couldn't imagine living outside of the city, huh?"

"I wouldn't go that far." Kandace nodded toward Kiana, who was crawling around on the floor. "She needs a swing set."

Dana instinctively touched her stomach. Kandace smiled. "Are you?"

Dana nodded. "The doctor confirmed it today. I'm six weeks."

"Oh, I'm going to be an auntie," Kandace said excitedly. "Now I will have a baby in New York to spoil."

"At least part of the time," Dana said as she watched Adrian and Solomon chat in a corner near the window overlooking the sparkling skyline of the city. "I don't think Adrian is going to become a full-time New Yorker."

"I'm glad to see that he and Solomon are working out this thing between them and are trying to be a family."

Dana nodded in agreement. "I'm sorry that it took Elliot's death for it to happen."

The doorbell rang before Kandace could reply.

"I'll get it," Solomon called out from across the room.

Kandace and Dana headed for the kitchen, where two caterers were about to send trays of appetizers and fresh fruit out into the main room. "I actually miss cooking," Kandace said. "Well, honestly, I miss getting food from the restaurant in Charlotte. But I do have a surprise." She crossed over to the refrigerator and pulled out a pink box. "Devon Harris shipped a cake from Paris."

"You know Devon Harris? I had a chance to eat at his restaurant when I did that photo shoot in Paris."

Kandace smiled. "Devon and I go way back. He designed the menu at Hometown Delights in Charlotte and he's Kiana's godfather."

"Wow."

"And," Solomon said from the doorway, "he's the reason this woman was single and waiting for me to sweep her off her weary feet."

Kandace rolled her eyes. "Don't believe him. And what are you doing in here?"

"Trying to figure out what's going on and give Richmond and Adrian a chance to talk." Solomon crossed over to Kandace. "If Richmond was smart, he'd realize that Vivvy leaving him behind this is a blessing."

"She left him?" Kandace asked, then brought her hand to her mouth.

Dana felt as if this was a conversation she shouldn't be privy to, but she didn't want to stroll into the living room and interrupt what she was sure had to be an explosive conversation.

* * *

Richmond paced back and forth in front of the window as Adrian stood in one spot. "You're a son of a bitch!" Richmond exploded.

"Yeah, I can be."

"You ruined my life with that damned stunt of yours. If it wasn't for the hooker being honest . . . Why did you do it?"

"Honestly, I wanted you and Solomon to suffer. And I wanted the construction of the hotel to be stymied by controversy."

"Why? Because of my father's actions? Like I had anything to do with that."

"I was misguided and I was wrong. Maybe you can explain to your wife what—"

"She gone," Richmond said, and dropped his head. "Before the news of my arrest was even public knowledge, she was gone."

"I'm sorry that happened," Adrian said. "I—"

"Can't really blame you for the loss of my marriage, but everything else I do hold you responsible for. The cost overrun on the construction of Crawford Towers and all the bad publicity, it's all your fault."

"We've been over this. But look, we're family and we're all we have left. I want to make a serious effort to get to know you and Solomon. Especially since I'm about to start a family of my own. I don't want my child to grow up around the bitterness and the fighting."

"And you think all is supposed to be forgiven because you said so?"

"No, but what other choice do we have? You already know I don't play fair. We can be enemies or we can learn how to be a family."

"What about my wife? What about the family I lost behind your bull?"

"If you really love her and if she loves you, then she'll be back."

Richmond walked over to the bar in the corner and poured himself a snifter full of scotch. "I wonder how Dad had two women, Solomon had so many and still found the one woman perfect for him, and I can't find someone to love me."

Adrian glanced at Dana, Kandace, and Solomon as they headed toward them. "There's someone for everyone. Maybe your wife wasn't the right one for you."

Richmond sighed as if he'd heard those things before. "Perhaps you're right," he said, then downed the glass of whiskey.

"Everything all right in here?" Solomon asked. "I see we're drinking my good stuff."

Richmond rolled his eyes and poured himself another healthy dose of liquor. "What are you going to do now that you're unemployed?" Richmond asked.

"File for unemployment," he quipped.

"You need to rethink resigning," Richmond said. "We have to present a united front now that Dad's gone."

"Maybe you ought to think about something more than work these days," Solomon said.

Richmond folded his arms and Kandace pushed his glass out of his reach. "And what should I focus on? I don't have a wife. I don't have kids. All I have is Crawford Hotels, so what do I need to focus on?"

"Not this alcohol," Kandace said. "Let's go sit down and eat."

Dana crossed over to Adrian and whispered, "Did everything go all right?"

"As well as can be expected," he said, then kissed her on the cheek. "He's mad."

"He has every right to be," Dana interjected.

Adrian agreed. "I know, but he needs to chill out. This could be a new start for all of us."

Dana glanced over at Richmond, who was scowling as he took a seat at the dining room table. "I don't think he's going to be chilling out anytime soon. Adrian, you ruined his life. Do you know his wife left him?"

"Yeah, we were discussing it. But from what he was telling me, his marriage was at the end anyway."

"Didn't mean you needed to help it along."

He wrapped his arms around Dana's waist. "Let's eat and then you can show me why this is the city that never sleeps."

"I like the sound of that."

After a quiet—at least when it came to this crew—dinner, Richmond turned to Solomon and Adrian and said, "We should run Crawford Hotels together. We can keep the media out of our business, assure the stockholders that the company is in good hands, and—"

"I don't know a thing about the hotel business," Adrian said before Solomon could reply. "And I have a business and a life in Los Angeles."

Dana sipped her grape juice slowly. She wished Adrian would've immediately agreed to joining the company and move to New York. But he was right; he had a business to run in Los Angeles and moving away so quickly wasn't going to be easy.

"What about the life you're trying to have here?" Solomon asked. "Even though I didn't want this to be a business dinner, Richmond makes a good point about us putting together a united front."

Kandace turned to Dana. "This is where we take our leave."

"No, I want to finish my cake."

Solomon turned to Dana. "I don't mean to put you in the middle," he began.

"But you are," Adrian said with a frown clouding his face.

"You did the same damned thing to us," Richmond slurred.

Solomon nodded. "At least we're up front about it."

"That hurts," Adrian replied with a laugh.

"But it was warranted," Kandace said as she returned to her seat and waved for one of the caterers. She whispered for him to bring cake slices and no knives.

"Listen," Solomon said. "Lost, and I mean Lost, Angeles is a great city to visit. But who wants to raise a family in a world of distorted body images and fake skyscrapers."

"Wow," Dana whispered. "That was a low blow."

"First of all," Adrian said, "I don't live on a movie set, and secondly, my son isn't going to have to worry about that kind of stuff."

"Son?" Solomon asked. "And you know this because?"

"Because I had a talk with God," Adrian replied.

Richmond groaned and reached for Kandace's full glass of wine. She snatched it away from him. "You're cut off," she said as the caterer placed cake slices on the table.

"I asked God for a son too," Solomon said, then nodded toward a portrait on the wall. "I was blessed with a little girl who will probably date men just like her dad."

"Not on my watch," Kandace said, and she and Dana broke out into laughter.

"Anyway," Solomon said, turning his attention back to Dana. "You know you can't get good hot dogs on the left coast."

"Please, don't remind me," she said.

"Do I need to remind you about the last time you had a famous New York hot dog?" Adrian asked.

Richmond groaned again. "Either we're going to do it or we're not. Why do we have to beg him to be a part of the family?"

"I thought family was about more than a business," Adrian said.

Richmond narrowed his eyes at Adrian. "What

do you even know about family? You're the reason why we need to do damage control."

"Richmond, calm down," Solomon said.

"And you! You walked away from the company when Dad needed you and I guess you think that teaming up with this guy will give you an edge?"

"You're drunk and you're about to get punched in the face," Solomon gritted. "And you brought this up."

"I'm tired of being the odd man out," he said. "Tired of being silly Richmond Crawford—who isn't really Elliot Crawford's son but cared about him a hell of a lot more than the two with his DNA." Richmond pushed away from the table, leaving everyone with their mouths hanging wide open. He stumbled to the sofa and dropped down. Adrian and Solomon exchanged confused looks. Seconds later, they heard snoring coming from Richmond's direction.

"Was that the rambling of a drunk man or is he telling the truth?" Adrian asked.

Solomon shrugged. "Maybe he found out when he tested to see if he was a match for Dad's DNA. What a twisted family tree we have."

Adrian dropped his head, not wanting to comment on Solomon's mother. Dana and Kandace sat in silence, watching as if they were viewing a big-screen movie.

"We're going to take off," Adrian said after a few moments of an uncomfortable silence.

Dana rose to her feet and exchanged a hug with Kandace. "Thanks for dinner."

"Anytime. Maybe we can do some shopping or something later this week," Kandace said, then shrugged.

"Give me your number. I get the feeling we're going to have a lot to talk about."

Kandace nodded and wrote her number down on a scrap of paper. "What are you all going to do about him?" Dana asked, nodding toward Richmond's sleeping form on the sofa.

"Sober him up and try to get him to realize that family is more than DNA." Kandace shook her head. "I've never liked Vivian, but I feel like that man needs her right now."

"Maybe not," Dana said. "I don't know her, but maybe he needs a fresh start without her. Even though Adrian set it up, no happily married man would willingly sleep with a strange woman in the backseat of a car."

"You do have a point there." The women hugged again as Adrian approached them.

Once the couple made it outside, Adrian was still taken aback by the way dinner had turned out. Richmond wasn't his brother, Solomon wanted him to move to New York and be a part of a business he had no interest in, and he still had a wedding to plan.

"Are you all right?" Dana asked as they got into a black town car that Solomon had called for them.

"I'm beginning to think that my mother had the right idea."

"Which was?"

"Leaving this city and never looking back. That Crawford family tree is twisted as hell."

"They're still your family."

"Family, yes, but unlike Richmond, being a Crawford isn't my entire identity."

Dana stroked his hand. "At least they want to include you in—"

"You really love this city, huh?"

"Not as much as I love you," Dana replied. "I know you have a successful business in Los Angeles and you're a hands-on business guy."

"Yeah, but more than anything else, I want to be a hands-on father. And I am going to be an extremely hands-on husband. So, you tell me, do you want to live in New York or Los Angeles?"

"Is Chicago still an option?" she joked. "Adrian, wherever we are together, we'll be happy. I can set up a second studio in Los Angeles. My base can be here and I can work with the studios more often."

"And have our baby grow up on movie sets?"

"Or in the office of a nightclub?"

They both broke out laughing. "So, we're going to be a bicoastal family?" Adrian asked.

"Sure, when little Adrienne is three."

"Adrienne? The female version, because you're so sure that we're having a little girl? I'm sure Daniel will enjoy spending his formative years in Los Angeles."

"New York."

"LA."

She smiled and climbed onto his lap. Dana nuzzled his neck and flicked her tongue across his earlobe. "I bet I can change your mind."

"Mmm," he moaned as he felt his erection stretch against his zipper. "I'm sure you can." He slipped his hand underneath her dress. The smooth skin of her bottom made his anticipation grow as well as his erection. Then she ran her tongue up and down the column of his neck while unzipping his pants. Dana stroked him, making him moan without regard to the driver, who was getting an ear show.

"Let's hear it for New York," she whispered in his ear before easing down his body and taking his throbbing erection between her lips.

"Oh yes!" he exclaimed. "I love New York!"

Epilogue

Three months later, Adrian was still struggling with being a New Yorker. Subways sucked; he didn't give a damn about the convenience. Traffic leaving Manhattan to get to Brooklyn every day was, at times, worse than the PCH at five o'clock. Cabs sucked. The drivers seemed to do everything to ensure the passengers had a heart attack while sitting in the back of a vehicle that smelled like a summer day in Beirut.

But what he loved about New York was watching his woman work. And watching his child grow inside her. Dana was showing only slightly, but she glowed like a Christmas tree every time she woke up in his arms. Even Imani had warmed up to him. She was also pregnant, and she was pretty, but Dana was the most beautiful woman he'd ever seen.

While Adrian didn't officially join Crawford Hotels, he did offer his services as a consultant for the LA project. He and Solomon got along as if they'd grown up together—most days.

He and Solomon were headstrong and always thought they were right. That led to a few arguments and threats of violence that usually ended when Solomon broke out the good liquor. Richmond, who had buried himself in work after learning of his paternity and the quickie divorce that Vivvy had gotten done in Mexico, tried to loosen up. He still had work to do. But Adrian was glad to see that he hadn't crawled into the bottom of a bottle.

Standing at the bay window in Solomon's office, Adrian smiled as he looked at the skyline. He really did love New York.

"Yo," Solomon said, breaking into Adrian's thoughts.

"What?"

"I said are you going to stare out the window all day or do you have some information for me about the opening party at Crawford Towers?"

"Yeah," he said. "It's in the file I e-mailed to you."

"I thought you said we needed to talk?" Solomon asked as he kicked his feet up on his desk.

"We do need to talk. But it's not about business."

"Okay," Solomon said as he flipped through some photos on his iPad. Adrian glanced over his brother's shoulder and saw the pictures were of his niece, Kiana. "You staring or you want to talk? I'm a busy man."

"Yeah, whatever. She's a beautiful little girl. Are

you ever worried about what happens when she grows up and meets a man of—"

"He'd better be a track star because if I get my hands on him, he's a goner."

"That's why I pray for a son every night. I hurt Dana in the middle of all of this. The fact that she agreed to marry me and have my child, it's unbelievable. I want our wedding to be magical. Something that will knock her off her feet."

"And you're doing it in New York, right? You know a divorce in California will cost you half."

Adrian raised his eyebrow at his brother. "Cynical much?"

"Yeah, when it comes to other people's marriages, not mine. I'm in it for the long haul and a few more kids."

"Anyway, no offense, but New York isn't that romantic to me. Between the subways and crazy cabdrivers, I have to get her out of this city to marry her."

"But what does Dana want?" Solomon asked. "She's the bride and the bride always gets what she wants."

"I want to surprise her."

"Bad idea."

Adrian stroked his chin and recounted Dana's hand in Imani's surprise Jamaican wedding. "I think her best friend would help with a little payback. The problem is, I don't want to take my pregnant fiancée too far away."

"I don't blame you on that. Kandace said I held

her hostage when she was pregnant, but that they don't get it. I felt so helpless when she was pregnant and that's not how I roll. But she was determined to go to Charlotte and Atlanta."

"You let her go?"

"I didn't have a choice. As quiet as it's kept, I just do what that woman says because her happiness means everything to me."

"The mighty Solomon Crawford is whipped."

"Yeah, pot, I'm whipped and proud of it."

They stopped talking when a scowling Richmond walked into the office and dropped a file at Solomon's propped up feet. "Here's the report from the resort in the Pocono Mountains."

Solomon picked up the report and then banged his hand on the desk. "This is it. You can get married here."

"What?" Richmond snapped. "Who's getting married?"

Solomon tilted his head toward Adrian. "He's trying to surprise Dana with a wedding."

Richmond rolled his eyes. "You'd be better off to forget a wedding."

"You two are some—" Adrian stopped short, remembering how bitter Richmond's divorce from Vivian Crawford was.

"Well," Richmond said, "there is a chapel at the resort and the property manager was planning to promote summer and autumn weddings."

"Hold up, my wedding is not going to be some marketing campaign."

"Of course not," Richmond said. "But there is a faculty there—you have a built-in excuse to get Dana there."

"Yeah, pretend we're opening a club in the resort and we have to check the place out," Solomon said.

"I like Dana," Richmond blurted out. "She's a really good woman and those are rare to find."

"Tell me about it," Adrian said. "Now I have to get Imani on board. Our relationship is just a thread. If I don't hip her to the plan, then she's going to hate me forever."

"All right," Solomon said, then nodded toward Richmond. "Good job."

"I used to be romantic and the like. I guess I got my balls back," Richmond said.

Solomon smirked and tipped his imaginary hat to his brother. "Then you can plan the bachelor party."

Richmond rolled his eyes and walked out of the office. He stopped at the door and turned to his brothers with a half-smile on his face. "Just let me know when I need to show up in Pennsylvania."

"Will do," Adrian said. "And thanks."

"Hopefully this is a favor I won't have to extend again."

It took two weeks for Adrian to get everything set up for his surprise wedding. Imani, who was finished filming her latest movie, had been more than happy to help Adrian.

"This had better work out," she said when he called her with instructions for the wedding cake.

"It's going to work out, I'm sure . . ."

"I'm not talking about the wedding, Mr. Slick."

"Are you ever going to call me Adrian?"

"Maybe on your seventy-fifth wedding anniversary—then I'll know it's real."

"It's very real, Mrs. Actress, and I have to say, I don't think *Fearless Diva* is that bad of a movie."

"See what I'm saying? Mr. Slick. That movie sucked ass. At least I can admit that now."

"I saw your last movie too. That was great as well," he said. "And that's the truth. Dana loves chocolate cake and—"

"Butter cream icing. I got this. I know what my best friend likes. And if you're smart, you'd better make sure there are some hot dogs close by."

"You two and these hot dogs."

Imani laughed. "You don't know how many dreams we discussed over those hot dogs."

"Or how many Broadway producers you two stalked?"

"Dang! Did Dana tell you everything?"

Before Adrian could respond, Dana walked through the front door of the brownstone. "All right," Adrian said as he rose from the sofa and crossed over to Dana. "I'll make sure to e-mail those details to you, Solomon."

"Tell Dana I said hello," Imani said before they ended the call.

"Hello, beautiful," he said as he took the camera bag from Dana's shoulder. She was a month away from the release of her book and had been finishing up a couple of sessions so that she would have a clear calendar for a short promotional tour.

"I wish I could see me through your eyes. I'm tired and annoyed."

"What's wrong with my baby?" he asked as he led her to the sofa. Adrian prompted her to stretch her legs on his lap. As he removed her shoe and massaged her feet, Dana told him about the Broadway cast she'd photographed that day and how annoying they'd been.

"I've dealt with some divas—hell, my best friend is one—but this cast took it to another level. Mmm, your hands are magical."

"You think so?" he said as his fingers danced up her calf. "I think you need to get away for a bit."

"Oh, I wish I could go with you on your next trip to LA." She placed her hand on her growing belly. "I might have one more ride in me."

"Yeah, no one is talking about going to LA, so you can keep that motorcycle in storage. Solomon and I are talking about beefing up the entertainment at the resort in the Poconos."

"The Poconos. I can't remember the last time I've been there. When are you guys going?"

"In a few days," he replied as he started on the other foot. "And there will be no motorcycle riding in the mountains."

She rolled her eyes and poked her bottom lip out as if she was upset. "You're no fun, Adrian."

He spread her legs apart and slipped between them. "I'll show you some fun," he said, then kissed her with a hot passion that made her forget about Broadway divas and motorcycles.

Two days later, Adrian and Dana arrived at the Crawford Mountain Resort. The first thing Dana did when she got out of the car was lift her camera and began snapping shots of the picture-perfect mountains behind the resort. As she walked around the side of the building and close to the edge of what Adrian thought was a steep cliff, he rushed over to her and grabbed her around her waist.

"What is wrong with you?" she snapped. "You know you messed up my shot!"

Adrian looked down and saw a two-inch drop, then kissed the back of her neck.

"You can't blame him," Solomon called out from behind them. "These first-time fathers think a woman can't walk when she's pregnant."

Kandace called out, "And he should know, because he was way worse."

Dana turned around and waved at Kandace. "I didn't know you were coming, but thank God you're here. Now I won't be bored while they talk business." She pushed past Adrian, just slightly perturbed about him messing up her picture. When he kissed her cheek, all was forgiven. Kandace and Dana headed into the resort, leaving Solomon, Adrian, and Richmond standing outside.

"So, does she suspect anything?" Solomon asked.

"If she doesn't, she will when she sees the three of us out here and no one's arguing," Richmond joked.

Solomon and Adrian looked at their brother,

then burst into laughter. Over the last few weeks, there had been a change in Richmond. He was relaxed and pretty funny. It was a good change to see.

"Well, let's wrap this up, then," Solomon said. "I got a message from the front desk that Imani and Raymond are checked in. Kandace and Dana should be heading to the spa soon."

Adrian nodded. "Is the cake here?"

"Yes," Richmond said. "The restaurant e-mailed me the menu for the reception."

"Then I guess it's time to get fitted for—"

"The monkey suits," Richmond said.

Solomon shook his head. "You're going to remarry one day and I'm going to remind you of how bitter you were today."

"Please, I wouldn't get married again if you paid me," Richmond replied as the three men headed for a room where the tailor was waiting.

"This is just the conversation I want to have before my wedding. Thanks, guys," Adrian quipped.

Three hours later, Dana stood in front of the full-length mirror in her suite, flanked by Imani and Kandace. The silver gown she wore was beautiful, strapless, knee-length, and way too much for a dinner with friends and family.

"What's going on? Because I know this is about more than dinner," Dana said.

"Why would you say that?" Imani asked. "It's the Poconos, a romantic place, and we want to impress our husbands." She twirled around in her beaded gold dress. Imani didn't mind showing off her baby bump, which had become the talk of Hollywood. Kandace looked at the pregnant women and took a step back.

"I need you two to keep your pregnancy dust over there," Kandace said.

"Oh, come on, Kandace," Dana said. "Kiana needs a little brother and I'm sure Solomon would be over the moon."

"He'd better focus on being a happy uncle. And I hope you have a boy. It will take the pressure off if Solomon has a nephew." The women laughed; then Kandace turned to Imani. "And are you going to be like the new Hollywood parents and sell your baby's pictures to *People*?"

"Raymond is not going for that and I think that's the dumbest thing that people do. Then cry about privacy. Besides, I'd like to see those photographers follow us to Harlem and try that LA crap."

Dana nudged Kandace. "My friend thinks she's as gangster as some of the characters she plays."

"Whatever," Imani said. "I keep telling you, I know people."

Kandace smiled and told them she couldn't wait to take them to Charlotte and introduce them to her friends, Jade, Serena, and Alicia.

"Charlotte sounds like a great trip," Imani said. "And we can leave the husbands at home."

Kandace shot Imani a cautioning look, and she shrugged in return. Dana looked from Kandace to Imani. "What is going on?"

"Nothing. Except we're going to be late for dinner if we don't hurry up," Kandace covered.

"That's right," Imani said as she slipped into a pair of ballerina flats. "I miss my heels but my feet are always swollen."

"It's about time you started wearing sensible shoes," Dana said as she applied a coat of lip gloss to her lips.

"Anyway, let's go." Kandace and Imani exchanged conspicuous smiles and Dana was about to question them again when there was a knock at the door.

Dana opened the door and saw a resort worker standing there with a bouquet of flowers. "Dana Singleton?" he asked.

"That's me."

"These are for you." He handed her the bouquet of yellow, orange, and pink roses. She looked down at the card, recognizing Adrian's handwriting immediately. She read the card and tears immediately sprang to her eyes.

Today, I want you to make me the happiest man in the world and become my wife. —A.B.

"What's wrong?" Imani asked.

"You can stop acting now," Dana sniffed. "I guess this was your way of getting me back for your wedding, huh?"

Imani shrugged and then nodded. "Yes, and that look on your face lets me know that it was worth it."

Dana turned around and hugged her best friend.

"Aww," Kandace said, then joined in the hugging. "Forget the pregnancy dust."

"Now let's go get you married," Imani said as she wiped a tear from Dana's cheek.

Candles illuminated the chapel. Adrian stood at the altar with Solomon and Richmond. All three men were dressed in black tuxedos with silver accessories. Adrian wrung his hands nervously as he watched the door. Part of him wondered if he could be this happy and lucky enough to have Dana in his life again. What if she didn't want this kind of wedding? What if the flowers sent her running? What if . . . He locked eyes with Dana as she appeared in the doorway with Kandace and Imani. His future wife was glowing. And the way she was wearing that dress made him want to get directly to the "you may kiss the bride" part of the ceremony.

Dana walked down the aisle and into his arms. Adrian couldn't help it; he could not wait to kiss her. The minister cleared his throat and Solomon tugged at the tail of Adrian's jacket.

"Too soon, bro, too soon," he said, causing everyone to laugh. Adrian and Dana broke their kiss and turned to the minister.

"Sorry, Reverend," Adrian said. "I couldn't help myself."

The older man nodded and began the quick ceremony. Adrian made a mental note to donate a butt load of money to his church when he said, "By the power vested in me by the state of Pennsylvania and our Father, the Lord our savior, I now pronounce you husband and wife. *Now* you may kiss your bride."

Dana wrapped her arms around Adrian's neck as he captured her lips in a hot, passionate kiss that left her weak and blushing in front of the minister because of the thoughts that were running through her mind.

"Let's get out of here," Adrian whispered, then scooped his wife up in his arms.

"Yes, let's do that."

The newly minted Mr. and Mrs. Adrian Bryant dashed out of the chapel and headed to their suite where they would begin their life of peace and love.

Don't miss

Forces of Nature

On sale now wherever books are sold.

Turn the page for an excerpt from
Forces of Nature . . .

Chapter 1

Crystal Hughes was mad as hell and the person behind this madness would feel her wrath, she decided as she ripped the notice she'd received in the mail to shreds. "Welco!" she muttered. Crossing the vast living room, Crystal grabbed her purse and keys from the coffee table. That company and its mysterious—at least from Crystal's point of view—owner wanted to own everything in town. Well, Hughes Farm was not for sale.

What was it that Douglas Wellington III had been quoted saying in the paper last week? *If Main Street can't keep their lights on, why should I have to share my bulbs?* How heartless! Crystal knew this man didn't give a damn about Reeseville. If he did, he'd know that helping, not buying, was the way people made it through rough times in this small town. Crystal wasn't even sure if old man Wellington even lived in Reeseville. If he did, he wouldn't want to destroy Hughes Farm. *Bastard!*

Dashing out of her plantation-style house, Crystal nearly bowled over two teenagers planting rosebushes near her steps.

"Miss Crystal, is everything okay?" asked Renda Johnson as Crystal placed her hand on her shoulder.

"Yes, I'm just in a hurry. What are you and MJ doing?" Crystal forced a smile at Monique and Renda, two sisters who lived in the Starlight House, a group home that sat a stone's throw from Crystal's house. No one else in Reeseville wanted the home for wayward girls anywhere near them. People said that the girls would be a danger to their neighborhoods and would lower their property value. But Crystal, who owned more than one hundred acres of land in west Duval County, subscribed to the notion that one good turn deserved another. "To whom much is given, much is required," Grandmother Hughes would always say. Crystal told the board of county commissioners that Starlight could have as much space as they needed. She treated the girls in Starlight just like the sisters she never had, and in return, they treated her to surprises like planting rosebushes in her yard, raking her lawn, and working in her community garden without any complaints.

Placing her hands on her hips and smacking a wad of gum, Monique stood up and looked Crystal in the eyes. "Well, it was supposed to be a surprise. But we found those orange rosebushes you were talking about. Why are you up so early?"

Nervously, Crystal twisted the green jade ring on her index finger. There was no way she could tell these girls about Welco's plans, plans that would level everything on her property. In their short lives, they'd seen so much disappointment and despair, and Crystal wasn't going to let evil Welco Industries add to it. She'd grown tired of watching this company buy up Reeseville as if they were playing Monopoly. In the last three years, Welco had purchased much of the land around Reeseville, building small factories that Crystal would bet her farm had been causing the increase in allergies around town. Did Wellington care? No. He simply said that people should take more vitamins.

But what she was most peeved with Welco about was the supercenter they'd built downtown, which caused the Fresh Food Market to close because they couldn't compete with the cheap prices of the supercenter. The Fresh Food Market had been the only grocery store in town where local farmers could sell their vegetables and fresh meats. When it closed, some of the smaller farms in Reeseville had suffered. Then Welco came along and bought them.

"Just some business in town, sweeties," Crystal replied. "Thank you so much for my surprise, though."

Mrs. Brooke Fey, the director and on-sight operator of the house, walked over to Crystal and the girls. "Ms. Hughes, I hope MJ and Renda aren't bothering you this morning," she said, surveying the scene in front of her.

"Oh no. These girls have given me something that I've wanted for a long time. Now, I really have to go." Crystal ran to her car, nearly tripping over her Birkenstock clogs and ankle-length rainbow-colored skirt. She started the car and peeled out of the driveway, leaving two black skid marks on the pavement. *This isn't going to happen. Welco isn't going to buy me!*

It wasn't nine a.m. yet and Douglas Wellington III, president and CEO of Welco Industries, was popping aspirin. His head throbbed like a heartbeat because the board was on his back, his assistant couldn't find the documents he needed for his ten-thirty presentation—and did she just say a woman was threatening to chain herself to the front door if he didn't meet with her immediately? This was not happening. Not today.

"Amy! Amy! I don't have time to meet with some kook. Call security or something. But what you need to do more than anything else is find my proposal!" he barked into the phone. From his desk, Douglas scrutinized Amy's small frame as she slumped over her desk. He knew he was too hard on her, but today wasn't a day for anyone to expect kindness from him. The board of directors was growing impatient about the time it was taking to get the business park project started. Douglas had no idea the owners of Hughes Farm would put up such a fight over that land. From what he understood, the farm wasn't a working farm with livestock and whatnot. Basically, they grew vegetables. In Douglas's opinion, there was enough dirt in Reeseville to plant a garden anywhere. It had been his great idea to hold off on any other projects until the business park was built. It wasn't as if Welco was losing money, but they weren't making money either. That was a problem Douglas had to fix—especially if he was going to keep Clive Oldsman off his back.

Twirling a silver ink pen between his fingers, Douglas picked up the phone and dialed Waylon Terrell's number. Waylon was his father's best friend and Douglas's godfather. In business, the only person Douglas trusted other than himself was Waylon. Were it not for his godfather, Douglas wouldn't be in the position he was in today. On days like this, that wasn't a good thing. He hadn't planned to follow in his father's footsteps. In fact, he'd spent a great deal of his life trying to be everything that Douglas Wellington Jr. was not, even if they were both coldhearted businessmen.

Luckily for him, he had Waylon in his life to control the board most of the time. Waylon had mentored him and guided him though some of his toughest business decisions.

"Hello, godson," the older man said when he answered.

"Waylon, the board is driving me crazy," Douglas

admitted. "I know they want me gone and I'm beginning to think Amy is working against me too."

"Calm down, son. These guys want you out of Welco, but your father groomed you your whole life for this. Don't let these old bastards push you around. Take a deep breath and show them who Doug Trey is."

Hearing his nickname brought a smile to Douglas's face. "All right, doc," he replied. "Did you take a look at my business park plans?"

"Uh, I haven't really looked over them. I'm retired, remember? I'll get back to you in a few days, but isn't this decision already made?"

Sighing, Douglas wished he'd gone to Waylon before presenting this business park idea to the board. What if he was going about building this place the wrong way?

I can't second-guess myself; that's what they expect.

"You're still there?" Waylon asked, breaking into Douglas's thoughts.

"Yeah, yeah. I'm going to go. We'll have to have dinner sometime this week," said Douglas. He said good-bye and hung up when he noticed Amy standing at his door. "What?"

"Sir," she said nervously. "That woman won't leave. She's handcuffed herself to my desk, sir. With her free hand, she keeps knocking papers off my desk."

Muttering a string of curses and profanities that would make a sailor blush, Douglas snatched his phone off the hook and dialed security. "There is a woman who needs to be removed from the building. You'll notice that she's wearing handcuffs," Douglas growled at the guard. Slamming the phone down, he walked over to the door and peered at the woman cuffed to Amy's desk as she dug in a huge brown sack. Thinking she might have a gun, Douglas immediately pulled Amy into his office and slammed the door. They ducked behind his desk, waiting for the woman to make her next move.

The artificial beauty of the Welco lobby grated on Crystal's nerves, from the potted silk plants to the shiny marble floors and the huge windows allowing bright sunlight to saturate the building. *But there's no life force here,* she thought as she looked around.

Crystal spotted a menacing security officer walking toward her, his massive hand at his side, gripping his flashlight. Dropping her bag to the floor, she sat down on the marble crossing her legs Indian style. This wasn't her first time standing up—rather sitting down—to corporate security. She and some of the girls from the Starlight House had protested at the local mall because security officers had harassed a number of young people for no reason. The Reeseville Mall ended up donating a hundred thousand dollars to the Starlight House to stop the weekly protests and the security guards were trained how to deal with diverse youth. Crystal's reputation as a community activist was born the day the settlement was announced. But she worried about living up to her family's legacy. Hughes Farm, which meant so much to the community, had been handed down each generation and she refused to be the one member of the family to mess things up and lose it.

She also didn't want to be viewed as some liberal nut either. Still, there was a right and a wrong way to do things. Many in the community already questioned if Crystal could handle running the farm and why she allowed the Starlight House to be built there. She'd heard the murmurs around town about her not doing as good a job with the farm as her parents. People questioned why she stopped raising livestock, accused her of being a hippie, and said she was going to ruin what took decades to build.

Maybe those whispers helped spur her anger toward Welco. People expected her to fail, and Welco buying out the farm wasn't going to prove her naysayers right. If she had to protest every day or sue to keep what was her family's, then she would. Douglas Wellington III was going to rue the day he tried to take over her farm. This was only the beginning.

The Welco security officer, who reminded her of an ogre from Greek mythology, snarled at her before saying, "Ma'am, unlock these handcuffs and leave."

Rolling her eyes, Crystal stood up to the towering guard. "If you want me to leave, get Wellington out here, otherwise, I'm camping out. What's right is right. I don't want to make a scene, but I will and the whole town will see it." Crystal threw her hand up, illustrating how close they were to the big bay window. Slowly, she returned to her seat on the floor.

The security officer ripped his radio from his hip holster as Crystal pulled a bottle of water from her bag. "All right," the officer said. "Show me that you don't have a gun in that sack and I'll see about getting Wellington out here."

Crystal looked at him quizzically as she opened up her bag to show him the contents: two more bottles of water and three apples. "Why the change of heart?"

Placing his hand on her shoulder, he smiled. "He ain't my favorite person, either. Hold tight." The officer waddled down the hall and disappeared behind glass double doors.

Crystal drank her water slowly, waiting for something to happen. *When is old Wellington going to appear?* she wondered, her frustration increasing, She'd already built an image of this monster in her mind—pencil thin, receding gray hair, a potbelly, and crooked teeth. Only a monster like that would want to displace people for the almighty dollar. Only a man with ice water in his veins rather than blood would view people as if they were a commodity to be bought and sold. Not Crystal—she wasn't for sale.

Moments later, a tall man, moving with the grace of a panther and the body of a Greek god, crossed the lobby and planted himself in front of her.

Crystal gazed up at him, momentarily speechless as he stared at her with slate gray eyes. His full lips seemingly beckoned her to kiss them and those hands—big and wide with long fingers—she wanted them on her body, caressing her breasts, thighs, and everything in between. Rapidly, she blinked and swallowed hard. She needed to get her hormones together; she wasn't here to lust after this man, whoever he was. She was here to meet with Wellington and she didn't give a damn if they sent Denzel Washington to the lobby to meet her—Crystal wasn't moving until she got what she wanted. Still, the man looking at her was fine as hell.

His face told a story of annoyance, with a scowl darkening his handsome features and his wide nostrils flaring with anger. "Are you going to just stare at me or do you have something to say?" His voice reminded her of a sensual sax, hypnotic and melodic. Her body was electrified at the thought of him whispering sweet words of passion in her ear.

"I'm not talking to anyone but Douglas Wellington." Crystal's voice wavered, but not from fear. Carnal desire described what she was feeling as she stared into his eyes.

"I *am* Douglas Wellington," he announced dryly.

Now on her feet, Crystal was dumbfounded. There was no way a man this beautiful could be as cold and callous as the man she'd dreamed up in her head. Where were his fangs, protruding belly, and horns? The scent of burning sulfur and brimstone? "What? You're Douglas Wellington?"

He folded his arms across his chest and shot her a look of irritation. "This is fascinating and all, listening to you repeat my name. But what the hell do you want, lady? Most people make a phone call and set an appointment to get a meeting. This is a distraction that's interrupting my workday."

Narrowing her dark eyes into slits, Crystal exclaimed, "My land is not for sale, you pompous ass. If you think for one second that I will allow you to come on to my property and just take over because you want to, you can forget it."

Douglas laughed and turned to walk away. "If you read the letter that was mailed to you about my company's plans, there was a number for my attorney that you can call. I suggest you do that," he said. "And uncuff yourself," he added, "otherwise, I'm calling the police."

"And I'm calling the press, jerk! Do you realize what you're planning to destroy all in the name of corporate greed? People need this land and I will fight you tooth and nail to make sure it stays in my possession. So, get ready to lose."

Douglas waved her off as if she were a gnat buzzing around his ear. "If you don't unshackle yourself by the time I get in my office, and then get out of this building, I will press charges when the police arrive."

GREAT BOOKS,
GREAT SAVINGS!

When You Visit Our Website:
www.kensingtonbooks.com
You Can Save Money Off The Retail Price
Of Any Book You Purchase!

- All Your Favorite Kensington Authors
- New Releases & Timeless Classics
- Overnight Shipping Available
- eBooks Available For Many Titles
- All Major Credit Cards Accepted

Visit Us Today To Start Saving!
www.kensingtonbooks.com

All Orders Are Subject To Availability.
Shipping and Handling Charges Apply.
Offers and Prices Subject To Change Without Notice.